'I shall go m...
here a day lon...

'Then you shan't.' ...
pocket and handed ... ... this is an
invitation to spend some time with Mama. She
has sent me with the coach to fetch you.'

'Oh, Robert, you are an angel!' She flung her
arms about his neck and kissed him joyously
on each cheek, as a child awarded a treat might
have done. He raised his hands halfway to his
shoulders and then, not knowing what to do
with them, dropped them again and stood
stiffly to attention.

Suddenly aware of his lack of response, she
realised she had embarrassed him and stood
back, her face a scarlet picture of mortification.
'Oh, I am sorry…'

Unaccountably pleased, he smiled and put out
his hand to stroke her cheek with the back of
one finger. 'Impulsive as always, my dear, but
you must remember that we are no longer
childhood playfellows. Society is like to be
shocked by such forwardness.'

Born in Singapore, **Mary Nichols** came to England when she was three, and has spent most of her life in different parts of East Anglia. She has been a radiographer, school secretary, information officer and industrial editor, as well as a writer. She has three grown-up children, and four grandchildren.

Recent titles by the same author:

THE RELUCTANT ESCORT
JACK CHILTERN'S WIFE

THE WESTMERE LEGACY

Mary Nichols

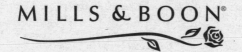

MILLS & BOON®

First published in Great Britain 2001
Harlequin Mills & Boon Limited,
Eton House, 18-24 Paradise Road, Richmond, Surrey TW9 1SR

© Mary Nichols 2001

ISBN 0 263 82726 7

Set in Times Roman 10½ on 11½ pt.
04-0401-85676

Printed and bound in Spain
by Litografia Rosés S.A., Barcelona

Chapter One

March 1816

'Sylvester!' William Huntley, second Earl of Westmere, could be heard bellowing as far away as the kitchens, where Bella was speaking to Cook about the day's menus. 'Sylvester! Damn your eyes, man! I want you here.'

'Oh, dear, his gout must be plaguing him again,' Bella said. 'Where can Sylvester be?'

There was the sound of hurrying footsteps on the landing above them and then silence. A few minutes later a tall gangly individual in a suit of black clothes and thinning hair of indeterminate colour appeared in the doorway with a large jug which he handed to Daisy, the kitchen maid, to fill with hot water. 'He is determined on dressing and coming downstairs,' he said.

'But he hasn't had his breakfast.'

'He says he will have it in the breakfast parlour in half an hour.'

'Oh, lor,' Daisy said, filling the jug with hot water from a huge kettle on the stove and giving it back to him. 'There's no fire in there.'

'Then you'd better put one there quick sharp.'

'And who's going to help me cook breakfast if the girl disappears, making fires?' Cook demanded. 'Can't you persuade him to have his breakfast in his room like he always does? I can't think why he should suddenly decide to come downstairs for it—it's years since he did that.'

'He says he's made a decision and he's going to set it in train today.'

'Oh, and what might that be?'

The valet shrugged his bony shoulders. 'How should I know?'

'You're privy to most things where he's concerned. I'll wager he's told you.'

'He has not and if he had, I wouldn't tell you, madam. I'm off before he starts yelling again.'

'Gout he might have, but it hasn't affected his voice,' Cook said, as they heard his lordship shouting again.

'No, but it does give him a great deal of pain,' Bella put in mildly, as the valet scuttled from the room with the hot water. 'He will feel better directly when Sylvester has given him his wash and shave and bound up his poor foot. Daisy, go and light that fire. I will help Cook with breakfast.'

The thirteen-year-old Daisy picked up a basket of wood, an old newspaper and a tinder box and left the kitchen. Bella found an apron in a drawer and rolled up the sleeves of her dress to help prepare the household's breakfasts. It was not an arduous task because although the Earl was hardly impecunious, he was very careful, some said mean, and kept no more staff than was necessary for his own comfort and the smooth running of the house and estate.

Indoors, there was only Sylvester Carpenter his valet, Sam Jolliffe the butler, Martha Tooke, housekeeper-cum-cook, Daisy the kitchen maid, a laundrywoman and two women who did not live in but came in from the village every day to make sure the east wing of the great mansion, which was the only part of it they used, was kept clean. It was not a convenient house, having the kitchens and pantries on the opposite side of the great hall to the reception rooms, but there were smaller, cosier parlours nearer to the hub of the great house, which were used now there were only three in residence.

This level of indoor staffing was considered adequate for a household that consisted of the Earl and Bella, and Ellen Battersby, Bella's maid and companion. The elderly Miss Battersby was away, visiting her sister who was ill, and Bella missed her.

Isabella, known to everyone as Bella, was the Earl's granddaughter, the only child of his son, Charles. She was seventeen years old and had lived at Westmere all her life. She did not remember her mother except as a rather ephemeral being who had always smelled nice and looked beautiful. She had died of fever after giving birth to a son who had survived her by only two days.

Bella's memories of her father were rather different. His smells were of tobacco and brandy, especially the brandy. Sometimes he had been exceptionally jovial and sometimes morose to the point of silence for hours, even days, on end. He had also had a violent temper, which had often led her grandfather to sigh heavily and declaim, 'I don't know where he gets it from, I am sure. I am the mildest of men myself.' Her father had died in 1805 when Bella had been six, and the event had hardly registered on her young mind except that she had suddenly found herself free of fear.

As for her grandfather, the Earl, he did have a temper, whatever he said to the contrary, but, unlike her father, he was never harsh with her. He had once been a very handsome man, tall and upright, with thick wavy hair and brown eyes beneath the finely arched brows which were the mark of nearly every male Huntley. He was old now, of course. Seventy-nine was a great age, and the hair, though still thick, was pure white, the eyes more often than not clouded with pain. He was always talking about 'kicking the bucket', which Bella found distressing.

Sometimes he would talk nostalgically of the times when he and his brother, John, had been boys and Westmere had simply been a bump in the fens, above the level of the fields that surrounded it, which had been frequently flooded in winter. It was hard to imagine that now because much of the marshy ground of the fens had been drained and culti-vated.

It was the death of his brother which had made him more crabby than usual, she decided. John had been the younger by three years and it must have made the Earl aware of his own mortality. 'Who would have guessed I would outlive him?' he had said, on hearing the news. 'He never had a day's illness in his life while I am plagued by gout and a bad heart, have been for years.'

Sir John Huntley, baronet, had died suddenly in his sleep at his home, Palgrave Manor in the county of Essex, just as the church bells had been pealing in the new year of 1816. He had outlived his wife and only son, just as the Earl had done, but was survived by two widowed daughters, a grand-daughter and four grandsons. Bella had been aware of un-dercurrents of feeling at the funeral they had attended two months before, though she could not exactly put her finger on why that should have been.

The church had been full, everyone dressed in deepest mourning, and during the committal they had obviously been distressed, but afterwards, when friends and distant relations had departed and close family had congregated at Palgrave Manor for refreshments and the reading of the will, there had been a certain tension and whispered comments about the inheritance.

'But I could not see there should be any dissent about it,' Bella said to her grandfather on the return journey from Palgrave to Westmere. 'I thought Sir John disposed of everything very properly. Edward has the title and the estate, which is surely as it should be, but he did not neglect the others. An annuity for the other three men and generous gifts to the ladies. Everyone was remembered, even the servants.'

It was a very uncomfortable journey with the roads deep in snow and the poor horses struggling to pull the heavy family coach through the drifts. And though they had hot bricks at their feet and warm rugs wrapped about their knees, Bella was still numb with cold and was quite sure her grandfather felt it even more than she did. It worried her that he had insisted on making the journey at all. He would have been excused his absence in the circumstances, she was sure.

'Of course they were,' the Earl growled. 'It's not John's estate they are concerned with, but mine.'

'Yours?' she queried in surprise.

'I have no son living and no grandsons. My brother was my heir. Now he is gone they are gathering like a crowd of vultures, waiting for me to stick my spoon in the wall, too. Got their eyes on my blunt, not to mention the title.'

'Oh, Grandpapa, I'm sure not,' Bella said, unwilling to believe any of her four second cousins were so mercenary. 'They are concerned for your health, that is all.'

'Oh, indeed they are,' he said with a chuckle. 'I've a good mind to live for ever to confound them.'

'I hope you may, Grandpapa.'

'Dear child, I do believe you are the only one who means that.'

And then he abruptly changed the subject, looking out of the coach at the bleak white landscape and saying how he would be glad when spring arrived and he could see the new lambs frolicking in the fields—the home farm had a large flock of sheep—and from that she deduced he was not expecting to die quite yet.

He did not mention it again and they resumed their usual humdrum routine. Every day he had his breakfast in his room and then followed a leisurely toilet, after which he made his way down to the little parlour and then, if he felt well enough, took a gentle hack round the estate and spoke to his steward about the work that needed doing. Sometimes she accompanied him on his rides or they would go out in the carriage together to visit neighbours. They would have dinner at three and supper at seven and he would retire early to his room.

Every Sunday morning, they went to the church in the village of Westmere, after which the Earl would stop and make some caustic comment to the parson about the sermon or the text and they would return home in time for an early dinner.

Apart from discussing the daily menus with Martha, Bella's only other duties were to write letters for her grandfather and read to him from *The Morning Post* and *The Times* which were sent down by mail from London every day. He also subscribed to Cobbett's *Political Register*, which often had him exploding with indignation. She wondered why he continued to require her to read it aloud if the author's radical views annoyed him so much. 'Tuppeny trash,' he called it, but, then, the Earl would disagree with almost everyone, just for love of an argument.

When not attending to her grandfather, Bella occupied her time with walks, charitable works, sewing and writing her journal. Not that she had a great deal to commit to paper, but she liked to observe people and their foibles and watch nature unfold, year by year, from winter to spring and into summer and autumn, to record the first snowdrop, the first cuckoo, the day the harvest began and the day the meres froze over and everyone took to their skates. She wrote about little domestic problems and news of the village—

who had been taken to bed with child, who had died, which young man was courting which of the village girls.

She read the *Ladies' Monthly Museum* and subscribed to a lending library so that she could read the latest novels. She had even begun to write one of her own, full of unrequited love, mystery, duels and dangerous adventures. It helped to relieve the boredom of a life that was mundane to say the least. She often longed for something exciting to happen to liven it up. And now it looked as though it might. Something was in the air. But what?

She did not have long to wait. As soon as they had finished their breakfast, the Earl stood up, pushing Sylvester aside when he ran to help him. 'Leave me, man, I am not slipping my wind yet.' Then he turned to Bella. 'Come with me, I want some letters written.'

She followed him to the library, where he sank into an armchair beside the fire. 'You don't look quite the thing, Grandpapa. Are you sure you want to do this today?' she asked. Spring was a very long time coming this year and the dismal days seemed to make him more and more tired.

'Yes, been putting it off too long as it is.'

'Very well, but you must stop if it becomes too much for you.'

'Will you cease fussing, child, and fetch out the writing things? I want four letters written.'

'Four?' she queried in surprise as she seated herself at his big leather-topped desk and took notepaper and pens from the drawer.

'Yes, one to each of my great-nephews. You know their directions.'

'Yes.' She dipped a pen in the ink and waited while he assembled his thoughts.

'Dear whichever of them you start with,' he began. 'It doesn't matter, they're all the same. You are requested and required to attend me at Westmere Hall on Thursday the 20th day of March at two in the afternoon…'

'Grandpapa, is that not a little abrupt?' Bella ventured. 'And very short notice. The twentieth is only three days away.'

He laughed. 'They will all come running with their tongues hanging out—you see.'

'Why do you want to see them all at once? It will exhaust you.'

'It will be far less tiring than telling them one at a time. And besides, they won't be able to argue among themselves about what I said to each if they hear it together.'

'Hear what, Grandpapa?'

'My will…'

'But surely that happens…' She stopped in dismay. 'Oh, please, do not tell me you are unwell.'

'I am old, Bella, and I have been thinking that I ought to make my peace with the past and ensure the future. Your future.'

'Mine?' she queried. It had never entered her head to wonder what would befall her after her grandfather died. She supposed, if it happened before she was married, he would leave her in the care of whoever succeeded, but until recently she had not given a thought to who that might be. Louis was the oldest of the great-nephews, but he was the son of a daughter. On the other hand, Edward was the elder son of a son and he bore the family name of Huntley, which Louis did not. She had no idea how these things were managed, but she could very well see quarrels ahead. No doubt her grandfather had seen them, too, and this was his way of dealing with them. But where did James, also on the distaff side, and Robert, Edward's younger brother, fit into it?

They were all honourable men and would make sure she had a roof over her head and did not starve. Suddenly she was filled with apprehension. Her grandfather must be having doubts about that or he would not be writing to them. She found herself looking at him, her heart thumping, the letters unfinished.

'Yes, my dear. You know when I am called to account, I do not want to be found wanting as far as you are concerned. You are a female and a very young and comely one.' He paused to scrutinise her from top to toe as if he had not looked at her properly for a long time. He saw large hazel eyes set in an oval face surrounded by dark ringlets, a proud neck, sloping shoulders and a trim figure dressed in a light green merino wool gown. She was taller and thinner than he would have liked, but he supposed she would fill out as she matured. He favoured women with a little more meat on them. 'And marriageable. You will need advice and instruction…'

'There is Miss Battersby, Grandpapa.'

'Pah! Her head is full of romantic notions. She would marry you off to the first young gallant with a ready smile and a twinkling eye.'

'She is not such a fribble and neither am I.'

'Perhaps not. But I am not going to take the gamble. I want to see you married before I go.' He paused. 'You know, being a female, you cannot inherit Westmere directly?'

'Yes, Grandpapa, and although I would rather not think about it, I am sure you will make provision for me. I am in no hurry to marry.'

'You may not be, but I am. That is why I have sent for those four. You shall marry one of them.'

'Grandfather!' She was shocked to the core. 'You are surely not going to instruct one of them to wed me?'

'No. The choice will be yours.'

The conversation was becoming more and more bizarre and her senses were reeling. She leaned back in her chair, the letter-writing forgotten. She could not imagine herself married to any one them. Although they were not first cousins, she had always looked on the young men as kinsmen, part of the family who came and went and sometimes stopped to chuck her under the chin and ask her how she did. The idea of being married to any one of them was past imagining.

'Grandpapa,' she said, trying to control the quaver in her voice. 'They are so much older than I and men of the world. I am persuaded not one of them will want me for a wife.' Indeed, she hoped and prayed that was the case.

'Oh, indeed, they will. I guarantee they will all be paying you fulsome compliments and begging you for your hand inside of an hour, if not before.' He chuckled suddenly. 'The one who comes up to the mark shall be my heir.'

'Grandfather!' She was horrified. 'I am to be bartered for a legacy?'

'Pity you weren't a boy,' he said, ignoring her outburst. 'You'd have inherited right and tight and no questions asked. I can leave the blunt to you, but where's the sense in that? You couldn't have the managing of it. It has to go to your husband and it were better he were one of the family.'

She could hardly take it in. She had assumed the estate was entailed, but it could not be if he could dispose of it as he had suggested. 'But I do not want any of them. I do not love them.'

'Love, bah! Old Batters been filling your head with nonsense, has she? Love has nothing to do with marriage.'

'I am persuaded you loved your wife.' Bella had never known her grandmother, the Countess, but Ellen had said she had been a beautiful woman but rather cold and haughty. According to Ellen, she had died of a broken heart, though when Bella had questioned her as to why, she had closed her mouth and refused to say another word. But broken hearts and haughtiness hardly went together, and Bella often wondered which was nearer the truth.

'No. Arranged marriage, hardly knew the woman, but we became comfortable with each other. That's the most important thing, you know, to be comfortable.'

'Well, I am sure Papa loved Mama.'

'And look where it got him. Dead himself a couple of years after her. A wasted life. All wasted lives…' His eyes clouded as if he were looking back into past unhappiness. 'His first wife was not at all suitable. I told him no good would come of it, that he was hardly out of leading strings and should see more of the world before he committed himself, but he would not listen. I let it go. I shan't make the same mistake with you.'

She had never dared to ask about her father's first wife—all she knew, and that was from Miss Battersby, was that her father had married the local doctor's daughter when both had been very young and that she had died after ten years of marriage and almost as many miscarriages. Begetting an heir had been more important than looking after her health. The heir had been the thing. Her father had married again with almost indecent haste and Isabella had been born a year later. It had been four more years before the longed-for heir had come and he had been dead in the space of a se'ennight, together with his mother. When her father had followed, Bella had been the only one left, except for her grandfather's great-nephews.

Louis was the son of Elizabeth, the elder of Sir John's daughters, who had married the French Comte de Courville and had lived in France until the Comte had been guillotined in 1793. Elizabeth had brought six-year-old Louis, now the new Comte, and her baby daughter, Colette, to live in England. Bella had seen very little of Louis as a child—his ambitious mother had been too busy making sure he was seen and noticed in Society. And she had succeeded all too well.

According to Miss Battersby, the fount of all gossip, Louis had made a name for himself as a rakeshame and a gambler and had a different woman on his arm almost every time he went out, but they didn't seem to mind that because he was generous to a fault. Where did his income came from? Bella was not at all sure. Did he need the Westmere inheritance? He was hardly husband material; she did not even like him much.

James Trenchard, the son of Helen, the second daughter, was a widower with twin daughters of six, Constance and Faith. James had inherited his father's fenland acres and was a farmer from the top of his low-crowned hat down to his mud-caked boots. He was sturdy and reliable but certainly did not excite her senses.

Then came brothers Edward and Robert, progeny of Sir John's only son. Edward—Sir Edward since his grandfather's death—cut a very fine figure, not foppish at all, but well dressed in a muted kind of way. He was tall, well built and dignified. 'Stiff-neck' was her grandfather's description of him but Bella thought that was unkind. She had always looked on him as a sort of favourite uncle. He was, in Ellen's words, 'a catch' but as Charlotte Mellish, a Society beauty by all accounts, seemed already to have caught him, he would not offer for her.

Robert she liked as a kind of common conspirator in their childhood scrapes. It had been Robert who had pulled her out when she had fallen through the ice into the dyke one hard winter when they had been skating, who had taken the blame on his own shoulders, though he had begged her not to be so foolish as to venture onto the slippery surface. She managed a watery smile, remembering how cold she had been and how he had wrapped her in his own coat and carried her home.

She had not seen much of him in the last few years because he had been away at the war. He had been a captain in the Hussars and had distinguished himself in the Peninsular War and at Waterloo. Her memories of him were of a tall, gangling youth with a ready smile, but last summer, after the war had ended, he had called at Westmere and she had discovered he had grown tall and well muscled, and heart-stoppingly handsome, with brown eyes that were full of wry humour. Of all the cousins she liked him the best, but Ellen Battersby said he had become somewhat footloose since his discharge. She could not imagine him offering for her, and if he did, she would have to refuse him—she had too much pride to accept him on her grandfather's terms. Besides, liking wasn't love, was it?

'I am sure I can rely on you to choose wisely,' the Earl went on. 'Running an estate like Westmere is a grave responsibility. There is not just yourself to consider but everyone who depends on the estate for a livelihood, and that not only means the immediate house and grounds but the villagers. I have always done my best for them…'

'I know that, Grandpapa, but would it not be best for you to choose your successor and not make it conditional on him marrying me? I would rather earn my living.'

'Don't be a goose, child, you are the granddaughter of an earl, not some peasant. And what do you know of the world of work?'

'I could learn. Grandpapa, please, don't do this.'

'My mind's made up,' he said. 'Now finish writing those letters and we'll send 'em off to the post.'

Bella picked up her pen again with a hand that shook. Could she delay posting them? But how could she? The Earl would expect the young men to arrive, and if they did not, he would send again for them. She wrote slowly and a tear escaped and slid down her cheek to drop with a plop on the letter she was writing. She was hardly aware of it. The old man, losing patience, rang the bell at his side. Sylvester appeared so swiftly she was sure he had been listening outside the door. Oh, what a tasty morsel of gossip this would furnish for the rest of the staff!

'A glass of brandy, man,' his lordship ordered. 'And pour Miss Huntley a cordial. I think she may need it. And then I want you to take my letters to the village and make sure they are put on the mail. Do it yourself, mind. If I find you have handed them over to some stable boy, I shall turn you off, do you understand?'

'Perfectly, my lord.' Sylvester poured the brandy from a decanter on a side cupboard, then groped beneath it for the bottle of cordial which was kept there for Bella on the few occasions her grandfather invited her to share refreshment with him. By the time her glass was at her elbow, she had finished the last letter and was dusting it before handing it to her grandfather to sign.

'Good,' he said, scrawling 'Westmere' on the bottom of each. 'You write a good hand.'

Hurriedly swallowing her cordial, Bella made her excuses and left her grandfather to Sylvester's mercies. She needed to get away from the stifling atmosphere of the house into the fresh air, to clear her head and think, to try and make a plan for her future, because assuredly she would need one. Oh, how she wished Miss Battersby would come back. Had her grandfather deliberately timed his announcement knowing she would not be able to turn to the old nurse for comfort and advice?

Grabbing a shawl from her room, she went out into the garden. She hardly noticed the daffodils and gillyflowers in the borders as she wandered across the lawns to the brook which ran along the bottom of the garden, or that the water was very high and lapping the grass. Her mind was on her dilemma. How could she face the men after they had heard what her grandfather proposed? It would be too mortifying to bear.

Would any of them offer for her? Would they show contempt or do as her grandfather said they would and fall over themselves to comply with his wishes? If they did, they would undoubtedly be doing it from the basest motives—money and power and a title—not for any feelings they might have for her. And if she were to accept one of them, her motives would be equally questionable. She needed a home and security and… Surely, her grandfather would not leave her penniless if she refused? Supposing she absented herself from the discussion. Would her grandfather abandon the idea? Supposing she left home? To go where? She did not have another relative in the world and no money. There was no alternative—she had somehow to persuade her grandfather to change his mind.

Bella turned back to the house and saw Sylvester hurrying along the drive towards the village, carrying the four letters which would seal her fate, and she knew it was too late. She had three days to wait and then she would learn the true colours of her grandfather's great-nephews. Three days and after that…

She did not want to think of that and forced herself to concentrate on preparing for their guests. The next two days she was busy opening up rooms long disused for their accommodation and trying to soothe the ruffled tempers of Cook and Daisy, who had to cope with all the extra work. By the morning when the guests were due to arrive, they were almost mutinous. 'Hire a couple of footmen,' her grandfather said when she told him of the problem. 'You shouldn't have any trouble—there's enough men out of work.'

She didn't bother to argue that most of the men who were out of work were labourers and would not have any idea of the duties of a footman. She hurried to her room, changed into a dark green riding habit and matching hat with its sweeping feather, pulled on her boots and went to the stables to ask for her mare, Misty, to be saddled, glad enough to be free of the stifling atmosphere of the house and enjoy her last few hours of independence.

The grey mare was sturdy rather than elegant but she was game and, because in the last few days the weather had been too inclement to go far, she was in need of exercise. Set to gallop, she responded immediately. As the horse took her across the park, Bella's thoughts went round and round in her head in time with the thundering hooves, but they always came back to the same thing. Her grandfather's ultimatum. He must surely have his own preferences about whom he would like to succeed him, but the choice had been left to her. It was an onerous burden she did not want. Was her happiness not to be considered at all? It just wasn't fair!

Beyond the park, the landscape was completely flat, broken only by an isolated house here and there, a few willow trees and some slowly turning windmills which were used to take the water off the fields and tip it into the dykes that criss-crossed the land. Because of the almost incessant rain since the snow had melted, very little ploughing had been done. Instead of the new green shoots of winter corn making an appearance, the ground was black and soggy and the windmills were kept busy, making sure the ground did not revert to marsh and mere.

She brought Misty back to a trot when she came to the Ely road. Ely was the nearest town of any size and until recently had been a thriving centre of commerce, its roads full of carriages and carts and stagecoaches which called at the several inns in the town, and its quayside busy with wherries and barges bringing in all manner of goods and taking out the produce of the area—grain, fish, vegetables, osiers. But now much of the produce rotted before it found a buyer.

In Ely, there were men loafing in idleness on almost every street corner. Two of them she recognised as coming from one of the farms on her grandfather's estate. They had wives and children to support but they laughed when she dismounted and asked them if they wanted two or three days' work in the house. 'We ain't bowin' and scrapin' for you nor no one,' they said, and turned away from her.

It was then she realised that there were more people about than usual and they were all making in the same direction, towards the market-place. Curious, she joined them, leading her horse. The open space was crowded with men and women, young and old, gathered around round a tall weather-beaten man with a shock of white hair who was standing on a flat cart, addressing them. It did not take a genius to surmise that this was a seditious meeting and Bella felt a frisson of fear, almost a premonition.

With the price of corn so high, the hungry labourers, unable to afford bread, together with soldiers and sailors who had been discharged without so much as a thank you for their part in the fight against Napoleon, were at the end of their tether. Already there had been disturbances—ricks and barns had been set on fire, mills and bakeries surrounded by mobs shouting, 'Bread or blood!'

'It would never have happened in my young day,' her grandfather had grumbled. 'The people knew their place and they kept to it, just as the landowners knew their responsibilities towards their tenants. Cobbett's right there—the new breed of landowners with money made from industry are only interested in the status their new possessions give them. They have no idea how to go on.'

Bella stopped to listen.

'You may shrug your shoulders and say, ''This is nothing to do with me'',' the man was saying. 'But we are all brethren together. If the labourer in the country goes down, then the town labourer will be next, the workers in the manufactories, the dockers and heavers of coal, all those who do not have a voice because Parliament denies it to them.'

The crowd was silent, listening intently as he went on, 'When the time comes, all men must rally to the cause against the despots who think property gives them rights over those whose only asset is the sweat of their brow and their strong right arm.' He paused as a rumble of assent went through his listeners. 'But those assets are of inestimable value, my friends. The country cannot exist without them. Are you ready to insist on your voice being heard?'

'Yes.' A roar went up and they looked from one to another, their eyes gleaming. 'Fair wages! Votes for the workers! Bread or blood!'

Bella knew she ought to leave, but she was fascinated and edged forward to hear more. And she wasn't the only outsider in the crowd. Not a dozen paces from her was a tall young man who was obviously not a labourer. He was wearing a riding coat of Bath cloth and fine leather breeches tucked into shining riding boots. His hair beneath his tall hat was dark and curled about his ears in the latest Windswept style. There was no doubt he was a gentleman, one of the hated upper classes. Almost as if he sensed her scrutiny, he turned towards her, shocking her into putting her gloved hand to her open mouth. It was her cousin Robert.

His dark brow lifted in surprise. 'Bella, what are you doing here?'

He was even taller and broader than she remembered him, more ruggedly handsome, though his expression, as he pushed his way through to her and stood looking down into her upturned face, was difficult to fathom. She thought it might be annoyance. But what right had he to be annoyed with her? And two could play at that game. 'I might ask you the same thing,' she retorted, refusing to acknowledge the swift beating of her heart and the flutter in the pit of her stomach as anything more than surprise at seeing him.

'You may ask, but that's not to say I will answer.'

She looked beyond him to the other men, some of whom had turned to watch the encounter with deep interest. Did they know who she was? Did they know who Robert was? 'No, because you should not be listening to sedition—that's as good as condoning it. What do you think Grandfather would say to that?'

'He may say whatever he wishes.'

'You are supposed to be on your way to Westmere.'

He grinned suddenly. 'Am I? I wonder why?'

She could tell him, she could tell him her grandfather's plan, warn him what to expect, but decided against it. His lordship wanted all the men to hear it together and he would be angry if she pre-empted that. 'If you want to know, you'll have to come, won't you?'

'No doubt it has something to do with the inheritance, and as I have no expectations in that direction I see no point to my presence.'

'It would be very discourteous of you to refuse...'

'Discourteous!' He laughed. 'And I suppose "requested and required" are terms of the utmost courtesy.'

'Oh, that's just Grandpapa's way, you should know that.' She paused. 'Why are you in Ely if not to see him?'

'I could say I came to see you.'

She was taken aback. 'Why?'

'Do I have to have a reason to visit a pretty young cousin?'

Bella laughed shakily at the compliment. 'Now you are bamming me.'

'Not at all. I was curious about that letter. The handwriting was not up to your usual standard and the paper was blotched. I detected a tear or two and was afraid his lordship must be about to hand in his accounts. Is he?'

She was slightly mollified to know that his concern had been for her and not the inheritance. 'Not at all. His gout troubles him, but that is all…'

'Then why?'

'He will tell you.'

'If I come,' Robert said curtly. 'Does he know you are out without a chaperone?'

'I do not need a chaperone. I have lived here all my life, everyone knows me. I am in no danger.'

'No?' He turned back to look at the crowd of men behind him. All were watching them warily, including the tall man with the white hair who had stopped speaking until he could regain his audience's attention. There was a murmur of anger. They were breaking the law by even congregating, and if they recognised Bella as the granddaughter of the biggest landowner in the neighbourhood, they would feel threatened. In their present mood they might even offer violence. He stepped in front of her to protect her, but there were far too many of them for that to be any more than a gesture. 'Go home, Bella,' he said. 'Forget you ever saw these people.'

'Why?' she demanded angrily. 'I heard what that man said and so did you. What do you think they mean to do?'

'I do not know.' He had been about to find out when Bella had arrived and now he doubted whether he would learn anything. And she was in danger. He grabbed Misty's bridle with one hand and, putting his other hand under her bottom, heaved her into the saddle. It was a most inelegant way to mount and she would have had something to say to him for taking such liberties with her person if she had not been so aware of the menace of the crowd.

'What about you? Are you coming, too?' she asked, as she settled her foot into the stirrup and picked up the reins.

'No.' Then he slapped the mare's rump hard.

Robert watched her cantering down the road until she was out of sight but by then the men had surrounded him.

Bella did not go back through the crowds to the main road but turned down the hill to the towpath and rode northwards along it, hardly noticing the barges which brought their goods up from the ports at King's Lynn and Wisbech to Ely, where they would add to the accumulation in the warehouses. Now and again she had to rein in and walk her mount round the horses which towed them but she did it automatically, her mind on her encounter with Robert. She had quite forgotten her original errand.

He had infuriated her. As if any of the local people would harm her! But that man on the cart hadn't been local and perhaps he was out to stir up trouble. Would Robert try and do anything about it? He undoubtedly thought listening to a man like that was more entertaining than obeying her grandfather's summons. Would any of them obey it? Whatever would Grandfather do if none of them came?

After two or three miles the towpath continued on the other side of the river and she turned away from it towards the village of Westmere where a few minutes later, she entered the gates of Westmere Hall. She reined in when she came within sight of it. It was a huge house, built a hundred and fifty years before, using a mixture of stone from a local abbey, destroyed during Cromwell's time, and Peterborough brick. Built on three sides of a rectangle, with steps up to a huge, very ancient oak door, also taken from the abbey, it stood four-square to the prevailing east wind, surrounded by mown lawns and flower-beds, its many windows gleaming in the sunlight.

Bella sighed, wondering how much longer it would remain her home if she refused to obey her grandfather, then spurred Misty round to the stable yard and left her in the care of a stable boy, before entering the house by a back door. In answer to her grandfather's enquiry, she said she had been unable to find any extra help in Ely.

'Why go to Ely? There are men in the village.'

'I'll send Jolliffe to see if he can find someone.' She said nothing of the meeting she had interrupted, neither did she tell him she had met Robert. It would be interesting to see if he put in an appearance later that afternoon.

James Trenchard, who lived at Eastmere, barely five miles away, was the first to arrive on horseback. He looked as though he had come straight off the fields. 'I hope this business won't take long,' he said, allowing Jolliffe to take his brown cloth overcoat and flat hat from him. But there was nothing to be done about his hard leather breeches, boots and gaiters, which bore signs of a recent excursion into the farmyard. Bella, greeting him, hoped it was only mud and not something worse. 'What's it all about, anyway? Old man's not ill, is he?'

'No, he is surprisingly well, except for his gout. Please, go into the drawing room. Jolliffe will serve you some refreshment while you wait.'

'Wait for what?'

'The others. The Comte, Sir Edward and Captain Huntley.'

'Oh, family conference, eh?'

'Something like that. Now, if you will excuse me…'

She escaped with relief. She would not be surprised if he were the first to fall in with her grandfather's wishes, perhaps the only one. Would she be obliged to accept him if he were? It had been two years since his wife had died and his two little daughters needed a mother. She felt sorry for them, but the idea of marrying him made her shudder. It wasn't that she had anything against farmers, especially when they worked as hard as James did, but he thought of nothing else.

He was utterly oblivious of his appearance and she

doubted if he had bathed in a twelvemonth. As for his house… It was a good enough house, old and solid, but as there was only a daily woman to keep it clean, it was in a sorry state. She would be expected to turn it round and take the girls in hand. There would be no love, no tenderness.

Bella went to the kitchen to see how Cook was getting on with dinner which would be served after the Earl had delivered his ultimatum, because ultimatum it was. She had a feeling it was going to be a miserable meal. By the time she returned to the drawing room, Edward had arrived.

He was standing by the window, looking out onto the garden, but turned when he heard her enter. He was not quite as tall as Robert, but he had the same dark good looks, except that his features were slightly heavier. He was dressed in a brown frock coat of impeccable cut and biscuit-coloured breeches tucked into tasselled Hessians, polished enough to be used as twin mirrors. His hair was cut in the Brutus style and his neckcloth tied to perfection. None of it was flamboyant, but was quietly elegant. 'Bella,' he said, bowing to her. 'I hope I see you well?'

'Very well, Edward,' she responded. Knowing what was to come, she felt very uncomfortable but did her best to hide it under the veneer of being a good hostess. 'Are your horses being looked after?'

'Yes, thank you. Took them round to the stables myself. James tells me we are all invited to this jamboree,' he said.

'Yes, I had thought you and the Captain might have travelled down together.'

'I did not know we had both been invited—the letter did not say and as Rob was in London when they both arrived, his was forwarded on to him. I doubt he will tear himself away from Society to come down here. I nearly did not come myself.'

'Then why did you?' He obviously did not know Robert was already in the neighbourhood.

'The letter was couched in terms that implied a certain urgency. I thought his lordship might be ill. James tells me he is not.'

She stopped herself from smiling; Edward had come to the same erroneous conclusion as Robert, that his lordship was dying, but he had not been so blunt in expressing it. 'He has the gout, but otherwise he is well.'

'Not touched in the attic either?' queried James, speaking for the first time. 'Old age sometimes puts people into strange humours. I remember when Sarah's mother was dying. Couldn't even remember where she lived at the end— used to roam all over the fens, talking to herself.'

'His lordship's mind is perfectly clear,' Bella said, wondering as she spoke if that might not be true.

'Where is he now?'

'Resting in his room until you all arrive.'

'Then we may wait an age,' Edward said. 'Louis has never been punctual for anything in his life and, as I said, I doubt Rob will come.'

They were interrupted by the sound of carriage wheels on the drive and Bella went to the window to see a magnificent equipage drawing up to the front door. The coach was brilliantly painted in red and green and had the arms of the de Courvilles emblazoned on the side. There were four horses, perfectly matched, and a postillion and a groom who jumped down with alacrity to open the coach door and hand out the occupants.

Bella gasped when she saw the Comtesse de Courville, dressed in a velvet carriage dress and a tall plumed hat, step down onto the gravel, followed by her ladyship's maid, her son's valet and, last of all, Louis himself. He was tall, as thin as a rake and dressed in green check pantaloons, yellow waistcoat and bright green coat with black velvet lapels. His collar points scratched his rouged cheeks and his cravat was a froth of exquisitely starched muslin.

'My God, will you look at that?' murmured Edward beside her. 'A dandy to out-dandy them all. I am surprised he can afford it.'

'I must go and greet them,' Bella said, wondering how they were going to accommodate everyone. She had never dreamed that her ladyship would come with her son and bring her maid, not to mention the coachman and postillion. She sincerely hoped Spooner, her grandfather's head groom, would be able to find places for the extra horses.

Bella arrived in the great hall just as her ladyship preceded her son into the house and an open-mouthed Jolliffe was moving forward to meet them. Behind them, the maid and valet were struggling with baggage enough to last a month.

'Your ladyship, this is an unexpected pleasure,' she said, aware that Louis had doffed his curly brimmed hat and was staring about him with pale blue eyes, as if summing up the value of everything he could see. 'Do come into the drawing room while I arrange for refreshment for you and for your rooms to be prepared. Did you have a pleasant journey?'

That was a mistake, she realised. 'No, we did not,' the Comtesse said. 'It was a great inconvenience. No time to pack properly, no time to arrange accommodation on the road and everyone most uncivil…'

'I am sorry to hear that,' Bella said, refraining from adding it was the lady's own fault—she had not been invited. Why she should have assumed that her presence was required, Bella did not know. What would her grandfather say? He had never dealt well with this particular niece.

Louis had completed his inspection and now turned his attention to Bella. He swept her an exaggerated bow and took her hand. 'Bella, your servant. Looking pretty as a picture, I see.'

Determined to make herself as unattractive as possible, she had chosen to wear a plain jaconet gown in an unbecoming grey, with a straight bodice and high neckline, lined with lace. Her skirt was full and stiff and hid her trim figure. Her hair was dressed simply and had no ornament. They would have to overcome an aversion to her looks before embarking on courtship. And it seemed that Louis was already learning to do this. Or else he was extremely short-sighted.

Bella led the way into the drawing room where the Comtesse stopped in the middle of another tirade against the ostlers at the last inn they had called at when she saw James and Edward. 'What are you two doing here?' she demanded.

'Sent for, same as you,' Edward said, bowing. 'How are you, Aunt?'

'Sent for?' she queried, not bothering to return his greeting. 'I did not know it was to be a party. Thought his lordship had asked for Louis to talk about his inheritance. Decided I'd best be here to hear it.'

'Mama, doing it a bit too brown,' Louis murmured, while he examined James from head to toe through his quizzing glass as if he were a prize animal at market. 'I say, coz, you could at the least have had a wash before presenting yourself. Insult to Mama and Miss Huntley, don't you know.'

'It's none of your business, sir. I earn my keep in honest toil and if our kinsman is so thoughtless as to give me no time to make other arrangements, then he must needs take me as he finds me.'

Bella thought it was time she intervened. 'Edward, if you are sure Robert is not going to come, I think I had better go and tell his lordship you are all assembled.'

She hurried from the room, glad to escape, though how her grandfather would react when he saw the Comtesse she did not dare to think. Nor what he would say when he realised Robert had not deigned to obey his summons. Perhaps she ought to tell him that she had seen Robert in Ely, but that would mean explaining what he had been doing there. But he had only been listening, as she had. It did not mean he was colluding with the dissidents, did it?

Chapter Two

Sylvester answered Bella's knock on the door of the Earl's apartments. 'Please, tell his lordship Mr Trenchard, the Comte de Courville and Sir Edward have arrived, but he does not think Captain Huntley will have received his invitation in time to obey.' She paused. 'And warn him the Comtesse is here, too.'

'Oh, is she?' came a bellow from an inner room. 'Well, I shall give her a right about, poking her nose in where it's not wanted.' He appeared at the door, dressed in a mulberry velvet jacket and matching breeches and clutching a walking stick. 'Take my arm, girl. Let's see what those young bloods are made of.'

'Do you need me?' she asked timidly. 'Could I not wait in my room?'

'No, you could not. Want to see their faces...'

'But I don't.'

'Yes, you do.'

To which there was no answer, and they made their slow and stately way down to the withdrawing room. Before entering, the Earl stood in the doorway and surveyed the company gathered there. Edward bowed slightly, James gave a curt nod and Louis flung out his arm in an extravagant gesture and bowed low. 'Your servant, my lord.'

The Earl grunted and, leaning heavily on Bella's arm, made his way over to a high-backed armchair and lowered himself into it. Then he turned to the Comtesse. 'What are you doing here? I do not recollect asking you to come.'

She dipped a curtsey. 'An oversight, I am sure, Uncle. How do you do?'

'Well enough. Not about to shuffle off, at any rate.'

'I should hope not!' she said with false brightness. 'But if you are about to settle your affairs, then I must tell you it is not before time.'

'What has it to do with you, madam?'

'Louis is your heir.'

'Is he? We shall see.'

'What do you mean by that? My goodness, if you mean to try and disinherit him, it is as well I decided to come, too.'

'You take too much upon yourself, madam. I wish you to leave us. Find something to amuse you while I talk to these reprobates.'

Elizabeth looked as though she were about to throw a fit, but then, realising he would not proceed while she stayed, flung her head up in disgust and sailed from the room. Bella, who was standing beside her grandfather's chair, bent and whispered, 'Should I go, too, Grandfather? She is truly upset and I could keep her company.'

'No, you will stay here. Sit on that stool.' He indicated a stool at his feet, then looked up at the three young men. 'Sit down, you will give me a crick in the neck from peering up at you.' And as they obeyed he added, 'Edward, where is that cork-brained brother of yours?'

'He was in Town when your letters arrived, my lord. I forwarded his, but he may not have received it in time to make arrangements to be here.'

'More likely demonstrating his independence.' He gave a grunt of amusement. 'And he the least independent of the lot of you.'

'He may yet come,' Bella ventured, wondering where Robert was. She would not put it past him to keep them waiting on purpose, doing as her grandfather had suggested and asserting his independence. Or proving to her he would not be coerced by anything she had said. She wouldn't put it beyond him to invite those argumentative labourers to join him in a glass of something at one of the many inns in Ely. 'We could wait a little longer.'

'I am not in the habit of waiting on ill-mannered jack-at-warts.'

'My lord,' Edward protested. 'There is nothing wrong with my brother's manners.'

'Well, we shall proceed without him.' He paused to look round at them, smiling slightly. 'What a gaggle of fine geese you are, to be sure. But you are all I have, bar Bella. You don't deserve her, not any of you, and if I had any choice I would not let her within a mile of you.' He sighed heavily. 'But my mind's made up. One of you shall have her.'

Bella, who had been sitting looking at her feet, risked a glance at them. She was confronted by three open mouths, though no sound issued from any of them. They had obviously been struck dumb.

'Well?' the old man said. 'Haven't you anything to say for yourselves?'

'What would you have us say?' Edward was the first to recover. 'Miss Huntley is a dear child. I am very fond of her but—'

'That, at least, is a start. But are you so blind that you cannot see what is before your eyes? She is no longer a child. While you have been sowing your wild oats, she has become a marriageable woman.'

Edward turned to Bella, smiling to soften what appeared

be a rejection of her. 'I beg your pardon, Bella, I meant no offence. You are beautiful and a man would have to be blind not to see that, but—'

'But you do not like being coerced,' she put in quickly, so that he might know it was not her idea. 'And neither do I. Please, do not consider it.'

'Then what is the point of this meeting?'

'I'll tell you, shall I?' the old man said. 'Isabella cannot have the management of a fortune, though I have no doubt she would make a better job of it than you, Louis.' He looked at the young man's extravagant clothes. 'Your tailor's bill alone would bankrupt the estate. I could appoint trustees until she married but I ain't keen on the idea. I want to see her married before I hand in my accounts.'

'Very laudable,' Louis said. 'But I shall choose my own wife.'

'Indeed, I hope you may,' Bella said, very near to tears, not at being rejected but at the humiliation of it all.

'Bella, please, do not cry,' Edward said. 'There is plenty of time for you to make a good match whatever the old greybeard says.'

'And I could rule you out for such impertinence.'

'I have already ruled myself out, sir, but you forget my brother is not here to speak for himself.'

'Who is to blame for that? I have told Bella she shall have her choice, but if she is sighing after that ne'er-do-well, she must find a way of bringing him to the mark.'

'Grandpapa, I am not sighing after him. I am not sighing after anyone and I wish you would not speak of me as if I were not in the room. I might as well go and bear the Comesse company.' It was unlike her to be so bold but she was being driven beyond endurance.

'Then it must be one of the others,' he said, ignoring her.

'I am your heir,' Louis said. 'But that does not mean you may dictate…'

The old man smiled. 'You are sure of that, are you?'

'No, of course he is not,' Edward said. 'The estate is entailed and must be handed down through the male line. And that means through Papa.'

'Is that so?' The old man seemed to be enjoying teasing them, although his tone was crotchety, as if he would quickly lose patience with them. 'You are very quick to lay your claim, but I have not heard you offer for Isabella.'

James, who had been listening to this exchange with a bemused look on his face, suddenly came to life and looked from Bella to the Earl. 'Are you saying that whoever marries Bella will inherit?'

'Yes, but he must make a push. I said there was no time to lose and I meant it.'

'You do not mean to say you have broken the entail?' Edward said, shocked to the core. 'You can't have done. The only people to gain by such a procedure are the lawyers. You'd be left without a feather to fly with.'

'And you are grasping at straws,' his lordship said.

'I don't believe it,' Louis said. 'The old man is trying to gammon one of us into marrying the chit.'

'I spoke first,' James put in. 'Miss Huntley, may I crave a moment alone with you?'

Everyone turned to look at the overweight farmer in his filthy clothes. He was not in the habit of making decisions in a hurry, but he knew that to be first in with his offer would be a distinct advantage.

'Oh, Bella,' Edward said, as Bella looked from one to the other, dismay written all over her face. 'You do not have to accept him, whatever his lordship says.'

Louis, who had been silently watching her through his quizzing glass for some time, let it drop to dangle on its ribbon from his wrist and turned to James. 'You do not, for a minute, suppose Miss Huntley will receive you looking like that,' he said. 'Or smelling like you do. Go home and bath and change.'

'While you insert yourself in my place.'

Louis laughed in a high-pitched, effeminate way. 'Lah, that is the last thing I would do. Insert myself anywhere you had been, I mean.' He fetched a lace handkerchief from his pocket and waved it before his nose. 'My lord, pray send him on his way.'

'Bella?' The Earl appealed to her. 'Do you want me to send him away?'

Before she could answer, they heard a commotion in the hall and Jolliffe's voice protesting loudly and another, even angrier, saying, 'I am come to speak to Mr Trenchard and speak to him I will.'

'Go and see what is happening,' the Earl instructed Bella. 'Tell Jolliffe to send whoever it is on his way. I will not have brawls in my house.'

Bella, thankful for the interruption, hurried to obey. A man of middling years in the working clothes of a labourer was standing in the hall, wringing his cap in his hands.

'What is it, Jolliffe?'

'He wants to speak to Mr Trenchard,' the butler said in aggrieved tones. 'I told him you were all about to go in to dinner…'

'And lucky you are to have a dinner to go to,' the man said, stung to anger. 'You don't think I wanted to come here, do you? It won't serve me well when they hear of it.'

'Who?' asked Bella.

'The Eastmere men, miss. They're all over the place. They said they'd pull the barn down and wreck the house if Mr Trenchard don't come and give them money.'

James had followed Bella into the hall. 'What is it, man? Can I not leave you five minutes but you must come running after me?'

'Mr Trenchard, sir, the men are rioting and they came to

the farm. They want money. Fifty pounds they said on account of low wages and the price of bread.'

'I wish I had fifty pounds to give them,' James said morosely. 'Tell them to go to the parish overseer—he is the one they should be applying to.' Since the parish had adopted the Speenhamland system, the shortfall on wages had been paid by the poor rates, a far from ideal situation which meant that the farmers had no incentive to pay a realistic wage and their men were forced to go cap in hand to charity. They salvaged their pride by calling it an allowance which they should have as of right.

'Sir, you must come, or they will burn the house down.'

'Faith and Constance?' he queried in alarm. 'Where are they? Are they safe?'

'Mrs Clarke is looking after them but she is afraid for her life…'

'James, you must go at once,' Bella said, appalled. Was this what the meeting in Ely had been about? The mob must have stopped talking in favour of action. But why pick on James? Where was Robert? Did he know about it? 'I am sure the Earl will excuse you.'

'Yes, I must.' Then to his foreman, 'I'll ride on. Follow as fast as you can, I might need you.' He was halfway to the door when he stopped and turned back to Bella. 'Miss Huntley, I beg leave to return to settle the matter we were discussing.'

She nodded without answering, wondering if she could have done anything to stop the trouble with the labourers. Perhaps she should have warned James about them, but her mind had been too full of the coming meeting with her cousins to connect a crowd of men in Ely with her cousin and his farm. She returned to the drawing room to acquaint the Earl with what had happened. He seemed not to be concerned for James's safety. To him it was inconceivable that a handful of unruly labourers could not be controlled.

'Can't think what the justices are playing at,' he said. 'I knew this would happen when they gave in to the mob in Suffolk last year. Now they are all at it. They should send for the militia to round them up—a spell in prison would soon bring them to a proper sense of their place.'

'Grandfather, they are starving and driven beyond endurance,' Bella said.

'What is that to the point? A few discontented labourers will not make me change my mind.' The Earl was more concerned with his own little drama than the greater one being played out in the villages and fields of East Anglia. 'And you would do well to consider your own position. You can assume you have had one offer, at least.'

James, she knew, was desperately pinched in the pocket in spite of his grandfather's small annuity, and if the mob destroyed his barn, it might well ruin him. She felt sorry for him, but she could not marry him. She could not. 'My lord, please, do not make me take James.'

'I am not going to make you, child. I should be unhappy if you had been too quick to say yes. He is not the only one.'

She was mystified. He knew whom he wanted to offer for her and yet he would not say. She looked at the other two men. Edward looked furious and Louis was smiling mockingly. What were they thinking?

Before anyone could give utterance to their thoughts, Jolliffe appeared again. 'My Lord, Cook asks if you wish to keep dinner back.'

'Oh, no,' Bella said. 'It will spoil if we do. Grandpapa, please, let us postpone this discussion.'

'Very well. We cannot continue until James returns. Tell Cook we are going to the dining room now. And send Sylvester to tell the Comtesse.' He allowed Edward to help him to his feet and then escorted Bella out of the room, across the vast hall to the formal dining room. It was a very big room and struck them as cold as they entered it. Bella shivered. She had wanted to dine in one of the smaller rooms, but her grandfather had overruled her. 'I am going to show those upstarts how an earl entertains,' he had said. 'One of them will have to become used to it.'

The Comtesse joined them as they seated themselves at the long refectory table, with the Earl at its head and Bella at the opposite end. Elizabeth took her place on his lordship's left. 'This place is as cold as a tomb,' she said, looking at the dismal fire. 'And just about as cheerful.'

'I am sorry, my lady,' Bella said. 'We do not often use this room and it is the first fire we have lit in here this year. I fear the chimney needs sweeping. I will see to it first thing tomorrow.'

'Uncle, you need a proper housekeeper,' Elizabeth said. 'Isabella is far too young for such a responsibility.'

'I think Bella does very well,' Edward said. 'I do not doubt that his lordship allowed her no time to prepare for such an unexpected influx of visitors.'

'That would account for the state of my room,' Elizabeth said, watching as Daisy, in a new dress and apron and shaking with nerves, brought in the first course with the help of a temporary footman from the village. 'It is thick with dust and the fire is so feeble it is no better than a peasant's.'

Bella did not think the Comtesse had any idea of what a peasant's fire was like, or that the poor man would not think of lighting one in a bedroom.

'Your own fault,' the Earl put in. 'We do not keep rooms ready against unexpected guests. It would be a criminal waste in these hard times. I suggest you change apartments with your son, whose rooms were prepared.'

'Of course, Mama,' Louis said, anxious not to quarrel with his great uncle. 'I'll have my things moved out as soon as we have finished our meal.'

Slightly mollified, Elizabeth turned to Bella. 'Where is

Miss Battersby? I would have expected her to have come forward to make me welcome if you were too busy, attending to everyone else's needs.'

'She is visiting her sick sister in Downham Market. I expect her back at any time,' Bella explained.

Elizabeth was shocked. 'My lord, surely you are not keeping a young unmarried girl here without companion or chaperone? There will be the most prodigious scandal if it gets abroad.'

'Fustian!' he said. 'I am her grandfather and this is her home. Always will be…'

'As to that, I am sure Louis is not such a pinchpenny as to deny her a home when he comes into his own, but it will hardly be proper for her to stay here while he is unmarried.'

'You presume too much, madam,' the Earl said, favouring her with a glacial look.

'Oh, Mama,' Louis put in. 'His lordship is determined on Miss Huntley bringing forth an heir before he dies.'

'What is that to the point?'

The Earl sighed. 'Tell her, Louis.'

'His lordship is determined on marrying her to one of us,' Louis told his mother, his usually pale complexion suffused with colour. 'It is to be a condition of inheriting.'

'You mean he is trying to force you to marry Isabella?' She looked at the girl as she spoke and her expression told clearly what she thought of that idea.

'Or Edward. Or James. Or Robert,' he said morosely. 'Her child will take precedence.'

'He can't do it,' she said. 'She is a female and the estate is entailed.'

'Would you like to put it to the test?' his lordship said.

'I own Edward might think he had a claim,' Elizabeth conceded, 'though he would be in error, but the other two…' It was past belief and her voice rose as she appealed to her uncle. 'I cannot conceive that you would ever consider them. One is a clodhopper and the other a scapegrace.'

'I said Bella may have her choice and I shall hold to that,' he said. 'James has already indicated his intention to offer for her.'

'You will never let her go to the muckraker? My goodness, you must be touched in the attic even to think it. James Trenchard in this house!' She laughed loudly, though her laughter was a little forced. 'Can you imagine it? He would keep pigs in the drawing room and chickens in the hall. I should hope Isabella has more sense than to consider such an offer. And as for you, Edward, you are already engaged to Miss Charlotte Mellish.'

'Not precisely,' he said laconically.

'How so, not precisely? Either you are or you are not, and I have it on good authority it wants but the announcement in *The Gazette*. You will be the worst kind of rakeshame if you renege on it and deserve to be cut dead.'

'For your information, ma'am, I have not yet made a formal offer and may be rejected.'

'Oh, so you mean to make yourself so disagreeable to Miss Mellish that she will have no hesitation but to end the affair. Very clever.' She turned to Bella. 'You would be making a fatal mistake if you were to take him on those terms, my dear…'

'I have not said I will have any of them,' Bella said in an anguished voice. 'I cannot think that all this quarrelling and argument can result in happiness for any of us. Grandfather, please, tell everyone you have been hoaxing them.'

'I shall tell them no such thing.' He turned to the footman who had brought in the second remove and signalled him to serve it. 'Now let us finish our meal in peace.'

The Comtesse opened her mouth to speak again but changed her mind and began eating her fish course with studied concentration. Bella knew she would have more to say as soon as the meal was over and she dreaded it.

She looked up and saw Edward smiling at her. She was not sure whether he was laughing at her or sympathising with her. Did he really mean to turn his back on Miss Mellish and make her an offer for the sake of the inheritance? What would it be like, being married to him under those conditions, knowing she was second best? It would hardly be propitious for a happy marriage. And would he be faithful to her? How long before he neglected her and sought the arms of Charlotte?

The interminable meal dragged on, as course after course was placed before them, picked at and taken away. The ladies remained silent, but Louis became increasingly foxed on his lordship's wine and even Edward seemed to have lost some of his haughtiness by the time they reached the fruit course. They seemed to have forgotten, or were ignoring, the reason they were there and spoke of every subject under the sun except the one uppermost in their thoughts. It was like a cat and mouse game. Bella was counting the minutes to her escape when Jolliffe came to tell his lordship that Captain Huntley had arrived.

'Then he may go hungry,' his lordship said. 'We have nearly finished. Put him in the drawing room to wait for us there.'

'My lord, he is…' Jolliffe paused. 'He is somewhat dishevelled. I believe he has met with an accident.'

Bella gasped and even Elizabeth looked startled. Edward put down his cutlery and rose. 'Is he hurt? Where is he?'

Robert himself appeared in the doorway behind Jolliffe. His beautiful cloth coat was torn and muddied, his cravat askew and he had lost his hat. What was worse, he had a bad cut over one eye which was encrusted with dried blood and a great purple bruise below it. He bowed to Elizabeth at the same time as he managed a quirky smile for Bella, who would have rushed forward to help him if the look he gave her had not halted her in her tracks. It warned her to be silent and not invite her grandfather's close questioning. 'A thousand apologies, ladies. I will take my leave until I am more presentable. Excuse me, my lord.' To Edward he said, 'Help me to my room, Teddy. Need a bath.' He limped out of the room on the arm of his brother.

'Well!' Elizabeth exclaimed. 'Been brawling like a prize-fighter and dares to show his face in the dining room. What is the world coming to? No manners any more, no respect. Is it any wonder the lower classes defy their betters when they have no good example to live by.'

'I am sure Robert has not been brawling,' Bella said, wondering just what had happened. 'No doubt he will en-lighten us when he is feeling more the thing.'

'Then let us retire to the drawing room, you and I,' the Comtesse went on. 'We shall have a comfortable coze, while his lordship and Louis talk business.' And with that she took Bella's arm in a very firm grip, curtsied to the Earl without relaxing it and almost dragged the girl to the draw-ing room.

'Now,' she said when they were seated and the teatray had been brought in, 'tell me what has brought on this cu-rious humour in my uncle. Have you noticed him behaving strangely lately? Not quite himself, eh?'

'He has been perfectly at ease with himself, except for his gout. It troubles him a great deal but he will not take the doctor's advice and refrain from drinking. He says gout has nothing to do with the claret and burgundy he consumes, but is caused by the wet weather we have been having. And he may be right. It has been the wettest spring anyone can remember and many of the fields are inundated, which does not make the labourers' plight any easier. Farmers like James are in sad straits themselves and cannot pay their men who have to apply to the parish…'

'Are you being purposely obtuse, Isabella? I care not a fig for the farmers, so long as they pay their rents on time. I am talking about this insane notion to marry you off for a legacy. I do believe old Hanson has put the old man up to it.'

Mr George Hanson was the Earl's legal man. 'Why should he do that?'

'To try and disinherit Louis. He has never looked on my son with any favour. He sees him as a Frenchman and therefore to be viewed with suspicion, which is very hard on my poor boy who has spent almost his entire life in England and renounced his lands in France.'

'Renounced them?' Bella queried, dragging her mind from what was happening upstairs to pay attention. 'I thought they had been taken from him by the Revolutionaries.'

'They were, but there are moves afoot to restore them. They will be ruined and worthless by now, of course, and I do not wish to go back.' She shuddered. 'And if we are not careful the contagion will spread and we shall have revolution here, on our doorstep.'

'Oh, no, surely not?'

'I saw evidence on our journey here—ricks burned, barns pulled down and posters pinned to empty shops. ''Bread or blood,'' they say. It is how it started in France. We need steadfast people like Louis at the helm to prevent it. That is why it is so important his legacy should not be put up to auction.'

Bella would not have described Louis as steadfast, but she let that go. She smiled crookedly. 'Is the notion of your son being married to me so distasteful, my lady?'

'Oh, you are a pleasant enough chit but, tell me, what have you to recommend you to a man of the world like Louis? Tucked away in the country, the companion of an old man who has forgotten what it is like to be in Society, how can you possibly know how to go on? Louis needs someone from the *ton*, someone with presence, not a timid little mouse. The court is full of beautiful women and Co-lette has the ear of the Regent, who will advise us.'

It was not only the Regent's ear Elizabeth's daughter had, Bella thought irreverently. By all accounts she had been possessed of other parts of his anatomy on occasion. And Louis must be a poor apology for a man to allow his mother and sister to choose his bride for him. 'I would not dream of coming between Louis and his aspirations at court,' she said.

'Good. Then we are agreed. You will refute this strange idea of the Earl's and not choose any of them. I can promise you, on Louis's behalf, that you will not be let starve.'

Bella supposed she was meant to be grateful for that, but before she could find a suitable reply his lordship and Louis had come into the room and she was obliged to busy herself, pouring tea for them. It was only when no one spoke that she realised both men looked furious. Louis was decidedly pink about the ears and the Earl's face was almost purple. Bella was afraid he was going to have a fit of apoplexy.

'Grandpapa, I do believe you have overtaxed yourself,' she said. 'Should you not go and lie down for a while?'

'I will go when I am ready. Where are Edward and Robert?'

'They have not come down again.'

He rang the bell furiously and sent the footman scurrying upstairs to summon the two young men. When they appeared, Robert had bathed and changed his clothes and was wearing a green frockcoat, pale brown pantaloons and tasselled Hessians, with a fresh shirt and a new cravat, though there was no disguising the injury to his face.

'Well, what have you to say for yourself?' his lordship asked when the young man had made his apologies for his earlier appearance.

'I was on my way here when I was set upon by a mob,' he said, seating himself and taking a cup of tea from Bella, who found her hand shaking so much the cup rattled in the saucer. 'They were the equal of any bloodthirsty French soldiers I met on the battlefield. And I had no weapon, not that a gun would have availed me, there were too many of them. They pulled me from my horse and demanded my money.'

'Where was this?' Bella asked.

He turned to look at her, surveying her slowly, taking in the homely grey dress and heightened colour and deciding that her obvious effort to appear unattractive had had the opposite effect. She was lovely. 'At the crossroads between here and Eastmere. They were marching and filling the whole road. I could not avoid them.'

'I should hope you did not give in to them,' Elizabeth said.

'I would not be sitting here if I had not, but I did not submit without a protest, which is why one hothead dealt me a blow with the club he carried.'

'Rabble,' the Comtesse said. 'Call out the militia. Hang the lot of them or we shall end up with our heads in a basket, just as it happened in France.'

'Oh, I do not think so,' Robert said mildly. 'The cases are very different. These are simple men driven to excess. When I expressed my sympathy with them, they took the money I proffered and bade me proceed very civilly. They did not take other valuables, or my luggage, which is a blessing or I would have had nothing to wear but what I stood up in.'

'Did you see Mr Trenchard?' Bella asked.

'No, should I have?'

'He was sent for to go home. His servant said the labourers were threatening to pull his barn down and wreck his house.'

'No, I did not see him. But he is not the only one to suffer—the mob I saw had been on the rampage for some time, most of 'em pot valiant. It will take the militia to make them return to their homes.'

'Oh, dear, I hope there will no blood shed,' she said. 'The poor have been sorely tried, what with the price of flour and bread rising so high and wages so low.'

'Your sympathy does you credit, Bella,' Edward said. 'But it does not give them the right to take the law into their own hands. Destroying the property of those they depend on will not serve.'

'Did you demand their names?' the Earl asked Robert. 'I can send for the constable to have them taken up and charged.'

'No, I did not. It is unlikely they would have furnished them if I had.' He put down his cup and stood up. 'Now, if you will excuse me, I am devilish hungry and as Edward has been so obliging as to replace the contents of my purse, I will repair to the local hostelry and bespeak me a meal.'

'Oh, dear, how thoughtless of me,' Bella said. 'Robert, please, be seated again and I will ask Cook to find something for you...'

'No need, my dear, no need at all. I shall do very well at the tavern.'

'But do you not wish to know why his lordship has called us all together?' Louis asked.

'Oh, as to that, Edward has acquainted me with the facts of the matter. I am sorry to say it, but I think the whole thing is a fudge and I wish I had saved myself the expense of the journey to hear it. I might still be in possession of my purse. And this...' He pointed to his eye. 'This might be its proper size and colour.'

Bella was delighted by his answer and found herself smiling. He swept her an elegant leg and then moved forward to take her hand and raise it to his lips. His brown eyes, looking into hers above the hand he held, were full of merriment. She was glad someone could find humour in the situation. 'My apologies, dear Bella. I do not mean to disparage you, but you must see that any marriage based on coercion will not serve. Besides, however much I might wish to, I cannot enter a contest against my brother. He has a right, I do not.'

'Right!' Louis exploded furiously. 'If anyone has a right—'

'Oh, please, do not quarrel,' Bella intervened. 'I cannot bear it. Grandpapa, please say something…'

He simply smiled and rang for Sylvester to help him to his room. As soon as he had gone Elizabeth bade Louis follow her upstairs to see if the servants had obeyed their instructions to change their rooms and, no doubt, to talk about what they would do next, leaving Bella facing Edward and Robert. She looked from one to the other in despair.

'I am so sorry,' she said. 'This is none of my doing. I cannot think what has got into Grandfather…'

'Touched in the attic,' Robert said. 'Must be. Not fair on you, not fair at all. Edward thinks so, too, don't you, Teddy?'

Thus appealed to, his brother agreed wholeheartedly. 'If he is thinking of your future, as he says he is, then he could easily secure that with an annuity or a good dowry.'

'But don't you see?' she cried. 'My dowry is to be Westmere.'

'I am not sure he can legally do it,' Edward said.

'Oh, how I wish Papa were still alive,' she said. 'There would be no argument and none of this would be happening.'

'If it is any comfort, you have our support,' Robert said. 'I promise you neither of us will offer for you.'

It was all too much and she fled to her room, where she flung herself across the bed and sobbed. How could her grandfather be so cruel? How could Robert think it would give her comfort to know that he would not offer for her? He still saw her as the young cousin he had sometimes condescended to amuse as a child, the little girl he had taught to ride and fish when he had visited Westmere on his summer vacation from Cambridge. But as her grandfather had pointed out, she had gown up and was now at a marriageable age. Oh, how she wished Miss Battersby would come home. She needed her.

Ellen Battersby was a little dotty, given to romantic notions and great sighings over the novels she read, and would insist on using their characters as examples of how to behave or not to behave. Bella humoured her, which was more than the Earl did. He was often so outspoken as to be rude to her and consequently the poor woman avoided his presence as much as possible. Perhaps that was why she had stayed away so long. But Bella needed her.

If Miss Battersby could not come home, then she would go to her and seek her out. It was only a short ride to Downham Market, and if no other remedy for her troubles presented itself, then she would stay away, find a way to earn her own living. She rose and changed into her riding habit. She did not want to meet any others of the household for they would surely want to know where she was going, so she carried her boots in her hand and crept along the upper gallery towards the back stairs.

It was gloomy and smelled damp in this unused part of the house, and she shivered a little, as if the ghosts of previous Huntleys were following her progress. She was glad when she found the small door at the back of the oldest part of the building and slipped out into the fresh air.

Bella stopped to put on her boots, gathered up her skirts in her hand and sped to the stables. The stable boys were all busy elsewhere and the head groom was, no doubt, sleeping off his dinner in the room above. She spoke quietly to

Misty to stop her snickering while she saddled her, then she led the mare out and, mounting from the block by the stable door, rode down the drive and out onto the road, where she turned towards Downham Market.

Absorbed by her own problems she had not given a thought to the riots or whether she might be riding into danger, but it became apparent the minute she entered the small hamlet of Eastmere, which was on the road to Downham Market. A crowd of angry men and women were marching down the street, carrying pitchforks and clubs. Two of them held a banner. 'Bread or blood,' it said in crude black letters.

She reined in and pulled Misty to one side to allow them to pass, but there were so many and they were so angry. They pushed and shoved and frightened the mare so much she snorted and pranced and was in danger of injuring those nearest to her. Her rider hauled hard on the reins but the horse, objecting to this unaccustomed harsh treatment, reared up so violently that Bella was thrown down among the trampling feet.

The first person she saw when she opened her eyes was Robert. He was kneeling beside her and she had her head in his lap. 'Thank the good Lord,' he said. 'I thought you were done for…'

'Misty threw me…'

'I know, it was lucky I saw it happen, though I could hardly believe my eyes. After what happened this morning, how could you be such a ninny as to ride out alone?'

'I am not a ninny.' Her hat had fallen off and her hair had come down. She was acutely conscious of the picture she must present and struggled to sit up but, overcome by dizziness, she collapsed back into his arms.

He looked down at her, torn between scolding her and comforting her. 'Are you hurt? Any bones broken?'

It was strange how warm and comforting his arms were

and how safe she felt, even though the tumult still raged about them and they were in grave danger of being trampled underfoot. 'No, I do not think so. My head aches.'

Robert put his hand gently behind her head. 'I am not surprised. There is a bump the size of an egg here and it's bleeding.' He looked about him, wondering how to get her safely away. The furious fenmen were out of control and he did not think it would serve to appeal to their better nature, especially if they recognised him. The encounter he had had with them earlier that day had been enough to convince him they meant business.

There was an inn across the road which had only minutes before been swarming with rioters but, having drunk it dry, they had now moved on. It was hardly the place to take a delicately nurtured young lady, but there was no help for it. He scrambled to his feet and retrieved her hat, which he put it into her hands, before stooping and picking her up in his arms as easily as if she were a child. Kicking the door of the inn open, he carried her inside and sat her on a settle, seating himself beside her. 'Better rest here until the furore has died down.'

It was a dingy, low-ceilinged room, its paintwork blackened by smoke and with an all-pervading smell of stale beer, which caught in her nostrils and made her choke. No one came to serve them, which was not at all surprising, but a young lad of eleven or twelve stood in the doorway of the back room, staring at them with curiosity. 'Sixpence if you catch the grey horse and bring it here,' Robert said. 'And another for bringing the black stallion you will find tethered in the yard of The King's Head.' The boy disappeared with alacrity.

'He might bring the rioters back with him,' Bella murmured.

'No, they are too intent on what they are doing.' He left her and returned with a glass of water. Sitting beside her, he helped her drink it. Then he took the glass away and fetched a bowl of water. 'I couldn't find a clean cloth,' he said, taking a linen handkerchief from his coat pocket and dipping it in the bowl. 'Let me see how bad that injury is.'

Robert's fingers were very gentle as he washed the blood from her hair and the back of her head. 'It's not as severe as I first thought,' he said, moving his hand from the back of her head and stroking her cheek with his forefinger. 'My poor Bella, you are as pale as a ghost.'

She tried not to think of what his gentle touch was doing to her, making her go hot and cold all over. Or was it the shock of being thrown from her horse? How fortunate it was that he had been on hand or she would have been trampled to death. 'I am only a little shaken,' she said. 'I shall be right as ninepence by and by, thank you.'

'My pleasure.' He was smiling, which made the purple swelling below his eye more pronounced. She wondered if it hurt him as much as her head hurt her. She supposed it did, though he gave no indication of it.

'Robert, what are you doing here?'

'Looking after you.'

'No, I do not mean that. I meant in Eastmere.'

'I came to see if I could be of any use to James. They were talking about him in The King's Head where I had my dinner. It seems they think he is the most likely to hand over money without putting up too much resistance on account of his children.'

'Do you think he is in danger?'

'Hard to tell, but he would be well advised to give them what they want.'

'Or they will give him a taste of what they gave you.'

He smiled ruefully, touching his bruised cheek. 'Something like that.'

'Did it happen in Ely, after I left?'

'Ely, Eastmere, what's the difference?' he said enigmatically. It would not help the situation if she felt she ought to be grateful to him. Gratitude was not what he wanted. 'The whole countryside is in ferment.'

'You don't think the Comtesse is right, do you? About revolution, I mean.'

'No, I do not. But as soon as I have seen you safely home, I will go and see James. I might be able to help.'

'I am not going home.'

'No? Where were you going?'

'I was on my way to Downham Market to find Miss Battersby.'

'Old Batters? Why?'

'I need her advice.'

'Oh, I see.' He knew what she meant and questioned whether the elderly servant would offer wise counsel, but he did not say so. He grinned impishly. 'Riding into a riot and being knocked senseless was preferable to choosing a husband, is that it?'

'It is no laughing matter.'

'The riot or choosing a husband?'

'Both.' Bella paused, wishing she did not feel so dizzy. 'I don't know what to do about it. Grandfather is not at all well, and if I defy him he might have a seizure. I am very fond of him…'

'Of course you are, my dear, but he has been excessively unkind to you. While other young ladies of your age are being taken to Town for a Season, going to balls and soirées and picnics, you are stuck in the country with an old skinflint who thinks more of preserving his lands and estate than the sensibilities of his granddaughter.'

'He is not a skinflint,' she said, staunchly defending the Earl. 'It is just that he is getting old and plagued by gout, which makes him crotchety. And he is worried about what will become of me when…' She could not bring herself to end the sentence.

'Loyal as always, my dear. I would not blame you if you damned the lot of us.'

'It is not your fault.'

'No, nor Edward's either. Fond of old Teddy, aren't you?'

She looked up at him, startled by his tone. 'Yes, of course, but I am fond of you, too…'

'Nice of you to say so,' Robert said laconically as the sounds of rioting faded. It was now uncannily quiet and he assumed the men had moved on. Soon it would be safe to leave and he would have to take Bella home. It would be the end of their delightful tête-à-tête. 'But I am persuaded there is a difference. He is the rightful heir and I do believe his lordship is being perverse just to amuse himself.'

'I do not find it amusing.'

'No, of course you don't. But stands to reason that he expects you to choose Edward. There is no alternative.'

'Edward is engaged.'

'No, he has not yet offered.'

'You do not mean he would repudiate it? Oh, Robert, I cannot believe that of him—he is an honourable man.'

'A title and great wealth are powerful arguments. I am glad I do not have to make the choice.'

She said nothing for a minute while she thought about what he had said, which only served to convince him he had been right—it was only Edward's previous attachment which was holding her back. 'You should think of yourself sometimes, you know,' he went on. 'Why don't you ask his lordship to give you a Season in Town, see you launched properly? You might meet someone else more to your liking. Someone eligible.'

'Oh, that would be wonderful. But how could I go? There is no one to bring me out.'

'Mama would do it,' he said. 'She is taking a house in Town for the Season.'

'Grandfather would not let me go. He will not let me go anywhere until I have said which one of you I will marry.'

'Then we are at a stand.'

Her head was clearing rapidly and she was suddenly possessed of an idea which was so audacious and yet so simple that she wondered why she had not thought of it before. 'There is something you could do for me,' she said slowly.

'Anything, my dear Bella. Anything in my power.'

'If Grandfather could be convinced I had made my choice, he would drop the subject.'

'Naturally he would.'

'Then, please, offer for me.'

'Me?' He could not believe his ears.

'Oh, do not look so shocked. I do not mean it to be a real engagement, but if we could only pretend…'

He was puzzled and intrigued, too. 'And what purpose would that serve?'

'What I need is time and it would give me that and…and a little freedom to be myself for a few weeks. If we told his lordship we had come to an understanding, he would agree to let me pay a visit to your mama, wouldn't he? If Cousin Henrietta would be so kind as to invite me. I truly cannot think properly while I am at Westmere. Being away might help.'

'Bella, I do believe that knock on your head has addled your brains. Have you thought about how you will bring it to an end, even if I should agree? I'm not the sort to make and break engagements, you know. It's just not the done thing. The whole *ton* will cut me dead as soon as it is known. I will not be received in any respectable hostess's drawing room. And Lord Westmere will be furious, not to mention Edward.'

'Why should he mind?'

'Bella, think about it. He knows he should be the heir and we both agreed we would not play his lordship's game.'

'Please, Robert. We do not need to make a public announcement of our engagement, then your pride will not be
hurt when it comes to an end.'

'Then what is the point of it?'

'To satisfy Grandfather.'

'To gull him, you mean.'

'There is no one else I can ask. James would certainly
not take me to London. He wants a housekeeper and mother
for his girls, nothing more. And if I went to London on the
arm of Louis…'

'Yes, I see your point,' he said, smiling a little. 'Be taken
for one of his ladybirds, I shouldn't wonder. Not the thing,
not the thing at all.'

'Then you will do it?'

'Bella you are a dear girl but…' He paused. The temp-
tation to gamble with his own happiness was there, but he
could not take it. He was sure the Earl meant Bella to marry
Edward and that was only right and proper. Edward could
give her so much more than he could and ensure that she
remained at her beloved Westmere. It was simply the Earl's
way of bringing the two together. He would not consider
Miss Mellish an obstacle. 'Do you think you can ride now?'

She felt immeasurably saddened. For one brief moment
she thought she had seen a way out, but he was right—it
was a hare-brained scheme. 'Yes, I think so.'

'I will go and see if that boy has brought our horses.' He
took his arm from about her shoulders and left her to her
muddled thoughts. And they were muddled. How could she
have made such an outrageous suggestion? It had put Robert
in an invidious position, and after he had been so kind to
her, too. He was right, of course, it would not answer. But
why could she not let it go? Why did she long to get away,
to have a little enjoyment?

She stood up and wandered round the room. At the window she stopped and looked out. The street was quiet; there

was no one in sight except Robert and the boy, who was leading Misty and the black stallion towards the inn. Robert was lucky it had not been stolen, she thought as she watched him give the boy a coin and take the horses from him. She went to the door as he approached. She was suddenly aware of how tall and muscular he was, how ruggedly handsome with his tanned face and laughing brown eyes. It unnerved her.

'Is the riot over?' she asked.

'The boy says they're all in the market-place, listening to the magistrates, but if they don't get what they want they'll be up in arms again, you can be sure. The sooner you are on your way home the better.'

'But Miss Battersby and James…'

'I will go and see how they are after I have seen you safely back at Westmere,' he said, helping her to mount.

'Thank you, Robert, but I do not need an escort,' she said more sharply than she intended, though she was more angry with herself than with him. How could she have been so forward as to ask him to offer for her? It was enough to give him a complete aversion to her. 'It is more important for you to find out what has happened. Fetch Ellen home. Bring her sister, too, if she wishes to come.'

'Nevertheless, I insist. There is no knowing what you will meet up with on the way.'

'Fustian! I have been riding these roads all my life.'

But it was only a token protest and they rode side by side in silence until they reached the outskirts of Westmere village. Here, the northernmost wall of the estate ran alongside the road. 'I am almost home now, Captain,' she said, stopping at a small gate. 'I can take a short cut through the wood. Thank you for your timely rescue.'

It was a definite dismissal and Robert thought about arguing but changed his mind. Bella was an excellent rider and he was confident that she would come to no harm on

Huntley land. Besides, he did not fancy going back to the leaden atmosphere of Westmere Hall and her silent reproaches because he had not seen fit to accede to her wishes. Secret engagement, indeed!

He dismounted and opened the gate for her to ride through. She smiled and bowed slightly from the waist as she passed him. He had no hat to remove but, instead, doffed an imaginary one, making her laugh. He watched until she was out of sight among the trees, then shut the gate and remounted. He did not think Ellen Battersby would leave her sister, but he would try to persuade her for Bella's sake. And there was James, who might need his help. Suddenly, with the prospect of a little action, he felt more cheerful than he had done since he had left the battlefield at Waterloo.

Chapter Three

The Westmere wood was the only substantial stand of trees in the area. It was here the Earl's gamekeeper raised pheasants and partridges for his lordship's sport, though he had not been out shooting for some time. Bella suspected that much of the game found its way into the local poachers' capacious pockets. If the birds went to feed the hungry poor then she, for one, did not begrudge them. Primroses grew in abundance in the early spring and there might still be a few late blooms under the shelter of the trees where the ground was less soggy. She would gather a few for her room—perhaps their sweet new growth would cheer her.

She had dismounted and was stooping to pick a few of the delicate blooms when she became aware that she was bring watched. She looked up sharply. A tiny old woman in a ragged black cloak, green with age, stood watching her. She had, Bella noticed, the clearest, bluest eyes she had ever seen, incongruous in such a brown, wrinkled face.

'Who are you?' Bella demanded. She was about to add that the woman was trespassing on Huntley land but decided she was doing no harm and was probably, like her, out to gather flowers.

The woman ignored the question. 'Want your fortune told, my dear?' she asked, holding out a bony hand.

'No, I do not think so, thank you.'

'You should. You have a decision to make…'

Bella gasped. 'How do you know that?'

'I have the gift of second sight.' In spite of her unprepossessing appearance, the old woman's voice was surprisingly cultured. 'Don't you want to know what the future has in store for you if you make the right choice?' She paused. 'Or the wrong one…?'

'I don't know…' She was wavering. What harm could it do?

'Come with me.' The old lady pointed to a tiny hovel which had once been a woodman's dwelling, but there was no woodman now that Bella knew of.

'You live there?'

'I do.' She held out her hand again. 'Come, you can rest awhile before you return home.' Without waiting for a reply, she took Misty's reins, tied the horse to a tree and led the way to the cottage, which was surrounded by a patch of well-tended garden.

Bemused, Bella followed her, ducking her head under the low lintel of the door. Inside was a single room, with an earth floor and a tiny window. It was furnished with a table, a couple of chairs and a bed in a corner covered with a multicoloured quilt. A dresser against the wall held stacked crockery and also rows of jars containing she knew not what. Bunches of herbs hung from a beam to dry. There were more on the tiny window-sill. Everywhere was surprisingly clean.

'Sit,' her hostess commanded. 'I will give you a herbal drink which will soothe you.'

It did not occur to Bella not to obey and she sat and watched as the tiny woman flitted about the room, picking up a bottle of this, a jar of that and adding some of the contents to a glass of clear water, stirring it with a thin stick. She had a kind of restless energy which defied her age. But how old was she? Fifty? Sixty? Seventy? More perhaps. She looked as though she had never had a square meal in her life, she was so thin. But her eyes! They were mesmerising.

'Who are you?' Bella asked. 'How long have you been living here?'

'How long?' the woman echoed. 'Time means nothing to me, means nothing to anyone. We are put on this earth for a short span to live and breathe, love, hate and procreate and then… Poof!'

'Oh, how cynical! Surely there is more to it than that?'

'Life is what you make of it,' the woman said, sitting down opposite her. 'Joy or sorrow—the choice is always there. Some make good choices, others bad.' She paused to look at the girl. It was an intense regard, as if she were looking right inside her past the flesh and bones to the person inside them. 'If I had made a good choice, I would not be here now, neither would you.'

'What do you mean, I would not be here?'

The woman laughed. 'Why, if I was not here, you would not be here talking to me, would you? Perhaps it is fate.' She paused and handed Bella the glass. 'Here, drink this.'

'What is it?'

'A few herbs, meant to soothe. I make it from a recipe the good nuns taught me.'

Bella sipped the cloudy liquid. It had a bitter-sweet taste but was not unpleasant. 'You are a nun?'

'No, I was never devout enough. I questioned things too much. The nuns and I parted when I came to my senses.'

'I don't understand.'

'No. It is of no consequence to you, who are young and innocent of any ill intent. But beware of others. You will be sorely tried before you find happiness.'

'But I will find happiness?' Bella wanted desperately to be reassured.

'Give me your hand.'

Bella held out her hand and it was taken in a firm grasp and turned palm upwards. She watched as the woman appeared to study it. 'Do I not have to cross your palm with silver first?'

'No. I do not make forecasts for money.'

'Then how do you live?'

'Curiosity is one of your traits, I see.'

'You see it in my hand?'

She laughed. 'No, I hear it on your tongue. Now, let me see. This burden you have to bear…' She was not looking at Bella's palm, but directly into her eyes.

'You know of it?'

'Only that there is one. You may tell me of it if you wish. It will go no further than these four walls. And I may be able to advise you.'

Bella longed to confide in someone, but this curious woman was a stranger she had never seen before. How could she admit what was troubling her? On the other hand, a stranger might be more objective. 'I have to choose a husband,' she said.

'I see nothing burdensome about that. For most young ladies, it is the best time of their lives, watching their swains making fools of themselves.'

Bella smiled ruefully. 'My choice is limited.'

'How many?'

'Four.'

'That is more than most young ladies have.'

'This is different.'

'Why?'

Bella hesitated. 'I do not think I want any of then. I mean, I am not sure… Oh, I am so confused. Besides, I do not think any of them will offer and I shall think the poorer of them if they do.'

'Oh, a conundrum. I like conundrums. How will you solve it?'

'I do not know.'

'You must be careful in whom you put your trust.'

'It is not a question of trust. I trust them all. It is a question of—'

'Happiness?' the woman finished for her, smiling a little. 'You think everyone has a right to happiness?'

'Why not? If it harms no one else.'

'Ah, but there's the rub. Every selfish act harms someone.'

'I should hate to be accused of selfishness…'

'On the other hand, to give in to moral blackmail might be unselfish, but it would be foolish in the extreme.'

'Moral blackmail? I do not understand.'

'Oh, I think you do.' She paused. 'There is money involved?'

'Yes, I believe so.'

'And a title.'

Bella looked up sharply. Did the woman know who she was? Now she wished she had not spoken. 'I do not believe you saw that in my palm.'

'No, I did not.'

'But you know who I am?'

'Oh, yes.'

'Then you have the advantage of me.'

'Yes.'

'Do tell me your name.'

'So that you may go to his lordship or his lordship's steward and have me turned off his property…'

'No, I will not betray you.'

'If you don't, you will be the first Huntley not to do so.'

'What do you mean? Do you have a grievance against the family?'

'No,' she retorted quickly. 'I am a silly old woman—take no note of what I say.'

Her retraction was so swift that Bella did not believe her, and for a moment she forgot her own dilemma in wondering what the Huntleys could possibly have done to the woman. But she knew that if she asked, she would not be told. She was beginning to wish she had not mentioned her troubles at all. 'You would not speak to anyone of what I have said to you?'

'Who would I tell? I see few people and those I do see are more interested in their own problems. They come for cures or favours or love potions…'

'There are no such things as love potions.'

'You may believe what you will—others would not agree with you. And as for William Huntley, what the eye doesn't see the heart cannot grieve over.'

'I will not tell him,' Bella said, surprised that the old woman should speak of the Earl in those almost contemptuous terms.

'Do you feel calmer now?'

'Yes, a little.' In fact, she felt rather sleepy, almost as if she were dreaming. What had been in that concoction she had drunk? Why had she swallowed it without demur?

'Good. It is time for you to go. If you take my advice, you will wait and see who offers and then make up your mind. But take your time, the old man is not about to die. Keep them dangling.' The old lady smiled, and the smile lit her face and made her seem years younger. Bella could imagine that she had once been beautiful. 'It might be quite diverting.'

Bella left her and walked slowly to her horse. As she mounted, she turned back, but although the hovel was there, nestling among the trees, there was no sign of the strange old woman. But surprisingly she did feel calmer, if not cheerful. Witch or not, she was right—there was no point in jumping her fences before she reached them.

She left the trees and crossed the park to rejoin the drive, where she stopped to gather her wits and shake out her skirts, so that when she approached the house she looked like a young lady back from a gentle hack. She had achieved nothing by her flight. Her problems were still there, still insurmountable, and if her grandfather ever heard about her attempted ride to Downham Market, he would be more determined than ever to see her safely married, and the Comtesse would brand her a hoyden.

She went up to her room and sat on the bed. Her nerves were on edge, she had a terrible headache from the bump on her head and there was a bruise on her side which hurt when she moved. She would much rather have had her supper in her room, but in less than an hour she would be expected to be the perfect hostess, bright and cheerful. Neither could she help thinking about her grandfather's impossible ultimatum. Somehow she had to avoid making a hasty decision. What had that strange woman in the woods said? 'Keep them dangling'?

But they weren't dangling, were they? Not one of them viewed the prospect of marriage to her with any pleasure, not even Robert. He had been unexpectedly sympathetic, but not enough to fall in with her plan. And yet it was a good plan.

Reluctantly she rose and changed for supper, putting on a pale blue silk gown, which had a full skirt and tiny puff sleeves and a neckline filled with ruched lace. It was hardly the height of fashion but, then, her grandfather disapproved of the flimsy apparel which was the latest mode. Slipping her feet into satin pumps, she made her way down to the kitchen to see that supper would be ready on time.

'Everything is going along nicely, Miss Huntley,' Martha told her.

'I believe Miss Battersby might be back and bringing her sister so, please, lay two extra covers.'

'Yes, miss.'

Returning to the drawing room, she took a book from a shelf to while away the time until supper and flicked idly through its pages. It was a small volume of poetry written by William Harrison, a young fenland poet who was making a name for himself locally, though his style was not one to commend itself to devotees of Tennyson or Shelley. There was nothing in it to bring her relief, but one short verse caught her attention. It was entitled 'Clod's Complaint'.

When war throughout all Europe reigned,
We farmers lived in clover
But now the friendly fiend is chained,
Our golden age is over.
Grant, O fate, ere 'tis too late
When men have had a blowing
War may revive, that we may thrive
And corn may pay for growing.

Bella smiled, thinking of James. He might almost have written it himself, except that he did not have a poetic bone in his body. And, on reflection, it was not amusing to wish for war as the answer to the country's ills.

She looked up as Louis wandered into the room. He was dressed for evening in black satin breeches, white stockings and a brocade coat decorated with rows of silver frogging. The frills of his shirt cuffs hung over his hands and his white muslin cravat was tied in some complicated knot which looked as though it might choke him.

'Ah, Cousin Isabella,' he said, putting up his quizzing glass. 'All alone?'

She shut the book with a sigh. 'As you see.'

'Good.' He dropped the glass and sat down beside her on the sofa. 'Hoping to see you alone. Need to speak to you.'

Her heart sank. 'I am listening.'

'Been talking to Mama about this idiotish plan of his lordship's.'

'Your mama has already spoken to me, Louis.'

'Yes, told me so. Said you were in accord.'

'Yes, we are,' she said. 'I do not expect you to offer for me.'

'That's the thing,' he said. 'Can't see it will serve. But…' He paused and searched her face. 'Pretty filly, no doubt of it. Pay for dressing.'

'Why, thank you, Louis,' she said, wondering why he spoke in that clipped way, as if he did not know how to string a whole sentence together.

'But if his lordship is determined on it…'

'Oh, he is, but Edward does not think he can legally do it.'

'Costly,' he said. 'Going through the courts, I mean.'

'Perhaps.'

'Got a solution.'

'Then, please, tell me, for there is nothing I would like better than a solution.'

'Like living at Westmere, don't you?'

'Yes,' she admitted doubtfully, wondering what was coming next. 'I have lived here all my life. But if I have to move, I shall do so.'

'No need for that. We can come to an accommodation, a *mariage de convenance*. You agree to stay in the country where you belong and don't interfere with me, and we shall get along famously.'

She was so dismayed that she hardly noticed that he had produced two complete sentences which sounded as though his mother had drilled him. 'But, Louis, how will that serve? Grandfather wishes for an heir…'

'Do my duty by you, naturally.' He sat back with a sigh of satisfaction. 'So what do you say? Make a marriage of it, shall we?'

She knew she was supposed to answer something to the effect that she was very sensible of the honour he did her but she could not accept his kind offer, but the words would not come. She was appalled. This was worse than James's clumsy attempt to propose.

'You mean I am to be the uncomplaining wife, hold house here and produce offspring as often as you deem necessary, while you continue to act the bachelor? No, thank you, Louis.'

'Plenty of fripperies when I come into my inheritance. All you need, not that you'll need a great deal, living as you do, quietly in the country…'

That was more of his mother. If Bella was capable of hate, she would certainly have hated Elizabeth, Comtesse de Courville, at that moment. 'Louis, much as I love Westmere, I cannot marry you,' she said.

He stood up. 'Persuaded you don't mean it. Too much to lose. You'll come about when you have had time to think about it.'

'She doesn't need to think about it,' said a voice at the door.

Bella looked up to see Robert leaning lazily against the jamb. How long had he been there? How much had he heard?

'Nothing to do with you,' Louis said, flushing scarlet. 'Not eligible.'

'Indeed I am,' he said, sauntering into the room. 'And Miss Huntley has already accepted my offer.'

'I don't believe you, it's a hum.'

'Not at all. We were about to see his lordship and tell

everyone over supper.' He turned from Louis to Bella, his brown eyes dancing with mischief. 'Isn't that so, my love?'

She was so relieved, she could have cried. Instead, she smiled. 'Yes. I was about to explain that to Louis, but he did not afford me the opportunity.'

Louis was obviously furious. He rose from his seat and advanced on Robert. 'Toad-eater! Jack-at-warts! Flat! You don't suppose that marrying the chit will give you the title and inheritance, do you?'

'You evidently did.'

'That's different. If his lordship is so set on her marrying the heir, then I'm happy to oblige him and Miss Huntley. But you're ineligible, whatever you may think. I shall fight you…'

'Oh, Louis, no!' Bella cried. 'Please, do not call him out.'

Robert's smile did not waver. 'Happy to accommodate you, cousin, but what the Earl would say to such a proceeding I do not know.'

'Wouldn't dirty my hands on you. Fight in the courts.'

'You may do as you please, sir, though I may tell you that my offer for Miss Huntley is not dependent on her sitting at Westmere in splendid isolation, nor, I may say, on hopes of a title or a legacy. It is not I you will have to fight but the Earl of Westmere.'

'Oh, Robert,' Bella breathed, her eyes shining. 'How very magnanimous of you.'

He stood before her and picked up her hand from her lap, stooping low to kiss the back of it so that his laughing eyes were on a level with hers. 'Not at all, my dear. We have kept our little secret long enough, don't you think?' He turned back to the sullen Louis. 'This is not a new thing, you understand, but an arrangement of some duration. You may offer your felicitations.'

Louis's answer was a loud snort as he hurried from the

room, no doubt to report to his mother, leaving the two young people convulsed with laughter.

Bella was the first to recover. 'Robert, I am grateful to you for saving me from Louis, but what do we do now?'

'Go to his lordship.'

'But you said you wouldn't, you begged me not to ask it of you.'

'I changed my mind when I saw that…that tulip daring to suggest what he did. I couldn't allow it.' He smiled. 'So we will put your plan into effect.'

'Oh, Robert, thank you, thank you.'

'But there will be no announcement,' he said firmly. 'Definitely no announcement.'

'Oh, no, I wouldn't dream of asking it of you. I promise you, Robert, you shall come out of this with your honour intact. Once we have arrived in London, I will make no demands upon you.'

'Then we are agreed.' He bent to kiss her cheek, wishing she would make all the demands she liked. 'Now, my dear, there are other things to be settled. I found Miss Battersby but her sister is not yet well enough to move and she would not leave her.'

'I was afraid she would not.' Bella's cheek was warm where his lips had touched it and she was sure he was aware of her confusion. She was being very silly, just because he had agreed to pretend to love her.

'I do not think they will come to any harm. Downham Market was perfectly quiet and so was Eastmere when I left.'

'You saw James?'

'Yes, he came back with me. We brought the children and Mrs Clarke, the housekeeper. I took the liberty of asking Jolliffe to instruct Daisy to find rooms for them all and they have gone upstairs to settle in.'

'Oh then I must go and make them welcome. The poor

little things will be frightened to death. Please, excuse me, Robert.' She hurried from the room, leaving him stroking his chin, wondering what he had let himself in for and what the Earl might have to say about it.

His chin felt rough and reminded him that he needed to wash and shave and change for supper. For Bella's sake he must carry off their masquerade with as much aplomb as he could muster, and he wished he had travelled by chaise and brought more than one change of clothes with him. Louis's foppery made him feel like a peasant.

Bella found Daisy scuttling from room to room with armfuls of linen and one of the daily women carrying wood and coal to the fires. Mrs Clarke was sitting on the bed in one of the bedchambers with her arms around the two little girls. They all stood up as she came into the room. On a nudge from the stout, middle-aged woman, the children curtsied.

'Oh, my darlings, you do not have to curtsey to me,' Bella said. 'I am so glad to see you safe and I want you to be comfortable. It is late, so I will have supper sent up to you and then Mrs Clarke will put you to bed. We can talk tomorrow.' She looked up at Mrs Clarke. 'It must have been terrible.'

'Oh, miss, I was in mortal fear. There was no reasoning with those men. They would have burned us in our beds if Mr Trenchard had not come back and given them money. I am sorry...'

'Sorry?' Bella queried, not understanding.

'For sending for him, taking him away from you.'

'Goodness, do not think of it. Looking after his family is much more important than paying calls.'

The woman looked startled and Bella wondered what she had been told. Surely not that Mr Trenchard had expectations of marrying her? She smiled. 'I will leave you to settle in. Please, ask Daisy for anything you need.'

But asking Daisy to look after the newcomers had a detrimental effect on the situation in the kitchen. Cook, deprived of the maid's help, said she could not possibly be expected to produce a supper of seven removes all on her own. Bella soothed her and stayed to help her, with the result that everyone had already assembled in the drawing when she made her way there an hour later.

'You are late, miss,' her grandfather said.

'Yes, I am sorry.' She stood just inside the door and surveyed the company. Her eye caught Robert's and she was rewarded with a wink, which made her already oven-warm face flare with more colour. Edward was standing by the window, gazing out onto the terrace. He was immaculately dressed in a black coat and trousers which were fastened under the instep of his polished shoes and made his long legs look even longer. His shirt was plain white and his cravat a huge black bow. He turned and bowed to her without speaking.

Louis, in his sparkling clothes, stood next to his mother, who had chosen bright pink satin decorated with white feathers for her gown. She had more feathers in her hair and diamonds about her throat. Neither could produce a smile.

Bella turned from them to James, who had changed into old-fashioned evening breeches which he must have dug out from the back of his closet for they, like his coat, strained across his portly front. But his face was scrubbed and his shoes clean. He smiled beatifically. 'Your servant, Miss Huntley. And may I say how much I appreciate you taking my two little girls under your wing…'

My goodness, she thought, surely he does not think I did it from any other reason but common humanity? She was reminded that he had said he would return to the subject of an interview and he must have taken it as a favourable sign that she had invited the children. Oh, he was in for a severe disillusionment when he discovered she had accepted Robert...

'They could not be left to the mercy of the rabble,' she said, hoping her answer might prepare him. 'They are welcome.'

'Been no children here since you were in leading strings,' his lordship said. 'I'm too old to be bothered with them.'

'I am sure they will not trouble you, Grandpapa,' she said. 'They have Mrs Clarke to look after them.'

'They have already upset supper. How long are we expected to wait?'

'I believe it is almost ready.'

'Then let us go to the table.'

They did not trouble to pair off and arrived in the dining room in a bunch, so that it was a minute or two before all were seated. Bella, at the foot of the table opposite her grandfather, found James on one side of her and Robert on the other. Both were determined to outdo each other in seeing that she had everything she needed.

'I believe the riots have been put down,' she said to James, watching as Daisy ladled soup from the tureen into the bowl in front of her.

'Yes, thank God. The magistrates heard what they had to say, not that they had any choice in the matter. The men surrounded them with pitchforks and guns...'

'Guns!' Elizabeth said in alarm. 'I knew it! It is the same as it was in France. We shall all be murdered in our beds.'

'I hardly think a handful of starving labourers constitutes a revolution,' Robert said laconically.

'What happened?' Louis asked James. 'I should hope the militia were sent for.'

'No, there was no need,' James said. 'The magistrates promised them an increased allowance which, I must say, I am heartily glad of, for I cannot afford to raise the wages of my men. Then the parson read the Riot Act and they dispersed.'

'It is a help, I suppose,' Bella said. 'But I am sure they would much rather have proper wages.'

'Shouldn't have given in to them,' the Earl said. 'You have to be firm with these people. It is a pity I decided to retire from the bench, or I'd have shown that lily-livered rabble who's master.'

'I do not suppose the bargain will be kept,' James said. 'Rioters cannot expect to have such agreements honoured, can they? The concession was made under threat of injury…'

'That's not fair,' Bella said. 'If the men were promised—'

'They should have arrested the ringleader, made an example of him,' her grandfather said, ignoring her outburst.

Bella was reminded of the man she had seen addressing the men from the cart that morning. Could it have been him? 'Do they know who he is?' she asked.

'Not difficult to find out. Put a few *agents provocateurs* among them, soon weed the troublemakers out. Parson's the magistrate at Eastmere, ain't he? I'll suggest it to him.'

She was about to protest that such tactics were unfair when she saw Robert looking at her, slowly shaking his head, almost as if he could read her mind. And on reflection she realised that arguing with her grandfather would hardly put him in a good humour to agree to her engagement to Robert. She smiled at him to show she understood.

'Do you think we could change the subject?' Elizabeth said. 'All this talk of riots and revolution has quite taken away my appetite.'

'Certainly,' his lordship said. 'It is not something that troubles my mind greatly. But if you do not like our conversation, I suggest you return to the Capital forthwith.'

'I shall be only too pleased to do so, once you have agreed that Louis is your heir.'

'Oh, has Isabella decided to take him?' he said, lifting one bushy white eyebrow.

'Oh, that is not at all fair,' James cried. 'I asked first. She said she would give me her answer…'

'Did I?' Bella asked, and then, catching Robert winking at her, spluttered into her soup.

'Oh, my dear, has it gone down the wrong way?' he asked, patting her gently on the back.

'No, no, it is hot, that's all.'

The Earl had been watching her. 'Well, child, it seems you have two suitors, ready to do battle for your hand…'

'Three,' said Robert.

'Then I must suppose that it is you who have entered the fray, for Edward says he has ruled himself out.'

'Indeed, I have,' Robert said. 'And been accepted, subject to your agreement, of course.'

'The devil take you!' Louis exclaimed, while James's jaw dropped open and Edward lifted his brows in a faint gesture of surprise, but he was too much the gentleman to make any comment.

'Well, I wish you both happy,' Elizabeth said. 'But it makes not one jot of difference. Louis is still the heir.'

'How do you come by that conclusion, woman?' his lordship asked reasonably.

'You know very well he is the oldest. And you have no right to throw away the inheritance on the whim of a miss hardly out of the schoolroom.'

'I may do as I wish.'

'I cannot believe anyone in their senses would hand it over to that young scapegrace. He will ruin the place in half a year. It cannot be borne. Louis, we will leave first thing tomorrow and speak to our lawyers. We shall see who has the right of it.'

'Speaking of rights,' Edward said, 'I do believe I have the prior claim, but I would not dream of pursuing it against his lordship's wishes. He has made those perfectly clear.' He stopped to turn to his brother who sat beside him. 'Rob, my felicitations. I wish you happy.'

His voice was quiet and controlled, so much so that Bella, looking up at him, was shocked to see a steely glint in his eye she had never seen there before. It was clear to her that he was angry. But with whom? Robert or her? Could he possibly be jealous? She dismissed that idea the moment it came into her head. He loved Miss Charlotte Mellish, not her.

His lordship was looking from one to the other and gave a wry smile. It was almost as if he was enjoying himself. 'Robert, we will speak together in the library after supper.'

That seemed to be the end of that particular discussion and Bella, who had been immeasurably cheered by the way things had gone, began to think about her trip to London. The Earl would allow it, wouldn't he? Oh, she prayed that he would.

'Cousin Elizabeth, do tell us all the latest *bon mot* in Town,' she said. 'And about the fashions.'

Elizabeth duly obliged, emphasising her own connections at court and what the Regent had said to Colette and how her daughter had put his other favourites' noses quite out of joint. She spoke of the coming Season. 'There was so much celebration and so many festivities last year, what with the end of the war and Wellington coming home and the French king parading with the Regent and then going back to France to claim his crown, the place was in a ferment the whole summer long. And this year, of course, everyone must needs flock to Paris. I am persuaded this Season will be quieter.'

'Oh, do you think so?' Bella asked, a little disappointed.

'Yes, but everyone of any consequence will be there, you may depend on it,' she said. 'I am going to give a ball for Colette and, no doubt, the Prince will put in an appearance.

And, of course, we shall be invited to the wedding of Princess Charlotte. Everyone will be in Town for that.'

'I shouldn't count on it,' Robert murmured so that only Bella could hear. 'Such pretensions! If the prince were not married to that eccentric Caroline, I do believe she would expect him to make a queen of Colette.'

'Surely not,' she whispered back.

'What are you two whispering about?' Elizabeth demanded. 'It is excessively ill mannered in company.'

'My fault,' Robert said, smiling. 'Sweet nothings, you understand.'

Elizabeth's answer was a sound that was very near to being a snort. Bella risked a glance at her grandfather, but he was sitting back in his chair, smiling benignly as if all was right with the world. Perhaps it was right with his world, but hers was decidedly topsy-turvy. She had no way of knowing if he was satisfied with her choice or not. She supposed she would find that out after he had spoken to Robert later in the evening.

When the long meal was finished, she and Elizabeth retired to the withdrawing room and the teacups. It was here that Elizabeth gave vent to her wrath with Bella and Robert. 'You are all run mad,' she said. 'And the Earl must be suffering from senility. Any court in the land would so rule.'

'Oh, my lady, I beg you do not go to court over it. It would upset his lordship so much and he is old.'

'The very point I am making, Isabella. He cannot be allowed to go on with this course of action and you had better resign yourself to being disappointed. Even if his lordship had been able to break the entail, no one in their right mind would think of Captain Robert Huntley as heir. He is a popinjay, a nobody, only a captain because my father bought him the commission. Otherwise he would never have risen above ensign.'

'He is not a popinjay and he served with great distinction. Why, Wellington himself commended him.'

'You defend him very hotly, miss.'

'Why would I not? We are, after all, engaged.'

Louis, James and Edward joined them almost at once and Bella supposed that Robert was closeted with her grandfather. She forced herself to sound normal as she asked them how they liked their tea.

Soon after that, Robert strolled into the room and told them his lordship had decided to retire, so if any of them had intended to resume the argument, they had perforce to postpone it until the following day. Elizabeth went off to the far corner of the big room and beckoned Louis to join her, where Bella supposed they were intent on formulating a plan to frustrate the Earl.

Bella attempted to begin a conversation with the other three men but gave it up when it became obvious they were not in the mood for idle chatter. And, to tell the truth, neither was she. She crossed to the pianoforte and sat down to play. Robert strolled across to stand beside her and began to hum the tune she was playing.

'I like this,' he said. 'Shall we sing it together?'

'Yes, if you wish,' she agreed, though she was longing to know what had passed between him and her grandfather.

They sang the duet and she discovered he had a very pleasing voice. When the song was finished, he bent down to whisper to her. 'All is well.'

Her fingers were still idly strumming a tune, which covered the murmur of their voices. 'What did he say about my going to London?'

'Didn't ask him.'

'You didn't?' Bella's voice was a squeak of protest.

'Shh. No. He would only think we had devised the plan between us. He isn't a fool, you know.'

'No, I know, but how shall we contrive?'

'I'll ask Mama to ask him. Most natural thing in the world she should invite you to spend some time with her.'

Her expressive hazel eyes lit up with pleasure. 'Oh, Robert, how clever you are! But will Cousin Henrietta do it?'

'Naturally, she will when I put it to her. She will want to get to know her future daughter-in-law.'

'But she will know that it is nothing but a ruse…'

'No, she won't. Mama is a dear sweet old thing and I love her, but if she has one fault it is an inability to keep a secret, so she shan't be told.'

'But she will have to know at the end of the Season when we call it off.'

'Naturally she will, but there's no sense in jumping our fences until we reach them. And Mama will behave more naturally if she does not know.'

Bella had not thought about extending the deception beyond Westmere when she had first mooted the plan, and now she was becoming a little apprehensive. 'Oh, Robert, I am not sure…'

'Do you want to call the whole thing off now? I shan't try and persuade you. It was your idea, after all, but if you stay here you will have to endure his lordship pushing for a decision and James and Louis importuning you all the time.'

She shuddered. 'No, I could not bear it. Thank you, Robert, thank you very much.'

He took her hand from the keys and lifted it to his lips, smiling at her. 'I shall go to Palgrave tomorrow,' he whispered, then added aloud, 'Goodnight, Miss Huntley.' He bowed to the Comtesse. 'My lady, excuse me, I am excessively fatigued. Gentlemen, goodnight.' And with that he was gone.

Left facing three aggressive people and Edward, who was looking at her as if he meant to quiz her the minute he could catch her alone, she excused herself, saying she, too, was tired and that was no less than the truth. It had been a long and eventful day and her head was throbbing.

She went to see that Mrs Clarke and the girls were comfortable and, finding that they were, sought the sanctuary of her room. She thought she would fall asleep as soon as her head hit the pillow, but it was not to be. Her thoughts went round and round in her head. Louis and his mother were going to be a problem. Would they respect the fact that there was to be no formal announcement of an engagement and keep the secret? At least she would be spared James's attentions while she was in London.

And there was Edward. Was he as indifferent as he pretended to be? He had been angry when he had first heard of it and, thinking back, he had been silent all through supper and afterwards, in the drawing room, had buried his head in a newspaper which was already two days old. But she must not worry about what Edward thought but concentrate on the plan she and Robert had devised. Robert was a dear man. The kindest of all her cousins. A gentle man, but strong, too. If only… She sighed. What a mull it all was. And sleep was as far away as ever.

Bella rose and went to the window and pulled back the heavy curtains. It had been raining again; the leaves on the trees close to the house and the roof of the stable block to her right glistened in the light from a feeble moon. A sound on the gravel below caught her attention. Someone was leading a horse from the stables. She recognised Robert as he mounted and cantered off down the drive. Where was he going? Surely he hadn't decided to ride to Palgrave in the middle of the night?

If he had, she would be left to face her grandfather and the others in the morning without his support. Feeling more alone that she had ever felt in her whole life, she returned to her bed and tossed and turned until sleep at last claimed her.

*   *   *

Fate was a strange thing, Robert mused as he rode. Before
he had received the summons from the Earl, he had been in
London in the company of two friends, George Fulbright
and Desmond Norton.

George was a giant of a man and companion of many a
military campaign. They had left the army together and
since then had been racketing about Town, doing little more
than enjoy themselves, which was all very well for George,
who had a small fortune and could afford to do nothing and
had the most amazing luck when it came to cards. He was
talking of buying a horse with his latest winnings. 'Tattersall's don't have what I want,' he had said. 'I've a mind to
go to Newmarket and take a look at what is on offer there.'

'Then we'll all go.' Robert had said. 'I fancy a ride out
of Town…'

'Being dunned, Rob?' Desmond had queried with a smile.
He was the oldest of the three by several years and was the
head of a successful publishing firm he had inherited from
his father. He had an inexhaustible supply of energy which
meant he could do enough work to make a good living and
enjoy his leisure, too. Robert, who was always pinched in
the pocket, envied him.

'No more than usual. I'll pay up as soon as my next
quarter's allowance comes through.'

The very next day he had received the summons to Westmere and as he would have been halfway there already, he
had decided out of curiosity to go and see what the old man
wanted with him. He had been even more curious after
meeting Bella in Ely, where he had stopped at The Club to
rest his horse and refresh himself. He had known he could
have no expectations, but he had been taken completely by
surprise by the Earl's pronouncement. Poor little Bella! She
was a pawn in the old man's game. The trouble was, he
was not sure what that game was.

He smiled as the moonlit road slipped by under his

horse's hooves. He had no idea where he was going, he simply wanted to be out in the open air to think. It had been the same when he had been in the Peninsula—a night ride had always cleared his head before a battle. Was he going into battle?

You would certainly think so, he told himself. Bella had almost as great a penchant for getting into scrapes as he had, and when he had seen her come off her horse and disappear under the feet of the mob in Eastmere, he had not hesitated to dash into the fray to rescue her. Holding her in his arms, he had discovered she was not little Bella at all, not a child but a beautiful young lady, and had been shaken to the core. He had had an almost overwhelming desire to kiss her, to taste those pink lips, to hold her close and protect her from whatever evil there was around her.

When she had put forward that impossible plan, his protests had been half-hearted and he had known he would comply, even before he had heard Louis talking to her. What had he let himself in for? How would they go on in Town? Why had he said he would not reveal the whole truth to his mother? It meant he would have to act the gallant. Not that he minded that, but it would put him in a severe case with his brother. They had made a pact and he had broken it. It would all end in tears, he was sure of it. His tears, if he had been a man given to weeping, which he was not. And he could see no way to prevent it short of going back on his word to Bella. And he could not do that.

He turned and trotted back the way he had come.

Chapter Four

Bella had been wrong about Robert. He arrived at the breakfast table before everyone else, wearing the riding coat and breeches he had arrived in the previous day which had been cleaned and pressed for him by Daisy.

Bella, who had slept fitfully and was glad to rise early and help with the breakfast, was already there, picking at a couple of coddled eggs she had no appetite for.

'Good morning, Bella.' He seemed uncommonly cheerful and none the worse for his nocturnal ride.

She sent Daisy back to the kitchen, before replying. 'Good morning, Robert. Did you sleep well?'

He helped himself to ham and eggs and meat pie and brought the plate to sit beside her. 'Yes. Should I not?'

'You had much to occupy your mind…' It was strange to be sitting beside him, almost engaged, and yet she did not feel any different. Perhaps she might have done if it had been real. She stole a glance at him as she poured him a cup of coffee. He seemed completely unconcerned, as if nothing had happened. She supposed that, to him, nothing had. It was all a sham and only in the company of the Earl and his cousins would he behave like a lovesick swain.

'Oh, as to that, I see no point in lying awake when the decisions have all been made.'

She wanted to ask him about his ride out in the dark, but decided that would not do. He would think her a scold and she had no right to quiz him. 'You have not changed your mind, then?'

'No, I am not one to go back on my word, Bella. As soon as I have had my breakfast, I shall take my leave of you and ride to Palgrave.'

'Robert,' she began tentatively, 'what will you tell Edward?'

He looked up from his food to search her face. 'What would you have me tell him?'

'Nothing.'

'Then I shall tell him nothing.'

They were interrupted by the arrival of James, once more dressed in his working clothes. They had hardly finished bidding him good morning when Edward came in, closely followed by Louis whose yellow and blue striped waistcoat dazzled the eyes. There was silence while they helped themselves from the sideboard.

Louis was the first to break it. 'Mama and I will be returning to London today,' he said. 'See no point in staying here. His lordship is clearly deranged. Got to see lawyers.'

'And I must go back to Eastmere,' James said. 'Bella, if you would be so kind as to keep my little girls a few days longer, I should deem it a favour. I am not at all sure that all danger is past.'

'Of course,' she said. 'Mrs Clarke is welcome to stay, too. I am sure Constance and Faith would be happier with her—they are used to her, after all.'

James, anxious about the state of the farm, which he would only have left in expectation of an interview and a favourable reply from Bella, took his leave, as disgruntled as a man could be.

'And I am off, too,' Robert said.

'So soon, brother?' queried Edward, mildly. 'I would have expected you would have stayed a little longer. It is not every day a man becomes betrothed, and to leave the lady the very next day might make an observer doubt the strength of his feeling.'

'There is nothing weak about my feelings, Teddy,' Robert said with a smile. 'But I must tell Mama the news—'

'Before she reads it in *The Gazette*. Quite right, too.'

'It is not to be publicly announced,' Bella put in quickly.

'Oh?' Edward turned to look at her and she felt her face turn fiery red. 'Why not?'

'Because…' She stopped. It was a question for which she had not prepared herself.

'Because people will think it very sudden,' Robert put in, understanding her difficulty. 'If the story of his lordship's disposition comes out, it will be supposed it was done for the inheritance which, I assure you, my dear brother, it was not. I have no expectations on that score.'

'You mean the Earl's *indisposition*,' Louis said. 'Yes, I can quite see your point. It will make you look a real noddicock when the lawyers prove he is not fit to be making a such a will.'

Robert did not argue with him but, having finished his breakfast, stood up to leave. Bella went with him to the door, where Jolliffe handed him his riding cape and a new hat. 'It's raining again, Captain,' he said.

'A little rain will not hurt me, Jolliffe.' He turned to take Bella's shoulders in his hands and look down into her face. Her huge hazel eyes were looking troubled. 'It will all come right in the end, I promise you,' he said in a low voice. 'I shall come back and fetch you myself in two days' time, three at the most.' And he bent and put his lips to her cheek. '*Au revoir*, my dear.'

Then he was gone and she was turning back to the breakfast parlour, rubbing her cheek where his lips had touched and wondering why she was trembling.

Soon afterwards, the Comtesse, having breakfasted in her room, came downstairs, followed closely by her maid and Louis's valet, carrying their bags and boxes. Louis called the coach to the door and they took their leave in a flurry of cantering horses.

The Earl did not come downstairs that day, but Edward asked for and was granted an interview with him in his room. What was said Bella never knew. He came down in a strange mood and said he did not see any point in prolonging his stay.

'Much as I like coming to Westmere and enjoying your delightful company, Bella, I must return to London. I have an engagement to go to the theatre with Miss Mellish and her parents.'

'Am I to wish you happy?'

'No, it is no more than an understanding at present,' he said, with a smile. 'But you shall be the first to know when it becomes official. Just as I hope I shall be the first to be told when you and Robert decide to make public that you are engaged.'

It seemed to her there was something barbed about the way he spoke, as if he knew the truth and he did not like it. She could hardly speak, but managed to whisper, 'Yes, of course.'

'In the meantime, it is a secret, is that so?'

'Yes. You see…'

'Oh, you do not need to explain all that again, my dear. I understand. Now, I must take my leave of you, little one. We shall see each other again very soon, I expect.'

Little one, she thought as she watched him drive away. He thinks I am a little one. Why, I am taller than most young ladies of my age and— She looked down at herself—my figure is certainly not childlike. He must be blind.

And now they had all gone and she was alone. Alone to dwell on what had happened, alone to wait, alone to despair. What had that woman in the woods said about trials before she found happiness? But she had assured her she would find happiness. How could that come about? And with whom?

Bella was not alone for long because Constance and Faith, escaping from Mrs Clarke, came rushing down the stairs, demanding to be amused. It was too wet to go out of doors and so Bella offered to show them round the great house.

'It has all sorts of treasures,' she said, taking each child by a hand. 'Let us go and explore the west wing. Goodness, I have not been there myself since I was a little girl.'

'Are there ghosts?' Constance wanted to know. Although the girls were twins, she was slightly the taller and more self-assured of the two.

'Not that I've heard of. Come, we will start downstairs.' She led the way across the hall and unlocked the door to the unused wing and passed through a small anteroom to the ballroom. It was a very large room and completely un-furnished, except for a few huge pictures of battle scenes and cavalry charges and another of a cavalryman on a pranc-ing black horse, a sword in his hand and a wild look on his face.

'Is that the Earl?' Faith asked.

Bella moved forward to read the inscription. 'Not the present earl, but his father. I own they do look very alike. It is something to do with the eyes, I think, the way they crinkle at the corner and the arch of the brows. I have no-ticed it in Sir Edward and Captain Huntley.'

'And Papa?'

'Yes, I do believe so,' she said. 'Though not in the Comte de Courville. He favours his mother.'

'Why is it called a ballroom?' Constance asked.

'Balls are very grand occasions, when everyone dresses up in their finest clothes and there is music for dancing and food and drink and everyone has a grand time,' Bella told her with a smile. 'I believe there were lots of balls here when my mother and the Countess were alive.'

'Did you go to them?'

'No, I was only a little girl. There have been no balls here for years. I believe his lordship does not care for them.'

'Papa said when he comes into his inheritance, he will hold a dance for us when we grow up.'

'Oh,' Bella said, startled. 'When did he say that?'

'Yesterday, when he said we were coming here. He said we were going to be rich and we should have new clothes and playthings and everything.'

'Then I hope you may. Shall we go upstairs now?'

Her spirits, which had begun to lift a little, plummeted again as the girls ran ahead of her. Poor James. She felt sorry for him, but she could not marry him. He really should not have said anything to the girls. They were going to be so disappointed. Or was he using them to put pressure on her?

At the top of the grand staircase, they found themselves in a wide gallery which seemed to go on for ever. 'These are all the state bedchambers along here,' she said, opening the first of the doors which lined the corridor.

They peered inside at a four-poster bed whose hangings were thick with dust, at dressing-tables with pitted mirrors and empty cupboards with their doors wide open. 'They are of little interest to you, I am sure,' Bella said, 'but just along here and up another flight of stairs, there is the nursery and the schoolroom. Let's go and see what we can find there. There might be some games you can play.'

The schoolroom was more interesting to the little girls because everything had been left just as it had been in Bella's father's day. Bella herself had never used it because by the time she had been ready for lessons, the west wing had been shut up and had already been gathering dust. She had been taught by a governess in a tiny room along the corridor from her bedroom in the east wing.

She watched as the two little girls explored the contents of the cupboards and found illustrated books of geography and plant life, several puzzles and slates, as well as a globe. Bella pointed out the continents and the oceans and places like Cambridge and Norwich and London, but they soon tired of that and went to explore the contents of a large chest. Leaving them to it, Bella strolled round the room, looking at maps and illustrations which had been pinned to the walls, and her eye was taken by two small portraits set side by side.

They depicted two small boys in the overdressed manner of thirty or forty years before. They were about eight or nine years old and as alike as two peas in a pod—dark hair, dark mischievous eyes and the well-defined brows of most of the Huntleys. She thought one was her father, but who was the other? The only other male of that generation she knew of was Richard Huntley, father of Edward and Robert, but he had been eight years younger than her father, so it could not be him. She was intrigued.

She could ask her grandfather but she did not think he was in the right frame of mind to satisfy her curiosity, but Ellen would know. However, thinking of Miss Battersby reminded her that she would probably be gone to Palgrave by the time Ellen returned and might not see her for some time.

'Miss Bella.' Constance's voice interrupted her reverie. She was holding out a box of spillikins and mother-of-pearl fishes. 'May we take these to our room to play with?'

'Of course.' Bella was not sure she had the right to lend out someone else's property but, no doubt, the Earl had forgotten their existence, if he had ever known about them.

'Take them and show them to Mrs Clarke. She will tell you how to play the games.'

They returned to the first floor and thence down the grand staircase to the ground floor. The girls scampered off as soon as they found themselves in familiar surroundings, and Bella locked the door again then turned to see Miss Battersby coming in the front door.

'Oh, Ellen! How glad I am to see you. But how did you get here? You surely did not walk. Why did you not tell Robert you would come today? We could have sent the coach for you.'

'Jethro Monk, the carrier, was going to Ely with his cart, so he brought me as far as the gate.' Ellen was in her mid-sixties, plump and rosy-cheeked and still very active. She would have been highly indignant if anyone had suggested she was too old to look after a spirited young lady. Bella was her baby, just as her father had been before her, and she would have died rather than admit she could not manage. 'The Captain intimated that you needed me…'

'So I did, so I do. But he said your sister was not well enough to leave.'

'She is recovering. And our cousin has arrived to stay with her for a while, so here I am.'

'And I am so very glad to see you.' And then Bella burst into tears.

Ellen put her bag on the floor and hurried to put her arm about the girl's shaking shoulder. 'Dearest child, whatever is the matter?'

'Everything. I never knew Grandfather could be so cruel.'

'Why, what has he done?' She started to lead Bella towards the stairs. 'Come, dry your eyes. We will go to your room and you shall tell your old Batters all about it.'

Once seated in her room, with Ellen's plump arm comfortably about her, Bella unburdened herself between sniffs and hiccoughs. 'It was all so horribly humiliating,' she said, after wiping her streaming eyes with the handkerchief Ellen had found for her. 'They don't want me, not for myself, but you can see them weighing up the advantages of a match if it happens that Grandfather really can do as he says he will. I feel like a cow at market…'

'Oh, you poor child, it must have been a shock.' Ellen paused. 'But, you know, it is time you were thinking of marriage.'

'You think I should fall in with Grandpapa's wishes? Oh, Ellen, how could you? I thought you, at least, would understand. Louis has suggested a marriage of convenience. His convenience. He says he is the rightful heir anyway and makes it sound as though he were doing me a favour to save him the trouble of going to law over it.'

'You refused him out of hand.'

'Of course I did. I am not so wanting in spirit or pride as to agree to that. And James wants a drudge and a mother for his girls. I will not take him either. In truth, I am determined not to have any of them, but I am afraid of the consequences of an outright refusal on Grandpapa. And so… And so…'

'So what, child? Out with it.'

'I have contrived a plot.'

'A plot, eh?' Ellen smiled to herself over the head of her young charge. 'Then let us hear it.'

By the time Bella had finished, the smile had grown wider, though Ellen did not let Bella see it. 'And Captain Huntley agreed to this?'

'Yes, after a little persuasion.'

'And how do you intend to bring it to an end?'

'I don't know. We shall just say we have decided we should not suit. It will be very amicable.'

'And then what? Do you imagine his lordship will simply forget it?'

'He will see that I am determined and change his mind. I do not care who inherits, and as for me…'

'The Earl might be angry enough to cut you off without a penny…'

'Oh, Ellen, he would never do that. He loves me and, apart from this one thing, I have never done anything against his wishes.'

Ellen did not comment. Used to having his own way in everything, she knew the Earl could be vindictive if he was thwarted, even against those he loved, and she did not want Bella to learn that the hard way. 'But, my dearest, you will have to marry sooner or later. It is what every woman wants—a husband and children—and if she is so lucky as to find a gentleman who is rich and powerful, she is doubly blessed.'

'You never had them.'

'No.'

'Did you never want to marry?'

'I never had the opportunity.'

'Never been in love?'

'Ah, that would be telling…'

'Then tell.'

'Oh, dear, no. It was all too long ago.' She smiled suddenly. 'I had the children without having to go through all the fuss of a marriage. Your dear papa and you were my family.'

'How old was Papa when you came here?' It made Bella feel better to talk about someone else, anything but what was really on her mind. She had expected Ellen to support her stance, but it seemed she was not going to. Her grandfather and Miss Battersby were the most unlikely allies.

'Less than a year old. He was such a weak thing, his arms like sticks and his head too big for his body. But, with my care, he became a strong, handsome man, and all the ladies swooning after him.'

Bella was astonished. She could not imagine her father other than the figure she remembered—tall and broad, his heavy features lightened by expressive eyes and the fine arched brows of the Huntleys. She had a feminine version of them herself. And he had not looked a weakling in that portrait in the schoolroom. Unless the artist had used artistic licence in drawing him.

'Speaking of my father,' she said, 'I took James's two little girls up to the schoolroom today and saw two portraits of little boys. I am sure one was my father, but who was the other?'

Ellen looked startled. 'Are they still there? I imagined that one had been destroyed when all the others went…'

'Destroyed—why? Who was the other boy? They could almost be twins.'

'Oh, dear, it is not my place to tell you of such things…'

'Who else is there to tell me? Shall I ask Grandfather?'

'Oh, no, whatever you do, do not speak to him of it.'

'Then tell me.'

'You are right, one of the boys is your father. The other is… Oh, dear, I am at a loss to tell it without upsetting you.'

'Go on.'

'He is Henry, the Earl's other son. He was two years older than your father, though smaller and more delicate which is why, at eight years old, there was very little between them in size.'

'Henry? I never heard of him. What happened to him?'

'He died in a tragic accident when he was nine. The two boys were playing in the woods and climbing trees. Henry fell and broke his neck.'

'Oh, how terrible. But why have I never heard of him? Why does no one ever speak of him? Why destroy his picture?'

'The tragedy affected the poor Countess so much she lost her reason. She could not look at your papa without bursting into tears over it and making herself ill, so he was kept away from her and all evidence of Henry's existence hidden from her.'

'But my father had lost a brother—could they not console each other?'

Ellen paused, wondering how much to tell. 'Although Charles was the younger, he was always the more adventurous of the two, even a little wild sometimes, and she blamed him for the accident. She said if Charles had not urged him on, Henry would never have climbed that tree— he was afraid of heights.'

Bella was appalled. No wonder her father had been morose and moody—he must have felt so unloved and probably blamed himself as well. Once, when she had been very small, he had taken her on his knee and told her never to put her trust in cold women. 'They have no heart,' he had said. Even at six, she had known he had often said strange things when he had been drinking and she had promptly forgotten all about it until today. Now she felt so sorry for him that her own troubles faded into the background. 'But what about the Earl? Papa was his son, too. Surely he did not condone the way the Countess was treating him?'

'Oh, he tried to do his best for the boy but, with the Countess so set against him, there was little he could do. I think that is why he is so concerned that you should be settled, my love.'

'When he told me of it, he said he had to make his peace with the past and ensure the future. Do you think he was referring to that?'

'Oh, undoubtedly, my dear. So, you see, you must be very careful how you deal with it. If he finds out you and Robert have been gulling him, he will be so angry…'

'He will not find out. It will all come to an end very naturally, after I have had my Season.'

'Why ask the Captain to help you? Why not Louis, or even Sir Edward?'

'I do not trust Louis. You said yourself he was a rake-shame and I would not wish to be seen on his arm. Why, everyone would take me for one of his ladybirds.'

Ellen laughed aloud. 'Where did you learn that name?'

'From Robert. That's what he said when—'

'Did he also tell you what it means?'

'No, but I deduce it is not very favourable.'

'You are right. So Louis is not to be considered, but what about Sir Edward? Now, that would have been the more logical choice and you need not go to the bother of breaking it off. He is eligible in every way and the one his lordship was thinking of, I shouldn't wonder.'

'Edward is on the way to being engaged to Miss Charlotte Mellish.'

'So, Captain Huntley it is by a process of elimination. Poor man—does he know what he is taking on, I wonder?' Ellen chuckled and was rewarded with a watery smile.

'I like Robert. He is the only one who is not mercenary. He almost did not come, you know. And he was very kind to me when I was frightened by the mob and Misty threw me.'

'Threw you? What is this? He said nothing of it.'

'No, he would not want me to be scolded.'

Ellen looked knowingly at her charge and decided not to comment. 'And the Earl has accepted your choice without a quibble?'

'He said he would and he can hardly refute it when I take him at his word, can he? And he agreed we need not publish the engagement until the end of the Season.'

'I'll wager he did,' Ellen muttered. 'He is a crafty old fox.'

'What do you mean?'

'Why, nothing, my love. I am sorry I spoke disrespectfully. Now, I must go down and fetch my bag and unpack. When do you expect Captain Huntley to return?'

'In two or three days, he said.'

'Then we shall see what transpires.'

Newmarket was roughly halfway between Westmere and Palgrave, and it was here that Robert turned into the yard of the inn and left his horse with an ostler, before going inside to order food. George and Desmond were already sitting at one of the tables, a huge dinner spread out before them.

'We had all but given you up,' Desmond said, as Robert threw off his rain cloak and lowered himself wearily into a chair beside them. 'You said you would not be gone above half a day.'

'If I had not known you were going to the country, I would have said you had been overindulging in the fleshpots of the capital,' George commented, looking at the slowly fading bruise on Robert's cheek. 'What have you been doing?'

Robert smiled. 'Listening to my great uncle throwing his orders about and my cousins quarrelling, not to mention my aunt ringing a peal over me and getting mixed up in one of those ''bread or blood'' riots...' He stopped short of mentioning Bella.

'Well, you're here now,' George said. 'Eat up and come and see the filly I've bought. She's a two-year-old chestnut and, I'll wager, a real goer. I'm going to let her try her paces in one of tomorrow's races, and if she's up to it, I'll enter her for the two thousand guineas next month.'

'Ain't that a mite ambitious?' Robert said, as the waiter brought more food and he tucked into it with the appetite of a hungry man.

'No. Wait till you see her run. We had her over the gallops this morning, didn't we, Desmond? She can really fly.'

Desmond confirmed the filly's speed but was intrigued
that Robert was less than enthusiastic. 'What's up, old fellow? Ain't like you to be blue-devilled. Old man not come
up trumps?'

They had assumed his visit to his great-uncle had been
undertaken to replenish funds and he had been unsuccessful.
He grinned ruefully. 'Not that. I'm afraid I'm obliged to
leave you again. Got to go to Palgrave.'

'Oh, I see. Perhaps you'll have better luck there. We'll
see you in Town at the end of the week.'

He did not bother to disillusion them, but finished his
meal and bade them goodbye. He had a feeling that his
carefree bachelor excursions with his two friends were going
to be sorely curtailed in the coming weeks, and though half
of him resented it, the other half was looking forward to
seeing more of his delightful cousin. Not too much,
though—that would start the tongues wagging and he could
not risk that if he were to come out at the end of it with a
whole reputation. Or so he told himself.

It was very late when he arrived at Palgrave Manor and
everyone had gone to bed. Rather than rouse them, he sta-
bled the horse and entered the house by a back door. After
helping himself to a cold chicken leg and a glass of wine,
he removed his boots and crept upstairs with them in his
hand. It would be time enough to talk to his mother after
breakfast the following day. Knowing him as she did, she
was going to take some convincing that he had decided to
settle down to matrimony.

And he was right. After he had brushed aside the questions about how he had come by a black eye, he told her
he had offered for Bella. She was so taken aback that she
could only stare at him in disbelief, a forkful of ham halfway
to her open mouth. 'You have done what?'

She was an indulgent mama as a rule, and used to the
unpredictable ways of her sons, but this was past everything.

Robert, unlike Edward, had never shown the least inclination to marry and settle down—he was more fond of galloping about the countryside, chasing foxes or taking part in curricle races or sparring at Jacksons to think of women. War had made him like that, she had decided, and he was still young and should be allowed to sow the wild oats he had been prevented from casting because of the war.

'Offered for Bella and been accepted,' he repeated.

'Robert, have you taken leave of your senses? How can you possibly support a wife? Where will you live?'

'Oh, there is plenty of time to worry about that,' he said airily. 'Not going to announce it until the end of the Season. It's to be a secret until then.'

'Why, Robert, why?'

He smiled and repeated the argument he had put forward to his brother, that he did not want everyone thinking he had done it because of the promise of a legacy. It had nothing to do with that…

'You are surely not saying you have developed a *tendre* for your cousin?'

'Why not?' he demanded.

'But she is a child and one that has been close confined. I do not believe she has ever been further afield than Cambridge or King's Lynn. How can she possibly be expected to make such an important decision? What does my uncle say? You did speak to him?'

'Oh, yes, indeed I did. We are in complete agreement.'

'Then he is as big a noddicock as you are.'

He grinned. 'That is Aunt Elizabeth's opinion, too. She is up in the boughs over it and thinks Louis has been slighted.'

Henrietta allowed herself a smile of understanding. Her sister-in-law was all pretension and ambition, if not for herself then for her children. Colette had been almost hurled at the Regent and Louis dressed so flamboyantly as to be instantly recognised at any society function. 'Louis would never offer for Bella.'

'He did, though, and in a most unflattering way.'

'Oh, I see, so you stepped in to save her from Louis…'

'And James.'

'Robert, that is not a good enough reason to offer marriage, you know. You will come home by weeping cross if you go on with it.'

'Mama, you are always telling me I should stop my racketing ways and settle down, and I like Bella well enough. I am very fond of her.'

'When have you seen her to form such an attachment?'

'When we went to Westmere as boys, when I came out of the army and stayed at Westmere for a night on the way back from Peterborough, and at Grandfather's funeral.'

'A little creature dressed all in black and not a word to say for herself.'

'She was overcome by the solemnity of the occasion. She is normally bright and cheerful and has a lively intelligence and the courage of a lion.'

'Such fulsome compliments as I never heard. I cannot wait to have these virtues demonstrated to me.'

'Good, because I have told her you will invite her to stay with you.'

'Naturally I will, but, Robert, have you forgotten I am removing to Town at the end of the week?'

'No, I had not forgot, but you could take her with you. Give her a Season. It will please her no end.'

'Season? You mean bring her out?'

'Yes, Mama, say you will, please. She is so looking forward to it.'

'What has the Earl to say on the matter?'

'I did not mention it to him. I thought it would be better if you were to invite her. He would not refuse you if you said you wished Bella to come and stay so that you may get to know her better.'

Henrietta smiled suddenly. So, it was all a ploy hatched to get Bella to London and had nothing to do with marriage at all. She breathed a sigh of relief. Robert was not such a souse crown after all. 'Very well, but should she not wait until I have settled in Holles Street?'

'No, you see, we could reach Palgrave from Westmere in a day but to go straight to London would mean an overnight stop and that might not be quite the thing...'

'We?' his mother queried.

'Yes, I promised to go and fetch her. If I bring her here you can take her under your wing for the rest of the journey.'

'Why are you always in such haste? Do you ever stop to consider the consequences of your actions?'

'If you could see the poor girl and the pressure his lordship is exerting on her, you would be in haste to fetch her away yourself.'

Henrietta sighed. She could not refuse her son anything that it was in her power to grant and she was curious to see what it was about Bella that had him in thrall. 'Very well,' she said. 'In truth, she will be company for me.'

Bella rode Misty along the road towards Westmere village. She was finding the time waiting for Robert to return tedious in the extreme. Her grandfather seemed to have shrunk into himself, as if he had expended all his energy on setting up the meeting with his great-nephews and had none left for ordinary day-to-day discourse. He made no secret of the fact that he did not like having James's girls in the house, though Mrs Clarke did her best to keep them in a distant part of the building. She was also making herself very useful in the kitchen, helping Martha, which left Bella with more time on her hands.

And so she had asked for Misty to be saddled and had gone for a ride. There was no danger. The rioters had dispersed, too afraid of retribution to continue with their protests, and Westmere had remained peaceful, mainly because the Earl, pinchpenny that he was over his own domestic expenses, did not ask more rent from the farmers on his land than he thought they could afford on condition they paid their workers properly.

Their wages were augmented by Bella who, encouraged by the Earl, took them food and outgrown clothes of her own to give their children. This old-fashioned paternal attitude of her grandfather's ensured loyalty and she did not think Westmere men would riot. But thinking of the rioters reminded her of Robert and the way he had rescued her, not only from the rabble but from her grandfather. She wondered how he was faring with his mother.

She had delivered her bounty and was returning home when she saw a bent figure walking along the road ahead of her and recognised the old lady from the woods. She was carrying a basket in which lay a single bunch of primroses.

'Good-day, mistress,' Bella said, reining in.

'Oh, 'tis you, miss. How are you?'

Bella slid from her horse. 'Well, thank you. How are you?'

'This cold and wet don't do for my old bones,' she said. 'But age is something there's no cure for.'

'I have a meat patty here,' Bella said, turning to extract the parcel from her saddlebag. 'Would you like it? It was fresh made this morning.'

'You think I am in need of charity?'

'No.' Bella was taken aback by the ungracious retort. 'I was being neighbourly.'

'What is neighbourliness if it isn't charity?'

'I am sorry, I shall know better than to offer it another

time. Not that there will be the opportunity, for I am going to London for a Season.'

'Is that so?' The woman seemed to show more interest in this piece of news. 'Then you made a choice after all.'

'No. I decided to follow your advice and take my time.'

'That's not what I heard. I heard you had accepted Captain Robert Huntley…'

'Who told you that?' Bella asked.

'A little bird.' The old lady smiled and, picking the bunch of primroses from her basket, handed them to Bella. 'I've been to Ely market and these were left over. Take them, call them payment for the pie.'

Bella laughed delightedly. The primroses had undoubtedly come from her grandfather's woods, but she would not argue the point of ownership. Instead, she handed over the pie and took the posy from the woman's gnarled fingers.

'Be on your guard, my little one,' the woman said, popping the package into her basket. 'There are those who wish you ill.'

And with that she left the road and struck off into the woods where she lived, leaving Bella to remount and ride home, musing on the strange woman who seemed to know everything that went on at Westmere Hall.

She rode Misty back to the stables where she discovered a dark green barouche in the yard and two new horses being looked after by a groom and a pimply youth who were both strangers to her. 'Whose are they?' she asked Spooner.

'Captain Huntley brought them, miss.'

Robert was back! She resisted the impulse to run and find him, to demand to know what his mother had said. Instead, she went up to her room to change out of her riding clothes and then make her way downstairs, demure and ladylike in spotted muslin and pink ribbons.

Long before she reached the drawing room, she could hear the twins squealing with pleasure and, on opening the door, discovered Robert crawling on his hands and knees, with the two little girls riding on his back, pretending to whip him. Seeing Bella, he collapsed in a heap with the girls on top of him.

'Bella, there you are.' He extracted himself and sent the children back to Mrs Clarke, before bowing before her.

She inclined her head in greeting, trying not to laugh at his tousled appearance. His hair was all over the place and his cravat crooked. 'Robert. How do you?'

'Well. And you? His lordship has not been scolding you?'

'No, I have seen little of him. He does not care for the children and has been keeping to his room.' She was aware of a certain stiffness in their manner towards each other, which surprised her. She had always been very easy with him before.

'His lordship's anxiety for a new heir does not extend to enjoying the society of children, then?'

'No.' She was not sure she wanted to be reminded of the reason for her grandfather's determination to see her married.

'Then it is his loss. They are delightful company.'

'I remember you and Edward giving me rides when I was small.' It brought home to her the difference in their ages. When she had been the same age as the twins, Robert had already been a gangly fifteen-year-old and Edward in his first year at university, quite the young gentleman.

'So we did. I had forgot.'

'Robert....' She paused.

'You want to know what my mother had to say?'

'Yes, please. I shall go mad if I have to stay here a day longer.'

'Then you shan't.' He took a letter from his pocket and handed it to her. 'I believe this is an invitation to spend some time with Mama. She has sent me with the coach to fetch you.'

'Oh, Robert, you are an angel!' She flung her arms about his neck and kissed him joyously on each cheek, as a child awarded a treat might have done. He raised his hands halfway to his shoulders and then, not knowing what to do with them, dropped them again and stood stiffly to attention.

Suddenly aware of his lack of response, she realised she had embarrassed him and stood back, her face a scarlet picture of mortification. 'Oh, I am sorry…'

Unaccountably pleased, he smiled and put out his hand to stroke her cheek with the back of one finger. 'Impulsive as always, my dear, but you must remember that we are no longer childhood playfellows. Society is like to be shocked by such forwardness, especially as we are to keep our betrothal a secret.'

'Oh, I will remember.' She was not at all sure she would know how to behave in Society—her grandfather had never seen fit to enlighten her and Miss Battersby's experience was limited. She hoped Mrs Huntley would set her right. 'Does my grandfather know of the invitation?'

'Mama sent a similar letter to him and I have had Sylvester carry it to him, so I assume he does. No doubt we shall hear what he has to say before long.'

They heard what he had to say at dinner. He waited until they had all been served from a dish of turbot in a cream sauce and then dismissed Daisy. Bella's heart was pounding because she was convinced he could see right through the ruse they had perpetrated and would be very angry.

'Well, miss,' he began, 'am I to assume you have received an invitation from Mrs Huntley to pay her a visit?'

'Yes, Grandpapa.'

'And you wish to accept?'

'Yes, Grandpapa. It is natural she would want to see me.'

'Can't think why. Knows you already. And what am I to do without you?'

'Why, I am sure you will manage very well. Miss Battersby can keep house for you.' She ignored Ellen's gasp of astonishment. 'And she has Mrs Clarke to help her. The house has never run so smoothly as it has this last week and I have done nothing at all. Oh, please, let me go.'

'But, dearest,' Ellen put in, 'if I am to stay here, who will chaperone you?'

She had not considered that. 'Do I need one?' she asked, looking from Ellen to her grandfather and then at Robert.

'Of course you do.' Ellen said.

'Well, I am not letting you both go,' the Earl put in. 'I need one of you here.'

'Then I shall take Daisy,' Bella said firmly. 'Miss Battersby can find another house servant from the village.'

'Yes, but—' the Earl began.

Bella sat back with a sigh of satisfaction. 'Then that's settled.'

Robert could only admire the way she had handled the old man and gave her an encouraging smile. 'We shall leave first thing tomorrow. Can you be ready?'

'Oh, yes. I can be packed in no time.'

'You will want to ride while you are with Mama, I have no doubt, so I brought a stable boy to ride your mare to Palgrave. He refuses absolutely to ride side-saddle so we will have to tie your saddle on the coach with the luggage.'

'Oh, Robert, how thoughtful you are! I love to ride and there is no one here to exercise Misty except me or one of the grooms. It is a capital solution.' The exclamation produced in him an unaccustomed flush of pleasure and drew from his lordship a wry smile which no one noticed.

The afternoon was spent in a flurry of preparation, with Daisy alternately elated and frightened at the elevation to lady's maid and the prospect of accompanying her mistress to London. But Bella had little baggage and it all went into one trunk and a small portmanteau.

Robert, watching his groom tying them on the boot of the

carriage next day along with her saddle, realised that if Bella was going to stay a whole Season in Town, she would need an entirely new wardrobe. When they arrived in London, he would make sure she was dressed in the latest mode and introduced to every eligible in Town. She was fetching enough with her mixture of sweet innocence and spirited defiance of convention to be a hit. He wanted her to forget her grandfather's unkindness and enjoy herself for a few weeks. She deserved that at least.

But, strangely, his lordship had thought about her clothes. When Bella, clad in a green jaconet carriage dress, topped with a three-quarter pelisse in a darker shade of the same colour, her dark curls peeping from under the brim of a velvet bonnet trimmed with pea-green silk, went to the library to bid her grandfather goodbye, he kissed her and handed her a package. 'You will need a new wardrobe—can't have the *ton* saying I can't afford to clothe you,' he said gruffly. 'Buy what you need. Do not stint yourself. And, Isabella…' He paused and looked down at her, for the moment unable to go on.

'Yes, Grandpapa?'

'Enjoy yourself. And write to me. I need to know how you go on.'

Overcome by emotion, she could not speak at first, though her eyes glistened with mixed tears of sadness and happiness. She reached up and kissed his cheek. 'Of course I will. Thank you so much, Grandpapa. Thank you.' Then she curtsied and left the room to join Robert who was waiting by the coach. The old man followed and stood beside Miss Battersby and Jolliffe at the door as she was helped in, her face alight with excitement.

Bella turned to wave at them as Robert climbed in beside her and told the coachman to proceed. The young groom, whose name she had learned was Danny, mounted Misty and the little cavalcade set off. She continued to wave until

the carriage turned out of the gate onto the road and the
house was lost to sight. And then it came to her all in a rush
that she had left her old life behind—her childhood, the two
people she loved most, the house and the village—and was
going into the unknown, and a future she could only guess
at.

Robert smiled at her, understanding. 'The die is cast, my
dear.'

Chapter Five

It was a long and bumpy ride. Much of the countryside through which they passed was sodden and in many places inundated by the recent rain, so that the roads were deeply rutted and they were frequently flung against each other as the carriage wheels dipped into the potholes. This slight physical contact was enough to make Bella's heartbeat quicken until she became quite breathless which, she felt, was very silly of her. She had known Robert all her life, had always looked on him as a favourite playmate, someone to ride and fish with, and here she was shaking at the thought of his firm thigh only separated from hers by a layer or two of cloth. Was he aware of it? Oh, she did hope not!

She made herself sit upright and hung grimly onto the strap to prevent it happening again, but one particularly bad lurch had her almost in his lap and he was obliged to put his arm about her to save her from falling on the floor. And having done so, he left it there, smiling at her without speaking. She knew it was highly improper and she should not have allowed it, but it felt so comfortable and it might hurt his feelings if she were to make a point of moving away. After all, they were supposed to be engaged, were they not? Why was she feeling so confused about that?

Daisy, terrified and suffering dreadfully from coach sickness, pressed herself in the opposite corner and loudly wished herself dead, but even though the maid was feeling ill, she could hear perfectly well and so Bella had little to say, afraid that by something she said, or the tone of her voice, she would give away their secret. Very little escaped the servants at Westmere Hall, and if the strange woman in the woods knew so much, she was sure Daisy was well aware that her mistress and Robert were secretly engaged. But what she did not know was that it was all pretence.

Newmarket Heath was open and bare but Bella saw some beautiful horses being exercised there, and when they left it behind they passed into countryside which was a little less flat and treeless than the fens which had been her home all her life. Here the landscape was patterned with fields and meadows, surrounded by hedges. The roads were a little better and they fairly sped along so that there was now no excuse to hold her and he sat with folded arms, staring silently out of the window.

Robert had bespoke several changes of horses and they were ready and waiting all along their route, so that there was no time to alight and stretch their legs, although at midday they did make a longer stop in order to have a meal. Daisy refused to go into the inn, saying the smell of food would make her stomach heave all over again, so Robert and Bella left her walking up and down in the yard and went inside, where Robert ordered a pork chop and vegetables for them both, ale for himself and cordial for Bella. Then he told the waiter to take something out to their coachman and young Danny who had just ridden Misty into the yard.

Half an hour later they resumed their seats but Daisy begged to be allowed to sit on the box beside the driver. 'I am sure I shall do better out in the air,' she said.

'Oh, Daisy, I am sorry,' Bella said. 'Of course you must sit outside if it will help you.'

The maid scrambled up beside the coachman who gave her a friendly grin and made room for her. 'I had much rather be up top on a fine day than anywhere else in the world,' he said, flicking the reins and calling to the horses to gee up.

Without the maid to hear every word, Bella felt less constrained. 'Why are we in such haste?' she asked Robert. 'You give us no time to look about and admire the scenery.'

'To do the journey in a single day, we have to crack on,' he said. 'I promised Mama I would have you at Palgrave by dark.'

'Oh.' She decided he was not enjoying the journey as she was. It was a boring chore to him and only undertaken because he had made her a rash promise he was probably already regretting. She sighed and then smiled. She had got her own way and was going to have her Season and she might as well put everything else behind her and enjoy it. 'When is Cousin Henrietta removing to London?'

'Two days hence, I think. She has taken a house in Holles Street for the Season, but I think she may decide to live permanently in London. Palgrave Manor belongs to Edward now, you know, and it will be his marital home. She does not want to stay after he is married and I cannot say I blame her.'

'Edward is going to offer for Miss Mellish soon, then?'

He looked sharply at her, unable to decide what had prompted the question. 'I expect so.'

'Does your mama not like Miss Mellish?'

'She has not expressed an opinion,' he said stiffly. 'It is Teddy's decision after all.'

'And the lady's.'

'Naturally.'

She did not seem to notice that his answers were a little short. 'Is there no dowager house?'

'There is, but it has been let for years and she does not want the tenants turned out. She says she doesn't like the place but I think she does not care to be too near.'

'Yes, I can understand it would be a wrench, handing your home over to another woman to manage. It never happened at Westmere because my mother died and the Countess remained in control, right up to the time of her death. After that there was only me.'

'It must have been hard for you to find yourself looking after that great barn of a place for your grandfather.'

'It is not a great barn—it is a lovely place and it is my home.'

'Is that why the Earl is so determined you shall stay in it—because he knows how much you love the place?'

'Perhaps. He only wants what's best for me, which is why I find it so hard to disoblige him.'

'Disoblige!' He laughed. 'Is that what you call it? He will call it something else when it comes to the end of the Season, unless you do as he asks.'

'You are already regretting your part in it, I can see. Do you want to turn the carriage round and go back? I shall quite understand if you do.'

'Don't be a ninny,' he said quickly. 'I said I would help and I will, but you should not blind yourself to the consequences.'

'I do not.' She paused, then went on after a moment's consideration, 'Did you know my papa had a brother?'

He turned to her in surprise. 'No, I never heard it. Are you sure?'

'Oh, yes, Batters told me, but he died when he was eight. You know, if he had lived, he would have been the heir, not Papa. And I would not be here now.'

'Would you not?'

'No, for there would be none of this fuss over the legacy, would there? My uncle would have married and his children would be in line, not any of us. Not me or you or Edward or Louis or James. Is that not strange to think of?'

'It is indeed.'

'I wonder what I would be doing now, where I would be living. My whole life would be have been different. Papa's would have been different.'

'No sense in speculating,' Robert said, disbelieving the story as a Banbury tale. Miss Battersby was known for her romanticism—she had probably read something like it in a book and imagined it was real. If there had been another son, there would have been talk, pictures of him, evidence of some kind about the house. 'You have to take life as it comes, play the cards you are dealt.'

'I collect you are a gambler.'

'No more than any man of my station.'

'Do you win?'

'Sometimes. Sometimes I lose.'

'But on the whole?'

'Mostly I win. Why do you want to know?'

'Because we are both gambling now, are we not? I am gambling that Grandpapa will change his mind about marrying me off and you are gambling that I will not make it difficult for you to come out of the whole affair with honour intact.'

'Something like that, to be sure.'

'I promise you, I shall break off our engagement in the most amicable way possible and no one will blame you at all.'

He laughed, but it was rather a cracked sound. 'Thank you, my dear.'

'But tell me, how shall we go on in London? Shall you be staying in Holles Street?'

'Oh, no, that would never do. I have a small bachelor apartment in Albany.'

'And Edward?'

'When my brother is in town he lives at Blandings House in Hanover Square.'

Blandings was his mother's maiden name, Bella knew, and the house had been inherited from her father. 'Oh.'

'You did not imagine we should all be cooped up together, did you? Heaven forbid!'

Bella was not sure how she felt about that last remark. Did it mean he did not like her company and was already regretting becoming involved with her? 'No, of course not. But will you visit us?'

'Naturally I will. Mama thinks we are engaged.'

'Are you sure you should not tell her the truth?' She was apprehensive about meeting his mother and worried that they were extending their masquerade beyond Westmere, which was not at all what she had meant when she had first suggested it. All she had wanted to do had been to lull her grandfather into thinking she had done as he had asked, simply to get away for a short time, not to deceive the world at large. 'It would mean we need not be seen so often in each other's company.'

He smiled lopsidedly at her. It seemed he had served his purpose in freeing her from her grandfather and now she wished to use that freedom to enjoy herself, unfettered by liaisons, real or imaginary. 'I shall contrive to be otherwise engaged as often as possible, my dear, and when we are together we shall, of course, be in company. You need not fear that I shall hamper your enjoyment.'

'Nor I yours,' she said waspishly. The last thing she wanted was for Robert to think she was wearing the willow for him and this was her way of catching him. Nothing could be further from the truth, she told herself firmly.

'Then we are agreed.'

There was nothing more to be said after that and they continued the journey in almost total silence, except when they stopped for a further change of horses and he asked if she wished to go into the inn for refreshment, which she politely declined, knowing it would delay them. Even so, it was almost dark by the time the coach clattered through the main street of a small village, which Robert told her was Palgrave, and turned through a pair of wrought-iron gates to draw up at the door of Palgrave Manor.

The house was less than half the size of Westmere Hall and more compact, being almost square. Its porticoed front door was in the centre of its façade and was flanked on each side by matching windows. A red creeper grew up its walls almost to roof height. A homely, comfortable-looking house, Bella decided, even before stepping inside.

A butler admitted them, but before he could conduct them to the drawing room a tiny plump woman came out to greet them. Still in mourning for her father-in-law, Henrietta was dressed in a gown of black mazarin silk, the bosom of which was filled with white lace. She wore a tiny scrap of black lace as a mourning cap. But there was nothing mournful about her smile. She came forward, both hands outstretched, and took both of Bella's even before she could pull off her gloves and divest herself of her pelisse.

'So here you are here!' She kissed Bella on each cheek 'Welcome, my dear, welcome. Did you have a good journey?'

Bella was overwhelmed and feeling quite dreadful over the trick they were playing on her. 'Yes, thank you, ma'am.'

'Oh, calling me "ma'am" makes me feel ancient. How about Cousin Henrietta?' She held her at arm's length and looked her up and down. 'You look tired, child. Has Robert been forcing the pace? He must do everything in a rush, you know. I never knew anyone like him for that. Not in the least careful that others might like to take life a little slower.'

'Mama, I protest...'

'No, ma'am...I mean cousin, he has been very careful of me,' Bella said.

Henrietta had put her arm round Bella and led her towards the stairs. 'Come, I will take you to your room myself and then you may rest and change and we will have a good coze over supper and you shall tell me how this whirlwind of a son of mine managed to stand still long enough to propose.' She turned back to Robert who was standing, completely bemused, staring after them. 'See the baggage is taken up, Robert. Supper will be in an hour.'

Now that she had lost the support of Robert and was alone with Henrietta, Bella found herself tongue-tied. She did not have a single thing to say, except to repeat her gratitude that she had been invited.

'My goodness, child, do not keep thanking me. It is perfectly natural that I should ask you. We need to spend some time getting to know each other. To be sure, I have known you almost since the day you were born, but we have not been often in each other's company, have we? And now you are a young lady and have done my scapegrace son the honour of consenting to be his wife, so we have a great deal to reflect upon.' As she spoke she opened a door on the gallery which ran round the upper floor. 'This is the room I have had prepared for you. I hope you find it comfortable.'

'Oh, I am sure I shall.' Bella was trembling with nerves and guilt, guilt most of all. She wished fervently that Robert had confided the truth to his mother, and the next time she spoke to him alone, she would insist on him doing so.

'And here is your maid and Peters with your trunk. I have ordered hot water to be sent up to you and a dish of hot chocolate which will revive you. Come down when you are ready. There is no hurry. I did not think you would wish for an elaborate meal tonight, so it will only be soup and a roast duck, followed by a light sorbet. I do find a heavy meal late at night plays havoc with the digestion, don't you?'

'Yes, indeed.'

'You are shy,' Henrietta said, smiling at her young guest. 'Robert said you were not, but what does he, a mere man, know of it?'

'I am a little overwhelmed by your kindness, ma'am.'

'Now, we will have no more of that. To be truthful, you are doing me a favour, bearing me company. I should find living alone in London quite daunting without you. Now I am looking forward to it. We shall go shopping and there are any number of places to visit. And when the Season begins in earnest, there will be invitations to musical and literary evenings, not to mention routs and balls, so that we shall be quite worn out with it all.'

Daisy had been unpacking the portmanteau while Mrs Huntley was speaking, and now there was a scratch at the door and another maid came in with a large jug of steaming water which she stood on the washstand. 'Now I shall leave you to make yourself at home.'

After she had gone, Bella looked about her. The room was delightfully furnished in rose pink and cream, even down to the bedhead, the doors of the large wardrobe and the jugs and basin on the washing stand. She crossed the pink carpet to look out of the window and discovered the room was at the back of the house and looked out onto a terraced garden and beyond that was parkland in which there was a lake with an island in the middle. Later she would enjoy exploring it. Now she must change and go down to face her hostess.

She turned back to her maid. 'Get me out of this dress, Daisy, and then pour the water into the bowl. I feel as if I had been in a mud bath. And then you can put out the pink muslin and my flame-coloured shawl.' It was not a difficult choice because she only had that and a white silk gown with a floss overdress which were at all suitable for evening wear. She smiled to herself. Grandpapa had given her five hundred pounds to spend and she would be able to buy what she needed when Mrs Huntley took her shopping. She was quite looking forward to that, though whom she wanted to impress she was not at all sure. Mrs Huntley? Robert? Or some unknown gallant waiting in the wings to claim her?

Robert, having obeyed his mama and ordered the footman to take Bella's trunk upstairs and directed Daisy to follow him, had turned into the book room where he poured himself a large brandy from a decanter and glasses on a side table and sprawled sideways into a chair to drink it, throwing his long legs over its arms.

He needed a drink because the next few hours were going to be the most difficult of the whole escapade. He had to tread the fine line between being too doting on his bride-to-be and too indifferent to be genuine. He had to satisfy his mother as to his intentions on one side and not complicate matters with Bella on the other. He was not in the least prepared for explaining himself to his brother, so when Edward strolled into the room he was startled and disconcerted.

He swung his legs over the chair arm and sat up. 'Teddy, I did not expect you to be here. Mama never said.'

'Why should I not be here? It is my home.'

'Yes, but I thought you had returned to London.'

'I do not have to give an account of my movements to you, brother, but since you ask, I came to see if there was anything I could do to help Mama with her move to Holles Street. The house is ready and I have engaged the staff, but there may be other commissions I can execute.'

'I beg pardon, Edward. Of course we should all help Mama.'

'Especially as you seem to have burdened her with a guest.'

'Bella is not a burden. I have no doubt she will be company for Mama and, in any case, she is one of the family.'

'To be sure, a second cousin.' He smiled. 'Soon to be closer, I collect. I must say I find your sudden change of heart difficult to believe, you know. Until we all went to Westmere, you had never given Bella a second glance. Not in the marriage stakes, you said often enough and repeated it while we were there. We both said we would not play his lordship's game, we agreed neither of us would offer. And what did you do as soon as you found her alone? Propose.'

'And was accepted. Do not forget that.'

'Yes, but James's manners and address are appalling and, no doubt, she had sense enough to see through Louis's affectations. I am persuaded she took you as the best of a bad bunch since I did not offer.'

Robert was acutely aware of the truth of this but he would not admit it to his brother because he had promised Bella he would tell him nothing. 'Not at all. We had formed an attachment before that.'

'When?'

Robert had been thinking of what he would say if that question arose and was ready with his answer. 'The last time I was at Westmere. I paid a visit when I first came home after the war. I had promised my sergeant that if he was killed I should visit his wife and she lives in Peterborough, and I used the opportunity to call at Westmere, which saved me a night's bed and board. And Bella and I...' He shrugged. 'Need I go on?'

'Did his lordship know of it?'

'Of course not. Not then. She was too young...' Not too young to capture his attention, he thought. Before he had gone away to war, she had been a child, a mischievous and delightful child, up to all manner of scrapes. When he had returned he had found a self-possessed young lady of extraordinary charm, one he was sure would turn many a head given the opportunity. She had already turned his.

'Still is, much too young to deal with the Earl of Westmere and an impecunious ex-soldier when they collude against her. But I tell you this, brother, if you play her false, you shall have me to answer to.'

They were almost quarrelling and they had not done that since they had been children and had squabbled over playthings. But Bella was not a plaything. She was flesh and blood, warm and caring, and her slight frame beside him on the carriage seat had sent him nearly crazy. He must remember it was all a masquerade and at the end of the Season she would fall in with her grandfather's wishes. And Robert did not have any doubt about what they were—they did not involve an 'impecunious ex-soldier', to use Edward's words. 'You may rest easy. We both know what we are about. Now, if you will excuse me, I must go and change for supper. Do you stay?'

'Yes, I would not miss it for the world.'

Robert had been afraid of that. He went up to his room, tore off his grubby travelling clothes and washed in the hot water put out by his man, Adam Gotobed, who had been with him throughout his army career and had stayed with him in civilian life. As a valet he was not outstanding, but as a faithful servant who knew every nuance of his master's mood and was not afraid of speaking his mind he was supreme.

'What will you wear, Captain?'

Robert considered the question. Should he dress to impress or assume a casual indifference to his appearance? He decided to take the middle road and selected black pantaloons, a white linen shirt, brocade waistcoat with silver buttons and a pale blue silk cravat. Having pulled on black buckled shoes, he allowed Adam to help him into a tail coat of dark blue velvet. He finished it off with a lace handkerchief peeping from the end of his sleeve and a quizzing glass on a ribbon round his neck. Not quite the dandy, but near enough. Then, humming to himself, he sauntered down to the withdrawing room.

Edward and his mother were already there, chatting amiably together about the new house. 'I shall need a carriage,' Henrietta was saying. 'I cannot continue to use the family coach—it is yours after all and you may need it yourself— but if I am to take Bella out and about and pay calls, I cannot be forever calling up a cab.'

'You may safely leave that to me, Mama,' Robert put in, before Edward could reply. 'I shall have more time than Edward and, besides, I am a better judge of horseflesh than he is.'

'You think so?' his brother queried, one fine brow raised in an expression that clearly said he did not agree.

'I am a cavalry man. Horses are part of my business.'

'You think Mama and Bella need cavalry horses?' He laughed. 'Can you imagine it? Why, they would be the laughing stock of the whole *ton*. And what would you have them ride in, one of those high-perch phaetons?'

'Don't be ridiculous.'

'Boys! Boys!' Henrietta said, laughing. 'Do not quarrel over it.'

'Just because he suddenly has prospects he never had before, he has become an authority,' Edward said. 'Well, I should not count on it, brother. Louis is all set to prove the old man is touched in the attic and not fit to make such a will.'

'Is he?' Henrietta asked in surprise.

'Touched in the attic? Who's to tell?'

'No, I meant Louis going to law.'

'He says he is, though how that will help him, I do not know. He has less claim than I have.' He grinned. 'But we shall see.' Then, catching sight of Bella hesitating in the doorway, he added brightly, 'Why, here is Cousin Isabella.'

Both he and Robert rose as one and moved forward to draw her into the room, almost knocking each other over. Bewildered, she took an arm of each and was escorted to sit beside Henrietta on the sofa.

'How charming you look,' Henrietta said.

She murmured, 'Thank you.' And then fell silent. She had come away from Westmere to escape that dreadful edict of her grandfather's and here they were, quarrelling over it. She could not believe it of Edward, who had up to now pretended indifference.

Standing just outside the door, trying to compose herself before entering, she had been taken aback to hear Edward's voice. But, more than that, it had not been the voice of the quiet, good-humoured man she knew. Its tone had been scornful and she was reminded of that brief expression of anger she had seen in him when he had first learned that she had accepted Robert. He did not like what she and Robert had done.

At first she had flattered herself that he might be jealous, but now she wondered if he might be driven by that legacy just as James and Louis were. She felt very hurt by it and was afraid her disappointment must show on her face, but no one commented on it. She was saved by the arrival of the footman who announced that supper was ready, and they all trooped into the dining room, Edward escorting his mother and Bella walking beside Robert, her hand lightly on his coat sleeve.

Bella had little appetite and only picked at the delicious food, answering briefly when she was spoken to but offering no contribution to the conversation unless directly addressed. She could not see how she could go on with the charade she was playing. It could have no happy ending.

'You poor child,' Henrietta said, as the meal ended. 'You

are exhausted and here we are, chattering like a flock of magpies. Would you like to retire?'

'Yes, please.'

She bade them goodnight and left the room, closing the door behind her. She was halfway across the hall when the door was reopened by one of the servants and she heard Mrs Huntley say, 'I own she must be fatigued after her journey, but I never saw anyone so quiet. Robert, I thought you said she was lively and intelligent.'

'Oh, she is, Mama. She is tired and a little nervous of you.'

'Then I am sorry for it…' The door closed again and Bella toiled up to her room and was helped to bed by Daisy, who bade her goodnight and went to her own bed in the next room. Bella did not expect to sleep, but she was wrong. She was slumbering as soon as her head hit the pillow.

She woke in the morning in a completely different frame of mind. She was young and away from home for the first time and she was looking forward to her Season and meeting all the eligibles. She might even fall in love with one of them, someone of whom her grandfather would approve. She smiled as she dressed. She would enjoy her Season and see what transpired.

Henrietta was busy all day, giving orders to the servants about what to take to her new home. Although it was furnished, there were a great many small pieces she wished to take with her and a wagon had been hired to convey everything to Holles Street. There was an escritoire, a chaise longue which she said she always used to lie on for an afternoon nap, a chair with low arms which was perfect to sit in when she wanted to sew, several pictures and ornaments, beside trunks full of clothes. Bella, unable to do anything to help, set out to explore her surroundings.

She was standing at the lakeside, looking at her reflection in the clear water, when it was joined by another. She looked up to see Edward standing beside her. He was the picture of quiet elegance in cream-coloured pantaloons, shining Hessians and a brown superfine frockcoat with velvet revers. His cravat was held by a diamond pin. 'Oh, Edward, you startled me.'

'I beg your pardon. But tell me, what is occupying your mind so totally you do not hear footsteps behind you?'

'Nothing,' she said. 'I came out for a walk. Cousin Henrietta is busy and I did not want to be in the way.'

'You are not in the way, little one. But I am sure that is not all that troubles you. It is monstrous of Great-Uncle William to force you to marry one of us, but are you sure your solution is the best one? Robert is a dear man and my brother, but he is hardly husband material.'

'Why not?' she demanded. 'And why should you think that it has anything to do with my grandfather?'

He smiled. 'Oh, come, Bella, I am not a greenhorn, you know. Robert never had the slightest intention of offering for you before he came to Westmere last week.'

'Neither did Louis or James, but that didn't stop them. And, no doubt, if you had not been already engaged, you would have jumped in, too. I do not like being used, Edward. It is hardly flattering.'

'And Robert is not using you?'

'No, he is not!' she snapped. 'He is a dear, kind man and not in the least interested in my grandfather's legacy.'

'Is that so?' There was an upward twist to his lips which could have been the beginnings of a smile. 'Then I wish you both happy.'

There was nothing to be said in answer to that except to thank him politely and they turned back to the house, walking side by side in silence. Robert, watching their approach from the drawing-room window, was seized with an inexplicable to desire to part them. Edward was so obviously the Earl of Westmere's choice but, knowing Edward was already on the way to becoming attached, the old man had devised this strange strategy of pretending to let Bella choose. He was playing for time, knowing Edward wanted the legacy more than anything, more than Charlotte Mellish. Was his brother even now sowing the seeds in Bella's mind? He hurried out to meet them. 'Hello, you two. Have you enjoyed your stroll?'

'Yes, thank you,' Bella said primly. 'I was walking by the lake when Edward came upon me. It is very beautiful down there.'

'So it is,' Robert said, falling into step beside them. Taking Bella's hand, he tucked it into the crook of his elbow. 'But the grounds are nothing like as extensive as at Westmere, and the lake is a puddle compared to some of the fenland meres and waterways with their great windmills and water birds. I hope you will not be homesick for it.'

She smiled. 'I shall be too much occupied to be homesick, I think.'

'I hope you may. I shall do my poor best to ensure you do not have a minute to repine.' It was a reply which, she knew perfectly well, had been given for Edward's benefit. And Edward, knowing it, smiled sardonically and said Robert's racketing ways would hardly serve to endear her to the *ton*. They were sparring with each other with words, she decided, and she did not like it at all.

She could not help comparing Edward's classical good looks and urbane self-confidence with Robert's overgrown boyishness and quicksilver movements. The one was the sort of man every young lady sighed over, the other a laughing companion who did not seem able to take anything seriously. But his offer had been serious; she did not think he was making a joke of it or he would not be taking so much trouble to hoax his mother and brother. Was Edward deceived? And did Robert have any other reason for it than simply pity for her? She hated the idea of being pitied and made up her mind not to rely on him too heavily from now on.

After nuncheon, the wagon was loaded with everything Henrietta had packed, together with Bella's trunk and saddle, and sent on ahead with a couple of servants, including Adam Gotobed who was going to Robert's apartment in Albany to make it ready for his arrival. Danny, the young groom, rode Misty.

Bella was left with her portmanteau containing sufficient baggage for another night at Palgrave. It was put on the coach as soon as they had breakfasted the following morning when Henrietta and her maid, Annette, and Bella and Daisy were handed in, the step put up, the door shut and they were off on what Bella confidently expected to be an experience of a lifetime.

Behind them rode Robert and Edward in Edward's curricle, though it soon overtook them. 'They will be there before us,' Bella commented as the back of the coach disappeared from view.

'Oh, they do not come to Holles Street,' Henrietta said. 'Edward will go to Blandings House and Robert to his apartments in Albany. But, no doubt, Robert will pay a call tomorrow and then we can make plans. You will find life in London very different from that of the country, my dear. It is governed by protocol and manners, which you must abide by, but so long as you are guided by me, we shall deal famously with everyone.'

'Tell me about it,' Bella said. 'I am very ignorant, you know, though I have read a great deal.' She gave a little sigh. 'There is not much else to do at Westmere. Grandfather goes out so little and then it is to meetings which he says are not of the least interest or use to me. Of course, Miss Battersby is very knowledgeable but I think perhaps that comes mostly from books, too.'

'Oh, there is not the least need for you to worry about it,

my dear. You will have me and Robert to help you and, no doubt, Edward will call frequently. He is a good son and most careful of me. He will make sure we are invited to all the right places and meet the right people. It is so long since I was in London, what with my husband dying so suddenly and then my father-in-law inviting me to keep house for him at Palgrave, that I have lost touch with my old acquaintances.' She turned and smiled at Bella. It was a smile of such warmth that Bella was drawn to her as she had never been to any other woman since her mama had died, not even Ellen Battersby. 'But I am persuaded we shall soon be in the thick of everything.'

Bella was beset by mixed feelings. She was eager to taste the pleasures London had to offer and very glad indeed to have such an amiable mentor, but it was Henrietta's amiability which made Bella feel more guilty than ever. She hated herself for the way she was using her. She ought to bring it to an end at once and confess her duplicity but that would leave her in the same coil she had been in before.

They reached Stevenage at three in the afternoon where they changed horses at The Swan and again at The Green Man in Barnet. After that there was Finchley Common which, she knew, was famous for highwaymen and she wondered, with a little frisson of fear, if they might be held up. But they passed over it safely and then topped the rise at Highgate and she found herself looking down on London with its sprawl of buildings and church steeples glinting in the afternoon sun. So this was her destination! She could not wait to get there.

The road dipped after this and she lost sight of the city as they made their way between the high banks of Holloway Road and came to the little village of Islington Spa with its pond on the green surrounded by tall elms. It was the last toll, Henrietta told her as they stopped to pay their dues.

It was early evening by the time they arrived in the middle of the capital and the roads were choked with traffic. The Huntley coach was obliged to slow to no more than walking pace and Bella was able to look about her as they made their way along Oxford Street. She had never seen so many different kinds of vehicle. There were carriages of every description—wagons, carts, cabs and chairs with link boys trotting beside them. And there were people everywhere, from the most modishly dressed ladies and their gentlemen escorts to hawkers with trays and barrows, ragged beggars and barefoot children, all of whom took their lives in their hands to cross the road.

And then the coach turned sharply right and they were in Holles Street and drawing up at the door of a tall terraced house. 'Home,' Henrietta said, and then laughed as the door was opened and Robert stood on the step. 'Oh, we have a welcome after all.'

He had come, he told them when they had gathered in the drawing room for refreshment, to make sure they had arrived safely and to make arrangements for the following day. Bella surprised herself with the pleasure she felt in seeing him. He was so solid and dependable. She could imagine his troops relying on him, even loving him, because he seemed to think of everything.

'Which is to be first?' he asked. 'The procurement of a carriage or shopping?'

'A carriage,' Henrietta said. 'But not until the afternoon. I shall sleep late and then there is bound to be a great deal to do, settling in and arranging my furniture. Come at two o'clock.'

Robert took his leave, saying it was only a five-minute walk to his apartment and he would call on them as arranged. He bowed to his mother and kissed the back of Bella's hand and was gone.

Bella regretted she had not had a single moment alone with him and had been unable to talk to him about ending their deception, so she was left to make conversation with Henrietta with that good lady still under the impression that they were engaged. But if Bella was a little quiet, Henrietta did not seem to notice as she went over their plans for the following day.

'I shall rise about half past ten,' she said. 'That will give me time to supervise the unpacking and the placement of the pictures before Robert arrives. What will you do? You may stay in bed if you wish.'

'Oh, no, I mean to explore.'

'Explore the house and the garden by all means, but you know you must not go abroad without a chaperone. I suppose you could take Daisy…'

'Oh, no, poor Daisy suffers dreadfully from coach sickness and I have told her to rest tomorrow. I will not leave the garden.'

'Good. I must go with Robert to Robinson and Cook to choose the carriage, for if I do not, Robert will buy a phaeton and whether it is low slung or high perched it will not serve. I do not think I should feel at all comfortable in one of those and we will need some shelter from inclement weather. This spring has been the wettest I can remember and I see no sign of it improving. I am determined on a barouche. What do you think?'

Phaetons were a rare sight in rural Cambridgeshire and all Bella knew about the latest carriages was what she had seen illustrated in her grandfather's *Gentleman's Magazine*. She had wondered what it would be like to ride in, but she thought it prudent to agree with her hostess. 'I am sure, you are right, cousin,' she said, a little wistfully.

'Shall you like to come with us?'

'Oh, yes, please.'

And so when Robert arrived promptly at two the following afternoon, he found both ladies ready and waiting. It was a pleasant surprise to find that Bella was going, too.

She was delightfully attired in a buttercup yellow pelisse over a lemon cambric walking dress which set off her dark ringlets to perfection. All three climbed into the Huntley coach for the short journey to premises of Robinson and Cook in Mount Street.

Bella was fascinated by the array of half-finished vehicles on offer. There were stately carriages, as well as curricles, tilburys, barouches and phaetons. 'I want something light for Town traffic,' Henrietta instructed Robert.

'A phaeton,' he suggested, listening to his mother at the same time as he watched Bella wandering round the vehicles on display in the yard. She really was looking very fetching and he could just imagine driving her out in one of the latest high-slung vehicles which at that moment she was inspecting. 'Sit in it, Bella,' he said, moving over to help her up.

'My goodness, it is so high,' she said. 'Are you sure it is safe?'

'In a good pair of hands, perfectly safe,' he said.

'Which is all very well,' Henrietta put in, coming to stand beside Robert and looking up at Bella. From the young lady's lofty point of view, she looked tiny beside her tall son. 'But old Walter would throw up his hands in horror if I asked him to drive one of those. Besides, I want something comfortably big enough to take four and with a roof we can put up or down according to the weather.'

Robert sighed and helped Bella down. 'Very well, a barouche it is.'

They looked over the barouches on show and one was quickly chosen, its colour decided and the deal concluded. It was going to take two days to finish with its final coat of dark blue paint and Mrs Huntley's coat of arms added to both doors and then it would be delivered. 'Edward has said I may continue to use the family coach until then,' Henrietta explained to Bella.

'Cousin Henrietta, I am putting you to a great deal of

expense,' Bella said. 'Grandfather gave me five hundred pounds to spend, but—'

'Goodness, child, think nothing of it. I would have had to buy a carriage in any case and I am not poor, you know. My own father left me a considerable sum in my own right, and my wants are so few it is more than adequate.' She smiled, catching sight of Robert still looking longingly at the phaeton. 'He still covets that but it would not have served, you know. Robert, do come away from there, we are waiting to leave.'

Smiling, he joined them and they went back to the coach. 'Now for Tattersall's,' he said. 'And I suppose you are going to insist on buying a couple of quiet nags, Mama.'

'No, you have boasted of being a good judge of horse-flesh, so I shall leave it you, but nothing too spirited. Remember, Walter is not as young as you.'

He laughed. 'Mama, he is ancient. I wonder you have not pensioned him off before now.' He turned to Bella. 'Walter is what you might call an old retainer. He taught Mama to ride when she was a little girl and she cannot bear to part with him.'

'He has what you call a safe pair of hands,' she said. 'I should hate the Earl to accuse me of putting his granddaughter's life at risk. And you should be thinking of Bella, too.'

'Oh, indeed I am,' he said, grinning at Bella and making her feel more guilty than ever. She was beginning to wonder if he had a conscience.

Robert was not as rash as his mother had feared and chose the horses with care. They were two perfectly matched bays which, though beautiful, they were assured were used to Town traffic and their temperament could be vouched for. They cost an astronomical sum, which made Bella gasp. 'Is everything so dear in London?' she asked, wondering how far her five hundred pounds would stretch.

'Quality is always worth paying for,' Henrietta said, as

they once more returned to the coach. 'Now, we will go home for tea. Tomorrow we will go shopping and the next day, when we have our brand-new equipage, we shall set out in it to leave calling cards and perhaps take a turn in the park. Robert, you will join us for that, I expect?'

Robert seemed to hesitate, as if riding with his mother and his bride-to-be was the last thing he had in mind for an afternoon's pleasure, and Bella was reminded of their bargain. He had not promised to dance attendance on her, and if she was going to meet other eligible young men, she did not want it. 'If you have other plans, please, do not put yourself out on my account,' she said.

'What is this?' Henrietta said. 'Not put himself out? My goodness, that is no way for an engaged man to behave. Bella, you must not be so self-denying. Of course he must come. You will, Robert, won't you?'

'It will be my pleasure,' he said, smiling at Bella and making her, for some inexplicable reason, want to hit him.

They had barely returned and settled in the drawing room over the teacups when the new butler announced Sir Edward Huntley and Miss Charlotte Mellish, and the next moment they entered the room to Bella's barely concealed consternation. She found it almost impossible to sit still and rose as greetings were exchanged between Mrs Huntley, Robert and the newcomers.

'Charlotte, may I present my cousin, Bella?' Edward said, drawing her forward. 'You may remember me speaking of her. She is bearing Mama company for the Season.'

'Of course, the little heiress.'

Though she was shorter than Bella by two or three inches, Charlotte's bearing made her seem far superior. She held herself like a queen, back straight and head so high that she seemed to look down her nose at everything. She had very pale hair which was piled on her head and topped with a scrap of a hat with a huge feather. Her aquamarine taffeta slip was worn under an open gown of transparent sprigged muslin. Her lace-gloved hands carried a matching parasol and reticule.

Bella became acutely aware that it was impossible for her to compete and it made her a little reckless. She drew herself up to her full height, so that she was the one looking down, and smiled. 'Not so little, Miss Mellish, or so much the heiress, for you must know that it is impossible for a female to control her own fortune, which is something I should change if I had my way.'

'Would you, indeed?' Charlotte sat down beside Mrs Huntley on the sofa and laid aside her reticule and parasol in order to pull off her gloves. 'I collect you are one of these modern females who think they are as good as men when it comes to business.'

'It depends on the man and the woman,' Bella said, sitting down again. 'All are different. There are some very poor men of business about.'

'You are right there,' Edward said, laughing.

'But not you, my dear.' Charlotte gave him a withering look, at the same time managing to smile sweetly as she spoke. Bella wondered how she did it. 'I am persuaded any lady's fortune would be safe in your hands.'

'Certainly safer than in Robert's,' he murmured. 'Robert, allow me to give you some good advice when you find yourself possessed of the Westmere legacy.'

Robert, who had been standing by the window, watching a couple of gardeners tackle the overgrown garden, turned and grinned at his brother but said nothing. The atmosphere was almost alive with tension. It made Bella uncomfortable, knowing she was the cause of it.

'Grandpapa may yet change his mind, Edward,' she said. 'I should hate to deprive you of your rightful inheritance.'

'Oh, you won't,' he said easily, making Robert look sharply at him.

'Do sit down and drink your tea,' Henrietta said, indicating the teacups she had just filled. As they obeyed, she went on, 'Charlotte, Edward tells me your parents are giving a grand ball for you.'

'Yes, we have not fixed on a date yet, but we think the middle of May, six weeks from now.' She smiled at Edward. 'We will be making an announcement. Everyone of note will be there. They will be sending you an invitation, of course. And I have no doubt we can add the names of Captain Huntley and Miss Huntley to it, if you would like it.'

'Thank you,' Henrietta said, while Robert and Bella looked at each other in dismay. Even without an announcement they were already being thrown into each other's company, which was all very well in private but at a public function like a ball, how would they go on? She had promised him he should come out of the affair with honour, but it was becoming more and more complicated.

And Robert did not make it any easier when he stood up and bowed to Charlotte. 'We shall be delighted, Miss Mellish,' he said, speaking for both of them. 'But now I must be going. Things to do, you know.' He bent to kiss his mother's cheek, then took Bella's hand and kissed that. 'Bella, do not forget we are going riding in the park tomorrow afternoon. It is time Misty had some exercise.'

It was the first she had heard of such an excursion, put forward for Edward's benefit, she did not doubt, but it was one that pleased her nonetheless—a ride was just what she needed. She smiled at him. 'I shall be ready at two.'

He hurried from the room, leaving Bella facing Edward and Charlotte and wondering what subject to introduce which would be safe. But she need not have worried. Having looked her over and having decided she was no threat to her peace of mind, Charlotte said they should go, they had other calls to make. 'We may see you at Lady Broughton's soirée perhaps,' she said, as she bade her hostess goodbye. 'Edward informed her you were in town and she said you and she were old friends and she would certainly invite you.'

'That was very kind of Edward,' Henrietta said. 'If we receive an invitation, we shall, no doubt, attend. I am going to have a little gathering of my own to introduce Bella— just a few friends and perhaps a little dancing, nothing elaborate for she is not yet out. I will send you a note of the date when it is decided.'

'I have a great many engagements, ma'am, but if I am free, then I shall be delighted.'

Charlotte bowed briefly to Bella and began to move away even before Edward had said goodbye to his mother and taken his leave of Bella which was brief in the extreme, being no more than a nod and the one word, 'Bella.' Bella watched them go and then sank back onto her chair with a huge sigh of relief.

'An ordeal,' Henrietta said. 'Charlotte can be somewhat overpowering, but I do not think she means it. Her papa, Sir George Mellish, has made his money from industry, one of the *nouveau riche*, which unfortunately has given him pretensions which he has passed on to his only daughter. But money is no substitute for true breeding. I should not say this, of course, and I beg you not to repeat it. She is, after all, to be my daughter-in-law.'

Bella assured her hostess she would not dream of telling anyone anything which had been told her in confidence, but it made her feel a great deal better about Charlotte Mellish and she supposed Henrietta knew that. It was also a warning to her that she should not quarrel with Charlotte. But that was the last thing on her mind. She would enjoy her Season, go to all the functions to which they were invited and take part enthusiastically in everything Mrs Huntley arranged for her. And tomorrow she would ride in the park with Robert. She was really looking forward to that.

Chapter Six

The following morning was spent in shopping for clothes. Bella would have enjoyed it a great deal more if she had not been so conscious of what everything was costing and how much she needed. According to Henrietta, the smallest daytime wardrobe she could possibly manage with had to consist of several day gowns for paying calls, two or three for riding in the carriage when it was vital to show off one's apparel along with the equipage, and at least one other good riding habit besides the one she already owned which, said Henrietta, was very fetching.

She and her hostess also expected to be going out in the evenings and there would be visits to the opera and the theatre when you were on view to the *haut monde*, and it was simply not done to appear in the same outfit more than once, not when you were going to be seen by the same group of people. And she must have no fewer than two ball gowns, more if they were so lucky as to be invited to more. All this as well as an undress gown for the house, underclothes, accessories, footwear and headgear.

Bella's five hundred pounds, which would have fed and clothed the whole village of Westmere for more than a year, was gone long before all these purchases had been made. It made her feel more guilty than ever because she had accepted it from the Earl under false pretences. He had always been frugal and had taught her to be the same.

'Isn't that just like a man?' Henrietta said, when Bella was forced to confess herself all but penniless. 'They have not the slightest idea of what it costs to bring a young lady out. Why, when I had my first Season my father spent thousands on clothes alone. Mind you, he did grumble a great deal when the accounts came in.' She laughed. 'He always paid them, though, not wanting anyone to think he was pinched in the pocket or too miserly to give his only daughter a good Come Out.'

They were returning to Edward's coach, which they were still using until the new one should be delivered. Their arms were full of packages and more were to be delivered to the house the following day. One or two gowns were being made up and Bella would have to go for fittings before they were finished. She was beginning to regret allowing herself to be persuaded to buy so much. 'I shall be able to manage quite well with what we have already bought, Cousin Henrietta.'

'Fustian!' the good lady said, handing her parcels to their coachman who had opened the door in readiness when he saw them approaching. 'Home, Walter,' she said.

With his arms full he was unable to help her in, but she did not seem to mind that in the least, and clambered in by herself, followed by Bella. The parcels were heaped on the opposite seat, Walter shut the door and climbed on the box.

'Going without or making do is not to be borne,' Henrietta said as soon as they were on the move. 'You only come out once and it should be a happy time, not miserable for want of the necessary. The Earl is no different from my father—he will pay up like a lamb when I write and tell him the high price of everything. And I am determined to give a ball at the end of the Season when we make the announcement of your engagement to Robert.'

Bella was appalled. 'Oh, no! Oh, you must not!'

Henrietta turned to Bella in surprise. 'Why not?'

'Oh, I do not think I should like a fuss and I am sure Robert will not.'

'Why should he not?'

Bella was confused and tongue-tied, not knowing how to explain herself. 'Everyone will be looking at us and wondering about…about…'

'Oh, you mean that edict of the Earl's. I doubt if it is generally known and even if it is, everyone will have forgotten about it by the end of the Season. And even if they have not, when they see how famously you deal together, they will see that it is nothing to the point.'

'I do hope so,' Bella said, wondering how she was going to persuade her sponsor against it. 'I should hate anyone to think ill of Robert for it.'

'You must not put too much store by it, my dear. I cannot think his lordship has broken the entail. Edward certainly does not think he has. Neither does Robert.' She smiled and patted Bella's hand. 'Think no more of it. Besides, I want an excuse to give a ball and as I have no daughter of my own, you must indulge me.'

There was nothing Bella could say without revealing her deception and she did not want to do that until she had spoken to Robert. They ought to confess together because they must tell the same story about why they had done it and she did not want his mother to blame him entirely. As soon as she had a minute alone with him, she would insist on a confession and that would be that afternoon when he called to take her riding in the park.

He arrived promptly at two, to find her already pacing the hall floor, waiting for him in her new riding habit of dark blue taffeta, its jacket fastened with rows of silver frogging. She looked so lovely that his breath caught in his throat and for a moment he could not speak, but stood looking at her, lost in admiration. He pulled himself together and smiled as he bowed to her. 'You are looking very fetching, Bella.'

She dipped a curtsey. 'Thank you, kind sir.'

'It is a grand day for riding,' he said. 'The rain has stopped at last and the sun is shining. Nelson is fresh as a daisy and ready to show Misty his mettle.'

'Then let us go,' she said, setting her plumed hat on her dark curls and drawing on her gloves.

She was being very prim and proper, which was not at all like the Bella he knew, and he supposed she had something on her mind. He smiled and put his hand beneath her elbow to escort her to their mounts, knowing he would learn of it soon enough.

She had had Misty saddled and brought to the door by Danny who was to follow at a discreet distance on a cob, and in less than five minutes later they were riding down Oxford Street towards Hyde Park. Because of the traffic it was necessary to walk their horses in single file and no conversation was possible until they turned in at the park entrance. Bella, who had been waiting for the opportunity to talk to Robert, was frustrated by the sheer volume of carriages and riders which filled the carriageway and the parallel ride.

It was obviously a social occasion. Ladies in barouches, attended by grooms or drivers, vied with those more adventurous females who drove their own curricles and others sat atop the world in high-perch phaetons beside their dandified escorts. There were tilburys and gigs being driven by the young bloods about town and they all went at the pace of a snail, stopping frequently to exchange pleasantries and blocking the way for several minutes at a time. And even the Ride was crowded and the horses doing no more than walk, as their riders seemed to spend more time in talking than in exercising their mounts.

By the time they had negotiated their way into an open space and the road before them was clear, all Bella wanted to do was leave it all behind and feel the wind in her face and so she spurred her horse and left Robert standing. He followed at once, galloping up alongside her, laughing, and they continued side by side for several minutes until they found themselves off the Ride and crossing open grass. They left young Danny far behind.

Bella felt free and exhilarated and she would have liked to have gone on for ever, but her horse had not been properly exercised for several days and she did not want to tire her so she reluctantly pulled up and dismounted without any help from Robert.

'My goodness, Bella, you are a bruising rider,' he said, springing down beside her.

She smiled as they walked beside their horses towards a small stand of trees. 'There is space in plenty at Westmere for a good gallop and there is nothing I like better.'

'Do you ride to hounds?'

'Sometimes. Grandfather used to go but his gout troubles him too much these days and he is reluctant to let me go without him, so I do not go so often now.'

'I am not surprised if you always ride like that.'

'Like what?'

'As if the devil were after you and you determined to outrun him.' He laughed suddenly. 'Unless you think of me with horns and a tail.'

'No, of course not.' She stopped beneath an oak tree and allowed Misty to crop the grass. 'Robert, I must talk to you, I really must.'

He grinned. 'You are talking to me.'

'Seriously.'

'Oh, then I think we should sit down. I cannot be talked

to seriously while standing, it is too much like having a peal rung over me.' He looped his horse's reins over a branch, took off his coat and spread it beneath the tree. Then he sat on one corner of it and patted the space beside him. 'Come, sit down.'

She obeyed, suddenly aware of his closeness; they were almost touching. She could feel the warmth of him and was torn between leaning towards him and putting her head on his shoulder, as she had done when he had rescued her in Eastmere, and hitching herself further from him to show him she was not entirely lacking in decorum. She did neither, sitting stiffly beside him and looking straight ahead, refusing to look at him, knowing his brown eyes were watching her. He had a way of looking directly into her eyes and making her feel trapped. That was it. Trapped.

'Now what have I done to displease you?' he asked.

'Did I say you had?'

'No, but I know that fierce look of yours and I cannot for the life of me decide what it is I have done or failed to do. Have I not been attentive enough for a potential husband? Have I neglected you?'

'No, quite the contrary.'

'Then what is the matter?'

'It is your mama. I do so hate deceiving her. I have become very fond of her.'

'She loves you, too. She told me it was far and away the best thing I had done in proposing to you.'

'Worse and worse,' Bella cried, turning to face him and wishing she had not. His brown eyes were boring into her, making her squirm. 'Robert, she is talking of giving a ball at the end of the season in order to announce our engagement.'

'The devil she is!'

'I think we should quarrel and break it off before we fall into an even greater coil.'

'What should we quarrel about?' he asked reasonably.

'Anything—it does not matter, so long as she realises we should not suit.'

'It would have to be something very serious, or she will threaten to knock our heads together and make us see the error of our ways. She will insist we kiss and make up.'

'We could tell her the truth.'

'No,' he said firmly. 'It is too soon. You will have to go back to Westmere. His lordship will be angry and Mama will be hurt and nothing will have been achieved. You know, she is so happy to have you here and enjoying your company.'

'But the longer it goes on, the harder it will be to end it. I promised you I would keep your reputation intact…'

'I think you should let me worry about my reputation,' he said. Then, because he liked to tease her and see her temper rise, had added, 'I tell you what. We will have the most monumental and public row at the Mellish ball, no holds barred. How's that?'

'Definitely not! It will make your poor mama swoon and quite spoil it for her. And I do not want to be made to look an idiot.'

'We must quarrel *sotto voce*, then?'

'I said I wanted to talk seriously,' she said angrily. 'And you are making a jest of it. How I ever came to agree to this charade, I do not know.'

'Agree to it! Why, the whole thing was your idea. You begged me…'

'I did not,' she insisted. 'I would never beg. It was simply something that crossed my mind, nothing of consequence at all, not meant to be taken seriously.'

'That's a whisker if ever I heard one.'

'It was you who told Louis we were… Oh, you know what I mean.'

'Oh, so you would rather be married to Louis.'

'No. You are twisting my words. Well, it will not serve. It was you who insisted on keeping the truth from your mama. I did not want to do that and you know it…'

'You know,' Robert said quietly, 'we are making a fair job of quarrelling now and there is no one to hear us and no Mama to tell us to kiss and make up. Such a waste.' He smiled suddenly. 'Come to think of it, that could be a very pleasant experience. Perhaps we should try it.'

'Try what?'

'Why, kiss and make up. In fact…' He stopped to take her chin in his hand and turn her face towards his, forcing her to look into his eyes. 'I've a mind to sample it now.' She was almost mesmerised, eyes wide, lips slightly apart, as he lowered his head and kissed her. His warm, moist mouth on hers made her stomach turn somersaults, his tongue, gently exploring her lips, set her limbs in a quiver of anticipation. She clung to him, lost to everything beyond their two selves, locked in each other's arms.

It was several seconds before she came to her senses enough to try and push him away, but by then it was much too late. Her peace of mind was in ruins. How could he do this to her? Kisses like that were for lovers and he had made it very clear he did not love her. And she did not love him. *She did not.*

He lifted his head and smiled down at her. 'My, you little siren! And I thought you an innocent…'

'You are despicable!'

'So quarrelling and making up are not to your liking?'

'Definitely not.'

'Then we are at an impasse.'

'You are laughing at me and that is not at all civil of you.'

He traced the outline of her bruised lips with his finger. 'Poor Bella, I am sorry. It will not happen again, I promise you.'

'No, it will not, for this masquerade must end and the sooner the better.'

'No, we will wait,' he said, the laughter gone from his voice. 'Fate has a way of turning up trumps, you know, and in the meantime we can go on as we said we would and take our chances.' He smiled. 'Have no fear, I have no more wish than you to be shackled in a loveless marriage.'

'Good,' she said, getting to her feet and grabbing Misty's bridle. 'But I would be obliged if you would find some pressing engagements which keep you from me as much as possible in future.'

'How can I? Mama expects me to escort you...'

'Isn't that just what I have been saying? We must tell her.'

'No. The time is not right.'

'Will it ever be right? The longer we deceive her the worse it becomes.'

'It was your idea. I told you at the outset you would have to live with the consequences and you said you were prepared for that. One of the burdens you will have to bear is my company, at least until the Season ends.'

He rose, shook out his coat and shrugged himself into it, before bending and holding out his clasped hands for her foot. She was so angry she ignored him and hoisted herself into the saddle unaided, then trotted Misty back the way they had come, meeting Danny, who had tactfully dismounted some way off to wait for their return. He jumped back into the saddle and resumed his position a few yards behind her.

Bella did not know why she was so angry—it was not Robert's fault. She had brought this situation upon herself and for that reason she must comply with his wishes. But, oh, how difficult it was. That kiss had opened her eyes to something she had only ever read about—the physical attraction between a man and a woman. But that wasn't love, was it? Love was something else. It was affection and mutual respect and honesty. She smiled a little grimly. He had certainly been honest. *No wish—to be shackled in a loveless marriage*, he had said, and she did not doubt he meant it.

As she turned back into the carriage ride, he came up alongside her and they walked their horses side by side in the cavalcade of riders for all the world as if they were enjoying it. But a close observer might have noticed the tightness of her mouth and the odd tear glistening on her lashes, threatening to fall, and they could not have failed to see the look of thunder on Robert's face.

It was then that Edward, driving Charlotte in his curricle along the carriage way on the other side of the rails, hailed them. 'Robert. Miss Huntley.' He pulled the carriage to a halt and there was nothing Bella could do, short of giving him the cut direct, but rein in and return his greeting.

'Sir Edward. Miss Mellish.' She bowed slightly from the waist, holding her horse in check.

'I see you have brought that mare of yours to town,' Edward said. 'Do you not find her a little spirited for the park?'

'No, for we do not have to remain on the bridle way.'

'So I noticed.' It was said with a tone of studied indifference, which did not deceive Bella. Just how much had they seen? Not that kiss, because they had been screened by trees, but they might have seen her emerging in disarray and riding out on her own. She blushed crimson with mortification. According to Miss Battersby, no honourable man would kiss a young lady unless he meant to offer for her, and if it was seen by others, he had no choice—it was as good as an engagement.

'It is a fine afternoon for a ride and the Captain was so good as to accompany me,' she said, forcing herself to sound cool and calm.

'And he is taking good care of you?'

She felt herself go hot under his scrutiny. Edward was the epitome of good manners and she could not, for a minute, imagine him forgetting himself so far as to kiss a lady against her wishes. 'Of course. Why should he not?'

'No reason,' he said vaguely. 'I am simply concerned that you should enjoy your time in London and if Robert should find himself otherwise engaged, I shall be pleased to escort you myself.'

'No need, no need at all,' Robert put in quickly. 'I am sure you have a great many calls on your time and I am happy to make myself available.'

They were sparring with each other, Bella realised, and she wished they would not—it made her feel uncomfortable. She smiled at Edward, trying to convey that the put-down was nothing to do with her. 'Thank you for offering.'

'My, how fortunate to have two men vying for your attention,' Charlotte cried, and there was a gleam of malice in her eye. 'It has something to do with that legacy, I collect. I should not count on it, though. It is not so easy to overturn an entail, you know.'

'Charlotte!' Edward admonished her, but she simply laughed.

Bella could find nothing to say and it was left to Robert to bring the conversation to an end. 'No doubt we shall see, in the fullness of time. I bid you good afternoon, Miss Mellish. Edward. Come, Bella.' He bowed to them and turned his horse to leave them.

Bella hesitated. It was not Edward's fault and she wanted him to know she realised that. 'Do you come to your mama's soirée tomorrow evening, Edward?'

He smiled. 'We would not miss it for the world, would we, Charlotte?'

Charlotte inclined her head without speaking. Bella bade them both goodbye and followed Robert. 'Miss Mellish does not like me,' she said, drawing alongside him.

'It is not you she dislikes but your prospects, Bella. She is the daughter of an industrialist, a man with no breeding. Being a Countess would make all her dreams come true.'

'But even if Grandpapa were to leave everything to the man I married, it would not affect the title, would it? He could not take that. Besides, Edward is already a baronet.'

'Ten a penny, they are. And the title without the great house would be a hollow victory. She wants it all.'

'Do you want it?'

'Want what?'

'The legacy.'

'Is that what you think of me?' he demanded, suddenly angry. 'You think I want to continue our masquerade in the hopes of a fortune?'

'There is no call to fly into the boughs. I only asked.'

'Then let me set your mind at rest. All the money in the world is not worth the misery of a marriage based on distrust and greed and lacking in the one thing that all good marriages should have.'

Miserable as she was, she could not help rising to the bait, keeping her voice light, forcing herself to sound cheerful. 'And what is that?'

'Love, Bella. Mutual love.'

'Oh. You think that is important?'

'Absolutely essential.'

'Then is it fortunate indeed that we have decided we should not suit, is it not?'

'Yes.'

There was nothing more to be said and they rode the rest of the way in silence, each smouldering with resentment that the other should be so thick-skinned. He had seen the look Bella had given Edward and it had jolted him. Was she wearing the willow for his brother? Was that why she had asked to come to London, in order to pursue him? If that were the case, there was no hope left for him. Edward was the heir to the home she loved so much—how could any young lady discount that?

Robert helped Bella alight outside the house and sent the boy to the mews with her horse and the cob. His own mount he tethered to a post by the door, meaning only to say good afternoon to his mother and then be on his way. Bella had made it perfectly clear she did not want his company and he was the last one to stay where he was not wanted.

But he was not to escape so lightly. His mother insisted he stay and take tea with them. 'The new carriage is to be delivered tomorrow,' she said, as she poured the tea, while he fidgeted to be gone. 'I should like you to be here and see that everything is as it should be and that the horses take to the shafts.'

'Mama, surely Walter can do that? I have another engagement. I am promised at George Fulbright's. We planned to go out of Town for a few days.'

'George Fulbright? My goodness, how you can speak of going out of Town with that scapegrace when Bella has only just arrived I do not know.'

'Mama, George is not a scapegrace, he has been a staunch friend and comrade in arms. And I collect his mama is your great bosom bow.'

'Oh, do not mind me,' Bella said, as fidgety as Robert. 'I would hate to deprive Robert of the company of his friends. He must do as he wishes.'

Henrietta looked from Robert to Bella. 'Bella, you do not look quite the thing. Are you well?'

'Perfectly, Cousin Henrietta.'

'Then you have quarrelled. Robert, I am ashamed of you. I cannot think how I can have raised you to be so insensitive. You will come tomorrow and you will be agreeable. And in the evening I have invited a few friends to meet Bella and I insist you attend.'

'Very well, Mama.' He turned towards Bella and smiled. 'Kiss and make up, my dear?'

Oh, she hated him, she really did. And if it would not have upset his mama, she would have told him so to his odious face. She held out her hand, plainly dismissing him, but he possessed himself of her fingers and raised them to his lips, gazing into her eyes as he did so and flustering her completely. 'Until tomorrow, dearest,' he said, acting the lovesick swain for all he was worth. 'We will give the new carriage and horses an outing and be the envy of the *ton* and I promise to be good.'

Henrietta gave a sigh as he took his leave. 'He used not to be so rag-mannered,' she said. 'I blame it on the army. Being so much in masculine company and having to fight in a war has coarsened him. But he is a good boy and you will soon have him tamed.'

Bella doubted that. She did not think he wanted to be tamed, or that she was the one to do it. Her reading matter had fuelled her imagination and she had often dreamed of being kissed by a handsome and gallant knight who knelt before her to tell her how much he loved her, begging her to marry him, and she being a little coquettish and telling him they ought to wait.

She had imagined the unknown swain kissing her, not in the way Robert had kissed her, never that, for she had never before had an inkling it could be like that, but giving her a chaste kiss with closed lips. That was pure fantasy, but Robert's lips on hers had been real. If she shut her eyes she could still feel them. And her body still ached with desire. Did he know that? Had he sensed her unthinking response and drawn his own conclusions? Oh, what a noddicock she had been!

There was nothing to do but keep Henrietta company and listen to her making plans which would mean being seen constantly with Robert, until in the end she was forced to protest. 'Cousin Henrietta, the engagement is supposed to be a secret and if we are seen too often in each other's company, the tattle-mongers will talk.'

'Does it matter?'

'To Robert, I think it does. He does not want to be labelled a fortune-hunter.'

'Oh, fustian! You are staying with me and Robert is my son. What should be more natural than he should escort you? But if you wish, I will contrive to introduce you to other young men and he may take his chances that you will not favour one of them over him.'

'I am sure he would prefer that. Other company, I mean,' she added hastily.

'More fool he, for you are very beautiful and are sure to take well in Society.'

'Thank you, Cousin Henrietta.'

Henrietta was no fool and she knew something havey cavey was going on between her son and his little cousin which had nothing to do with the legacy or being engaged, but she decided to say nothing. Sooner or later one of them would tell her. It was a great pity for anyone with eyes in their heads could see the pair were made for each other. She smiled and patted Bella's hand. 'Now, I think I shall lie down for a while because we are going to Lady Broughton's tonight and she never has supper brought in before midnight and we shall be very late home. I advise you to do the same.'

Bella did not want to rest; she was too tense even to lie down. Instead, she went to her room and wrote to her grandfather, describing her impressions of London, making it sound as if she were happy and interested. She knew he would require Miss Battersby to read it aloud and its contents would be all round the servants' quarters and the village in no time. Her feelings, her strange mixed-up emotions, her guilt and her anger with the man who had enabled her to escape, she committed only to her journal.

Having nothing else to do until it was time to dress to go out, she opened the novel she was writing and began a new chapter. In the story, coloured by her own situation and her indiscriminate reading, the heroine lived with her guardian and knew nothing of her own history. In trying to uncover her beginnings, she was involved in mystery and intrigue, with duels and dangerous adventures and lovers' trysts on almost every page. It was great fun to write, but she did not suppose she would ever find a publisher for it.

After struggling for several minutes, writing and crossing out what she had written, she sighed and laid aside her pen to stare unseeingly out of the window at the clouds gathering above the rooftops. The muse had left her. Her once vivid imagination was barren of everything except the dreadful coil she was in. If they were not very careful, she and Robert would find themselves so deeply involved there would be no way out. He would hate that and so would she.

She was interrupted by Daisy bringing her hot water to wash. Sighing, she put the writing things in a drawer and locked it. Then she turned and began her preparations to go out for the evening. Tonight, at least, there would be no Robert to upset her equilibrium.

In spite of that, or perhaps even because of it, the evening was a dead bore. The matrons did nothing but tear absent friends to shreds and the girls giggled over the inane jokes made by the young dandies. Bella was glad when it was time to take their leave.

It rained heavily again overnight but by the next afternoon the sun was shining, though it was a little blustery. Robert arrived about noon, delivering the new carriage and horses himself. Henrietta was as excited as a child and, in spite of the clouds, was determined to go on the planned outing as soon as they had had a light nuncheon. 'A barouche has the advantage over some of these more fashionable equipages,' she said. 'It has a sturdy hood we can put up against the rain.'

And so they set out, with Henrietta and Bella sitting side by side and Robert in the facing seat. Bella could hardly look at him. Their quarrel sat like a stone upon her shoulders, weighing her down. The strange thing was that he did not seem to be the least affected, but smiled easily at her, as if that kiss had never happened or he had forgotten it. That was probably the truth of it, she thought as they bowled towards the park gate. He was so accustomed to taking young ladies in his arms and kissing them that it made no impact on his memory.

The park was a little less crowded than it had been the day before, probably because of the threatening weather, but even so, they met several people of Henrietta's acquaintance and stopped to exchange pleasantries and for Bella to be introduced, which resulted in several invitations.

'There!' Henrietta said, as they turned at the end of the carriage way and started back the way they had come. 'That was very satisfactory. We dine with the Howards on Friday, go to the theatre with Mr and Mrs Fulbright next week and Lady Collison has promised to come to my soirée. That is good, for she will bring her son, Peter.' She risked a glance under the brim of her bonnet at Robert, though she was speaking to Bella. 'I am persuaded you will like him, my dear. Such a pleasant young gentleman.'

Robert, who knew very well what his mother was up to, smiled. 'A little green, I fancy, Mama, and a tulip to boot, but harmless enough.'

Bella did not comment; her opinion of Robert at that moment was not fit for Henrietta's ears. Two minutes later they drew up at the door in Holles Street. Robert saw them safely inside then left Walter to put the carriages away and see to the horses, before setting off for Gentleman Jackson's boxing emporium where he had arranged to meet George and Desmond.

He was in a foul mood and before he and George had been sparring many minutes he was hitting with more than usual aggression and landing some furious punches on his friend's head and body. 'Rob, it's me, your friend, at the end of your fists,' George cried, backing off and dabbing at the blood streaming from his nose. 'If you want to take out your ill temper on someone, find another punch bag.'

'Sorry, George, got carried away.'

'What's up? Didn't the old lady come up trumps?'

'What?' He was puzzled and then laughed. 'Oh, you mean Mama and my empty pockets. Couldn't ask her—she has too many demands on her purse already, bringing out my little cousin. And it's not of any consequence, not dished up yet.'

'Glad to hear it. What's she like, this cousin of yours?'

'Like?' he repeated vaguely.

'Yes. How old? Fat or thin, dark or fair. Bright or dull as ditch water.'

'Not dull, certainly not dull. She is the most exasperating chit you could ever wish to meet.'

'Oh, I see.' George grinned. 'Do you hear that, Desmond? Our Robbie has fallen in love at last.'

'If you were not my friend I would draw your cork for that,' Robert said angrily.

'Only bamming,' George said. 'When shall we meet her?'

'Your parents have invited her and my mother to the theatre next week, I believe. They arranged it this morning. Do you go?'

'I will now. Will you join us?'

'Not if I can help it,' Robert said firmly.

'Oh, come, man, it cannot be as bad as that,' Desmond said. 'Why don't we all go? I can think of a couple of little bits of muslin who would be only too pleased to have an outing.'

'Not in my mother's box,' George said emphatically.

'Then let us take another. We can observe this far-from-dull, exasperating chit from a distance.'

'Bella would hate that if she knew of it.'

'Bella, eh? Pretty name. Is she pretty?'

'Yes, she is, in an immature way.' He tried to sound off-hand and failed.

'Young, then. Oh, Rob, I despair of you. We shall have to take you in hand.'

'And I am still of a mind to tap your claret,' Robert said. 'I do not need taking in hand. The young lady is my second cousin, granddaughter of the Earl of Westmere, and as both her parents are dead, she is under the protection of my mother who has undertaken to bring her out. Does that satisfy you?'

'I will reserve judgement for the moment,' George said. 'Now I am more concerned with my stomach. I am devilish hungry. What say we adjourn to find something to eat?'

'Did you say the Earl of Westmere?' Desmond said, as they left Jackson's premises and repaired to a nearby inn.

'Yes, he is my great-uncle—why?'

'I have heard of him. He was something of a rake in his young days, full of jest and scrapes, the despair of his father.'

'How do you know that?' Robert asked, intrigued in spite of his ill humour. He could not imagine his lordship as a wild young man.

'My father was acquainted with him.' Desmond, who was older than the other two by several years and had been born when his parents had almost given up hope of having a child, often came up with juicy bits of gossip from an earlier generation, thus perpetuating scandals that might otherwise have died. 'He was older than my father and by that time had settled down and married, but you know how it is—give a dog a bad name and he has it for life. There was a story that he got the wife of his father's steward with child and somehow she disappeared, murdered, some said.'

'Oh, be blowed to that for a Banbury tale,' Robert said, laughing. 'I never heard it.'

'Well, you would not, would you? These things are always kept from the family. But when old John—begging your pardon, Robert—your grandfather died this year, the last person who knew the whole truth was gone. It was reading his obituary that brought the story to my father's mind. He said that for all his wealth the old reprobate had never prospered, never had an heir that lived. I mean the Earl, of course, not your grandfather.'

'What happened to the child, then?'

'What child?'

'The one you say he fathered on the steward's wife.'

'No one knows. If she was murdered before it was born, it would never have seen the light of day, would it? On the other hand, it could be anywhere—adopted, rich, poor, famous or infamous… Intriguing, wouldn't you say?'

'If there was a child and it was a son, would it affect the inheritance?' George asked.

'No, of course not,' Robert said.. 'You know by-blows do not inherit or heaven knows who would be sitting in the House of Lords.' He laughed, his discomfort making the sound unnatural. 'Or on the throne for that matter.'

'What happened to the steward?' George asked Desmond.

'Given the bag, of course. Like his wife, never heard of again.'

They had arrived at the inn by this time and the conversation was dropped in favour of finding seats and ordering a meal. Robert dismissed the story as a fribble and put it from his mind.

'Are you coming to White's tonight?' George asked him. 'I am feeling lucky.'

'Then I shall certainly not come. I cannot afford your luck.'

'It cannot last,' Desmond put in. 'Rob, you might as well come and help me break it.'

'Sorry, old friend, I am engaged to attend my mother's soirée and she will skin me alive if I do not go.'

'Or is it the delectable young cousin who draws you there?'

'Not at all,' he said, trying to control the exasperation in his voice. His friends often roasted him, and he rarely let it bother him, but the mention of Bella touched him on a raw spot.

He smiled wryly to himself, remembering that kiss. It had taken him by surprise, not that he had kissed her at all, but the fact that she had responded so ardently and he had found himself wanting to do it again. But in a flash she had turned into a virago and bitter words had been said, so that it had become impossible to explain himself. 'I will have to put in an appearance,' he said. 'But I will join you later and you had better pray your luck holds, George, for I mean to win.'

Henrietta had invited so many people for the evening that her small drawing room was crowded and the guests, clutching glasses of wine, spilled out into the hall. Robert had been right about Peter Collison, Bella decided, after spending ten minutes listening to him talk about his passion for antiquities. He held forth for some time about the debate in Parliament on the merits and value of the marbles and other ancient Greek artefacts Lord Elgin had acquired while Ambassador in Constantinople, which was being hotly disputed by others who claimed they were second rate and were so badly damaged as to have little value. 'They are displayed in a private museum in Lord Elgin's garden in Piccadilly,' he told Bella. 'It will be my privilege to escort you to see them, if you would do me the honour.'

'I thought it was decided their value lay in the public domain,' Bella said, remembering reading the long report of the debate to her grandfather. 'Are they not yet in the British Museum?'

'I do not know if a date has been set to move them.' He seemed surprised that she knew so much, but ploughed on, the high points of his collar scratching his red cheeks every time he moved his head. 'I am a connoisseur myself, you know. On a recent trip to Greece, I brought back some statuary from a temple dedicated to Bacchus.'

'The god of wine and good living,' she said.

'You know?' Peter queried in surprise. 'The carvings are especially good, with the god sitting on a bank with his hair and loins tangled with vines and a goblet to his lips. All about him are handmaidens feeding him grapes and holding more goblets. I have set it up at the end of the rose arbour at my country home where the evening sun catches it. You must come and see it for yourself. The Society of Antiquaries tell me it is very fine and superior to the Elgin marbles, being complete in every detail.'

'What is?' demanded Robert, joining them. He had seen Bella apparently listening intently and had been filled with an urge to hear what was being said. He might pretend indifference to his friends, but he was very far from it. The more he saw of his pretty cousin, the deeper became his predicament.

'Mr Collison was telling me of his travels to Greece and the figure of Bacchus he has brought home,' she said. Though she was smiling, her heart was thumping in her throat and she knew it was Robert's presence at her side which was doing it to her. How she was going to survive several weeks of it, she did not know. It was like being pulled in two directions at once, wanting him near because he made her feel gloriously alive and wanting him gone in order to ease her laboured breathing. 'I think it is clothed in nothing but vine leaves.'

'Strategically placed, I trust?' Robert said, one eyebrow raised in a kind of mockery.

'Of course,' the young man said, furious with Robert for interrupting him just when he thought he had the little heiress's attention. 'I would not insult Miss Huntley by mentioning anything that was not in the best possible taste.'

'I am pleased to hear it for, you know, Miss Huntley is under my mother's protection and, by that token, mine also.'

'Oh, Robert, do not be so pompous,' Bella said. 'We were having a perfectly proper conversation about Greek antiquities.'

'I will not tell you my opinion of people who remove priceless artefacts from where they belong simply to gratify their covetousness.'

'Sir, I protest,' Collison said. 'I did not invite your opinion and neither did Miss Huntley.'

'No, Robert, I didn't,' Bella said. She secretly agreed with him, but not for a minute would she have let him know that.

'Then I am sorry I intruded.' He bowed and left them.

Bella watched him go with a sinking heart. She had been glad of his interruption. Mr Collison's gaze upon her was a little too intent and she had the uncomfortable feeling he was undressing her with his eyes, perhaps imagining her as one of those handmaidens of Bacchus. Why had she sent Robert away? She saw Henrietta on the other side of the room and, telling him her hostess had beckoned to her, excused herself and escaped before he could repeat his invitation to take her to see the marbles.

Henrietta was preoccupied, talking to a very fat man in old-fashioned breeches and clocked stockings whose corset creaked with every move. Unable to keep from laughing,

Bella moved away and wandered into the hall where it was cooler.

She heard raised voices in the book room whose door, on the other side of the hall, stood ajar. Curiosity drove her forward so that she was near enough to identify the speaker and hear what was being said. She knew she should not eavesdrop, but when she realised the subject of their conversation she could not help herself.

'No, Charlotte, that would not serve. His lordship will not change his mind, he told me so.'

'You did ask him, then?'

'Naturally I did.'

'In other words, he intends you to marry the little mouse of a cousin.' Miss Mellish was obviously furious.

'Only if I offer for her.'

'And will you?'

'Of course not! I am engaged to you.'

'So you are. You know, I had thought you might have forgot that...'

'Now you are being foolish.'

'Am I? You like her well enough and a fortune is a great inducement to overlook her imperfections.'

'What imperfections?'

'Oh, there are none so blind as those who will not see. She is a hoyden to say the least. You saw her in the park, galloping about with her hat all askew and Robert looking sheepish. And she has no idea how to converse in polite Society. Twice I have heard her offer an opinion about the troubles in the countryside. As if anyone were interested in her opinion, especially when it is at odds with what everyone else thinks. She is much too forward.'

'She is young.'

'Too young for you, Edward. You would do better to find some other way to possess yourself of your great uncle's fortune.'

'And how do you suggest I do that?' There was a sharp edge to his voice which told Bella he was becoming very cross.

'Why, prove that the entail was never broken. It is not a simple procedure, is it? There are bound to be documents. A good lawyer would soon find something amiss in them. And if there are no documents, then the Earl has been having sport with you.'

'Why should he do that?'

'To secure the future for his granddaughter.' She laughed harshly. 'You would feel a great noddicock if you married her and found that, after all, there had been no necessity.'

'I have no intention of marrying her. I am engaged to you.'

'So you are. And if the *haut monde* thought you had broken it off to submit to that old man's fancies, you would be cut dead. Do not think I will release you without everyone knowing why.'

'Charlotte,' he said wearily, 'we are quarrelling about nothing. There is no need for you to get on your high ropes. Please, leave it to me. This thing must be done carefully.'

'You will do something?'

'Naturally I will do something. I will not be bullied by that old man.'

'Oh, Edward, you darling!'

There was silence and Bella risked a peep through the crack in the hinge side of the door. The curtains had not been drawn and they were standing in front of the window, outlined by pale moonlight. Charlotte had her arms about his neck and he was holding her close. They were kissing. Bella fled upstairs to her room and flung herself across the bed.

Edward was no better than the others, only cleverer. And with Charlotte urging him on, he would do his best to disinherit her. Well, she did not care. She did not care if she never received a penny. She would earn her own living and let them fight among themselves. How her grandfather must be laughing at them! He was playing with them all as if they were puppets dancing to his tune, and it was extraordinary how the prospect of wealth made them twist and turn so willingly to his music. But she would not.

She rose from her bed and sat at the escritoire in the window alcove. Taking her writing materials from the drawer, she dipped her pen in the ink and wrote on a clean sheet of paper, 'Chapter Six.' Then she looked up at the clouds scudding across the uncurtained window and imagined her heroine, clothed her in flesh and blood, felt her anguish, shared her despair and began to write...

Chapter Seven

For her visit to the theatre, Bella wore a pink silk gown, trimmed with darker pink ribbon threaded through under the bust and puffed sleeves. Her dark ringlets were topped by a scrap of pink material decorated with tiny feathers dyed to match and tied under her chin with a ribbon bow. About her neck she wore a string of garnets her father had given her which had once belonged to her mother. Although she was tall, the effect was one of feminine delicacy.

She and Henrietta, in deep purple as a change from mourning black, rode to Covent Garden in the new coach which deposited them at the door of the theatre so that their senses were not assailed by sounds and sights which might disgust or upset them in the mean streets that surrounded the theatre. But Bella did notice a man haranguing the theatregoers who were making their way on foot. He had gathered a little crowd about him and she found herself wondering what he was saying to them.

But he was soon forgotten in the excitement of her very first visit to a London theatre. It was a glittering occasion with everyone dressed in the first stare of fashion, which meant they intended to be stared at. And stare she did. As soon as they had joined Mr and Mrs Fulbright and taken their seats in the box, Bella settled down to drink it all in.

Below her in the stalls, theatregoers who did not have the privilege of a box sat reading their programmes or looking about them through opera glasses. Those in the front of the balcony were noisy and laughing as they called out to friends and acquaintances in nearby seats. High up in the gods sat those who could not afford better seats and who would be hard put to hear the dialogue on stage, but who obviously had every intention of enjoying themselves. Directly opposite Bella were other boxes and it was in one of these she spied Robert, wearing a black evening suit, white figured waistcoat and a purple cravat in which, even at that distance, she could see a diamond pin glittering.

She had not seen him since the night of his mother's soirée and she supposed that was hardly surprising since she had as good as told him to go away. And even before that she had said he would be doing her a favour if he absented himself, so she could hardly blame him if he took her at her word. Not for a moment would she admit that she had missed him.

And here he was disporting himself with two other young men and three young ladies, all of whom were laughing uproariously at something one of them had said. He suddenly caught sight of her and before she could look away bowed deeply. Then he turned back to the young lady at his side and said something which had her shrieking with laughter.

'There's Robert,' Bella said, pointing him out to Henrietta.

'So it is. He did not tell me he meant to come tonight. He could have accompanied us if I had known.'

'I think, Cousin Henrietta, he is otherwise engaged,' Bella said, trying unsuccessfully not to sound hurt.

'So I see.' She pressed her lips together in a straight line of disapproval. 'I shall have something to say about his rag-mannered treatment of you. I thought you had made up that quarrel.'

'We did. Please, do not say anything to him.'

Henrietta did not answer because at that moment the orchestra began the overture and the curtain rose. Bella, determined not to let Robert's presence spoil her enjoyment, turned towards the stage and pretended to become lost in the performance. She did not look towards the other box until the interval and then she was surprised to see that it was empty.

All about her people were moving about, joining friends, visiting other boxes, and Mr Fulbright left theirs but he was soon back, accompanied by George, Robert and Desmond whom he had found in the corridor.

'You are acquainted with my son, George?' Mr Fulbright said, addressing Henrietta.

'To be sure. How do you do, Mr Fulbright? May I introduce Miss Huntley?'

'Mrs Huntley. Miss Huntley.' He bowed towards them. 'May I present Mr Desmond Norton?'

Bella saw a man in his late thirties, thin and wiry, with sharp ascetic features and probing grey eyes. They acknowledged each other with a bow, then George laughed and waved his hand in the general direction of Robert who was standing behind them. 'This scapegrace I believe you know.'

'Yes, to my shame,' Henrietta said. 'Robert, I shall expect you at Holles Street at noon tomorrow. I have something I wish to say to you.'

Bella felt considerably discomfited and wished she had never pointed Robert out to his mother, but undoubtedly she would have seen him in any case. Mr Fulbright would surely have visited his parents' box and Robert would have accompanied him. But what had happened to the young ladies?

'Mama.' Robert bowed to her, then turned to Bella. 'Miss Huntley, your obedient.'

'Captain.' She inclined her head, wondering what else she could say. 'Are you enjoying the play?'

'Oh, it is great fun,' he said, proving he had paid not a scrap of attention to it, for it was meant to be a tragedy. His fun, she presumed, came from the company of the young ladies.

'How do you find London, Miss Huntley?' George asked.

'Interesting,' she said. 'It is a city of contrasts, do you not think? Rich and poor, wide avenues, dirty alleys, drabness and colour, magnificence and squalor. And very noisy.'

'Well put, Miss Huntley,' Desmond said. 'I think you do not find it dull.'

'Oh, no, not dull.'

'Miss Huntley is interested in everything about her,' Robert put in. 'I heard her discoursing the other day about antiquities and she is equally at home with the troubles of the agricultural labourers.'

It was a barb meant to hurt, Bella realised, but she would not let him see it had gone home. Instead she directed an arrow of her own. 'If people who have been privileged all their lives were to take more note of the world about them, they might be more tolerant of others' misfortunes. And they might realise that there is more to life than enjoying oneself.'

George laughed. 'Round one to you, Miss Huntley. What do you say in reply, Robert, my friend?'

Before Robert could answer a bell sounded the end of the intermission and everyone began returning to their seats. 'Saved by the bell,' George said, linking his arm through Robert's as they left to return to their own seats.

Bella watched the box opposite and two minutes later the young men reappeared and so did the ladies. She heard Mrs Huntley click her tongue disapprovingly beside her as the lights in the auditorium were turned down and the curtain rose for the second act.

This time Bella found it difficult to concentrate because she had seen one of the women fluttering her fan in Robert's face and whispering in his ear and had seen him laugh in response before seating himself close beside her for the rest of the performance. The little green god was sitting on Bella's shoulder and she was fuming. Jealousy was an emotion hitherto unknown to her and she did not recognise it for what it was.

Robert hated himself and he could not bear the attentions of Kitty, who had until then been a good friend and lusty lover. He was acutely aware of the young lady in pink, sitting rigidly on the other side of the auditorium watching the performance, chin tilted defiantly, fluttering her fan so vigorously he thought everyone else in the box must feel the disturbed air. He deserved her disapproval. And tomorrow he would have to endure a jobation from his mother. And he would deserve that, too.

Why had he insisted they carry on with their little game? Bella wanted an end of it. 'The sooner, the better,' she had said. That was why he had put on that show of independence and it was one he bitterly regretted. She would never forgive him. Before the final curtain he excused himself and left. He needed time to think and that could not be done in present company. Instead of calling up a cab or a chair, he set off on foot, head down, deep in thought.

Why, in heaven's name, had he agreed to Desmond's proposal to take a separate box and, worse, to invite the three young ladies? It was not what he had wanted. He wanted to declare himself, to ask Bella to forget that legacy and share his life. He could find something interesting to do to earn a living. She might not be the Countess of Westmere, but he would do everything in his power to make her happy.

But she was making it impossible and the more time he spent in her company, the more he realised what he had let himself in for—heartache and anguish. Now he had made matters a hundred times worse.

He arrived home without realising how he had arrived there, or where he had been. He let himself in, undressed and flung himself into bed. Tomorrow—no today, for it was almost dawn—he had to go to Holles Street and face his mama. And Bella. Bella. He fell asleep with her name on his lips.

As Henrietta was 'at home' the following morning, several people called. Some merely left cards, others stayed for refreshment. Bella, sitting beside her patroness, making light conversation and listening to the gossip, some of which she thought very shocking, found it very difficult to concentrate. Henrietta had summoned Robert and she knew he was in for a scold, and though she thought he deserved it for embarrassing his mother at the theatre, the situation in which they found themselves was not entirely his fault. Not his fault at all. It was hers. It was time for a confession. Or it would be as soon as Robert appeared and all these people went away.

She kept looking at the clock, her insides bubbling with agitation. This time tomorrow, she was sure she would be on her way back to Westmere in disgrace. At five minutes to noon, as some of the callers began drifting away, the butler appeared and Bella's breath caught in her throat. However, it was not Robert he had come to announce, but Edward and Charlotte.

They stood for a moment in the doorway, looking round at those of the company who remained, before Edward hurried forward to bow to his mother. She rose to greet him and afterwards kissed Charlotte's cheek. 'How nice to see you, my dear. You know everyone, do you not?'

'Why, yes, ma'am.' She looked round and, spotting Bella, said, 'How do you do, Miss Huntley?'

'I am well, thank you, Miss Mellish.'

Having done her duty in acknowledging Bella's presence, Charlotte turned her back on her to speak to Henrietta. 'I have brought the invitations to my ball, Mrs Huntley. It is to be on Friday, the seventeenth of May, and, as I intimated before, there is to be an announcement.'

'Thank you, my dear. I wish you both happy.'

Charlotte suddenly swung round to Bella. 'What about you, Miss Huntley? Do you wish us happy?'

Bella, whose every fibre was concentrated on the door for the arrival of Robert, found herself being scrutinised. Charlotte was looking at her as if she were issuing a challenge. Bella forced a smile. 'Of course I do. My felicitations.'

'How is your grandfather?'

Bella was taken aback by the sudden switch in the conversation, but showed no sign of it as she answered. 'I have heard from Miss Battersby and she tells me he is well, apart from the gout.'

Charlotte smiled the smile of a contented cat. 'And one does not die of the gout. Let us hope he lives for a long time yet.'

'Amen to that,' Henrietta said, because her young relative seemed to have been struck dumb.

Bella found herself looking covertly at Edward. He was just the same very handsome, well-turned-out man he had always been. His smile, as he had greeted her, had been just as friendly as ever but she could not help thinking of that conversation she had overheard in the book room and she felt again the animosity and the greed of Charlotte and heard Edward's voice saying, 'Leave it to me.'

Instead of repudiating his interest in the Westmere legacy and scolding Charlotte for her cupidity, he had condoned it; instead of rebuking her, he had kissed her, had held her so close to his body they had seemed melded into one. What was he planning? The old lady she had met in Westmere woods had warned her to be careful about whom she trusted. Had she meant Edward? No, of course not. The very idea was ludicrous.

'Captain Robert Huntley, ma'am.' She heard the butler's voice as if from a long way off and then Robert was among them, dressed in a frockcoat of brown superfine, his long legs encased in strapped trousers, bowing and saying good-day, laughing pleasantly, bandying words with his brother. But Bella was shocked to see the white, pinched look on his face and the dark shadows beneath his eyes, and the eyes themselves had lost their customary humour. She had done this to him.

Having made a tour of the room and having spoken to everyone else, he stopped in front of Bella and bowed from the waist. 'Miss Huntley,' he said formally. 'I trust I find you well?'

She replied with a curtsey. 'Quite well, thank you.' And then an imp of mischief sat on her tongue and she allowed it to have its way. 'I am persuaded you enjoyed the entertainment last evening, judging by your jollity.'

He smiled, almost wearily. 'Looks can deceive.'

'Yes, indeed they can. I am sorry if the play was not to your liking, but undoubtedly you enjoyed the company. For myself, I found the acting somewhat overdone. One does not shout when one dies of unrequited love, surely? The anguish would make speaking of it difficult.'

He was tempted to ask her if she spoke from experience, but decided against it. But she was right—it was impossible to speak of it. 'I doubt the actor could be heard up in the gallery if he had not raised his voice.'

'True. But the end was very disappointing, don't you think?'

'I did not stay to see the end. I lost patience with the hero's weakness.'

'Dear, dear, so bad?' The voice was Charlotte's. 'Edward and I had engaged to go, but perhaps we shall not bother. I do so hate weakness in a man.'

'Sometimes,' said Bella, 'it is not weakness but sensitivity. One should not confuse the two.'

'No, but sensitivity can be misplaced. Some people take advantage of it, you know. Edward is a case in point. He is sometimes so sensible of others' supposed feelings he is completely taken in by them and refuses to act in his own interests.'

'Then I am glad he has you to put him right, Miss Mellish,' Bella said, while Robert turned aside to change his chuckle into a cough.

'And I shall do so,' Charlotte said perfectly seriously. 'Do not make the mistake of thinking I will not, Miss Huntley. You will never be the Countess of Westmere.'

'Charlotte!' Edward, who had been talking to his mother, had returned to her side in time to hear her last remark. 'That was uncalled for.'

'She needs to be told.'

'Bella is well aware of the situation,' Robert said, moving to stand beside her. 'She does not need you to refine upon it.'

'Oh, we are the staunch lover now, are we? It is not what I heard. I heard a certain Kitty O'Donovan was proving more entertaining.'

'Lover?' queried Robert, one eyebrow raised, which made him look very like his brother, standing only a foot or two away. Bella had not noticed it before, but told herself that being alike in looks certainly did not mean they were alike in character and temperament. The one was urbane, unruffled, the other volatile. 'That word implies an insult to Miss Huntley and to me.'

'I think Charlotte meant suitor,' Edward put in hastily. 'You are engaged, after all.'

'Edward, it is supposed to be a secret,' Bella said, horrified that he should have spoken of it to anyone else.

'Secret!' Charlotte cried. 'It is the worst-kept secret in the world. The whole *ton* is talking of it and speculating on how much you are worth. Some say twenty thousand a year at least, others, who know better, say nothing at all for the old Earl has windmills in his head and cannot order his own affairs. And that is not to mention other rumours of a less salubrious kind. Shall I tell you what they are?'

'Charlotte,' warned Edward, putting a hand on her arm, 'you have said more than enough.' He turned to Bella, obviously embarrassed by Charlotte's outburst. 'I am truly sorry, Bella. In my own defence I must say it was not me who betrayed your confidence.'

'I do not wish to speak of it,' Bella said.

Charlotte laughed, not in the least put out by Edward's remonstrance. 'You do not suppose that tulip, the Comte de Courville, would keep his mouth shut, do you? He told his sister, Colette, who told Lady Boston and you know what a gabble-grinder she is. No, of course, you don't, you have only recently arrived in town, but I can tell you there is nothing that lady does not know and what she does not know she can discover.'

'Oh, no.' Bella was appalled. She had forgotten all about Louis, and yet it had been Louis's clumsy proposal which had made Robert agree to bring her to London. 'Is Louis in Town?'

'Where else would he be?' Charlotte countered. 'He is saying you will get your comeuppance but, then, so will he, for he will never be the Earl of Westmere either.'

'Charlotte, it is time we took our leave,' Edward said before she could enlarge on what she was saying. 'Come along.' And he grabbed her arm and propelled her towards the door.

'What is the matter with Edward?' Henrietta asked, joining them. 'One minute he is here and showing every sign of staying, the next he is almost running out of the door.'

'I believe Charlotte is not well, Mama,' Robert said. 'Overcome by the heat.' He glanced at Bella and saw an answering gleam of amusement in her hazel eyes.

'It is not at all hot in here,' his mother said.

'No, Mama, perhaps not. I meant the heat of argument.'

'You have not been quarrelling with her as well? Whatever is the matter with you?'

'They were not quarrelling,' Bella said, defending him. 'It was a little misunderstanding, that is all.'

'Oh, that legacy, I collect. You know, I begin to think that the gossips may be right and his lordship is a little out of his mind to have caused such a furore.'

'You have heard it, too?' Bella asked.

'Oh, it does not signify. Some people's lives are so empty they must fill it with talk of others. Do not let it agitate you. Now I must say goodbye to the rest of my guests and then, Robert, I wish to speak to you.'

She turned away, leaving Robert and Bella facing each other. Only by clenching her fists in the folds of her skirt and refusing to look into his face could Bella control the shaking of her limbs. Of all the people she had met since coming to London, only Henrietta had showed any cordiality. To the rest she was an object of resentment, of derision, at best of curiosity. It seemed everyone knew she was being sold to the highest bidder.

'Bella, I am sorry you had to hear that,' he said softly.

'You knew about the rumours?'

'There are always rumours. Mama is right, some people have nothing better to do.'

'What are they saying?'

'Oh, refining on the state of his lordship's mental health, the kind of thing Louis said when he was at Westmere.'

'But there is nothing wrong with Grandfather's mind, you know that. It is sharp as a razor.'

'Oh, yes, none sharper.'

She did not detect the irony in his voice. 'I think I will go home tomorrow. Nothing has turned out the way I imagined it would and I can see no way out except to return to Westmere and tell my grandfather I cannot comply with his wishes.'

'Don't be such a goose.'

'I am not a goose,' she hissed, afraid Henrietta might hear them. 'I cannot marry any of you and Grandpapa will not change his mind. He told Edward so.'

'How do you know that?'

'I heard Edward tell Charlotte. That is why she is so angry. Robert, I do not want to make people angry. I must go home and throw myself on my grandfather's mercy.'

'That would make the tongues wag even harder, don't you think? Where's your pride?'

'*My pride!* My pride doesn't come into it.' But it did. She had been so wrong about everything. It was not the polite, polished Edward but Robert, the jester, who had stood by her, Robert who had apologised, tried to soften the hurt done by Charlotte's malicious tongue. But he had made no secret of the fact that he did not love her and would be glad when the Season came to an end.

'Mine does,' he said. 'You will make me look a noddicock…'

'You are in a fair way of doing that entirely by yourself,' she snapped. 'At the first setback you are off, disporting yourself with another young lady in full view of half the *ton*. And if Charlotte is right and our engagement—our *supposed* engagement—is an open secret, such behaviour is unpardonable.'

'You wanted us to quarrel, so now's your chance. Tell Mama you will never forgive me. Break it off. I dare you to.' He was taking the biggest gamble of his life, though his expression gave nothing away.

Bella hesitated, staring down at her feet, encased in soft kid slippers which matched the pale green of her simple muslin gown. Had he purposely flaunted those young ladies at the theatre to give her the opportunity to quarrel with him? She could not look at him, knowing that if she did she would be reminded of that kiss and the memory of that always set her limbs in a quake whatever she happened to be doing at the time, even when he was not in the same room.

When he was standing facing her, so close she could almost feel his warmth and power, it was impossible to keep still. This was not what she had expected would happen and she had no idea how to deal with it. Her legs suddenly refused to support her and she sank onto the sofa beside which she had been standing.

He remained towering above her. 'Well?' he demanded.

'Your mama would think me very hard-hearted if I broke it off because of one mistake.' She managed a wintry smile. 'She would insist we kiss and make up.'

He flung up the skirt of his frockcoat and lowered himself to sit beside her. 'Is that what you want?' His voice was no more than a whisper.

Was he teasing her again? Did he mean he would kiss her if she said yes? But she could not. She would give herself away without a doubt. 'I could blame your disreputable friends for leading you astray,' she suggested.

'No one leads me, astray or otherwise,' Robert said firmly, but his heart gave a sudden leap that she had not jumped at the opening he had offered. 'And disreputable is not a word I like to hear applied to George Fulbright, who has been a staunch comrade in arms. And it is hardly fair to his parents when you were their guest only last night. As for Desmond Norton, he is a gentleman. He owns a very respectable and profitable publishing company, besides inheriting a fortune from his father.'

'A publisher?' she queried eagerly, setting aside their quarrel. 'Oh, you must introduce me to him, Robert.'

'George did last night as I recall,' he said dryly.

'Properly. I mean properly. Please, Robert.'

'Why?'

'I must earn my own living and I thought I might write.'

'Earn your own living? I never heard such nonsense.'

'It is not nonsense. I have been thinking of it for a long while. If I am independent I do not have to marry at all, do I?'

'Fustian! You have no idea how hard it will be.' She had given him hope, only to dash it again.

'Of course I do, but I must try. Please, Robert…'

'And then?' He spoke softly.

'Then what?'

'What do you expect me to do? Shall I fall at your feet, shall I be allowed to address you? Or will you be too rich and famous to deign to acknowledge me?'

'It is not kind in you to tease me so.'

'What makes you think I am teasing?'

'I know very well you are,' she said, fighting tears. 'Go away and leave me alone.'

He sat on, undecided, wondering whether to try and change her mind or if it might make matters worse between them. The last of the guests had left and he looked up to see his mother coming purposefully over to join them. He rose and offered her his seat, which she took, settling herself beside Bella.

'Now, Robert, I wish to know what you have to say for yourself,' Henrietta said. 'To bring those…those…'

'Ladybirds?' Bella finished for her, giving Robert a barbed look which would have made a lesser man squirm.

Henrietta gave her a startled look and then continued to harangue her son. 'Sit down, for goodness' sake. I shall have a crick in my neck, looking up at you.' She waited until he had folded his long length into a small chair opposite her, then went on. 'It was the outside of enough to bring those…those demi-reps to a place where you knew I would be, and with Bella, too. Have you no consideration? I wonder she agreed to marry you, I really do.'

'So do I, Mama,' he said mournfully.

'It would serve you well if she were to break off the engagement. No harm would be done, seeing you have not yet announced it, but I hope it has not come to that. Bella, for my sake, will you forgive this scapegrace and give him another chance?'

What could she do? She could not say she wanted to break it off now, could she? She could not say she was tired of London already and wanted to go home. Besides, there was now the added incentive of meeting a real live publisher if she stayed. 'Yes, of course,' Bella said. 'It was only a little scrape after all. It would be churlish to hold it against him, wouldn't it?'

Henrietta gave a sigh of relief. 'There you are, Robert, you are forgiven and I can think of many young ladies who would not be so magnanimous.'

'Thank you, my dear.' His voice was penitent as he reached across to seize Bella's hand and put it to his lips, but he was grinning so much she felt like slapping him.

Henrietta rang the small handbell on the table at her side, and when a maid came in answer to the summons she directed her to serve nuncheon. 'After we have eaten, Robert will take you riding,' she told Bella, giving her no opportunity to dissent. 'And make sure you are seen. It is the only way to silence the wagging tongues.'

'Should we not take the barouche?' Bella suggested, not trusting herself to be alone with him. 'Then you could come with us.'

'No, I need the carriage myself. I promised to visit Lady Jersey. With luck she will provide vouchers for Almack's and Robert can escort us there.'

'Oh, Mama, I cannot think of anything more boring,' Robert said. 'Dressing up in breeches and stockings and dancing all those country dances and nothing to drink but lemonade.'

'Nevertheless, it is the place to be seen if you wish to be noticed. Vouchers are not given lightly, you know.'

It seemed Henrietta was determined to throw them together and Bella sat through the light meal, listening to her hostess talking about Almack's, which was a weekly supper dance arranged by five of London's leading dowagers, and wished herself anywhere but where she was. And the worst of it was that Robert was infernally cheerful. How could he be so light-hearted? He no more wanted to be given a second chance than she wanted to give it to him.

She was not prepared to enjoy their ride. Her heart was too heavy and Robert's cheerful chatter made her want to scream and rail against the unkind fate which had catapulted her into this situation. They walked their horses down the Ride, bowing this way and that, stopping to say a few words here and there and generally obeying Henrietta's instruction to make sure they were seen.

'It is all very well for your mama to say that riding together will silence the tattle-mongers,' she said, after they had acknowledged Lady Boston in her cumbersome town coach with its liveried flunkies front and rear. 'But I think we are playing into their hands.'

'It is either that or displease Mama.'

'We have done as she asked. Now we can go home?'

'Very well.' He was tight-lipped as he turned to go back

the way they had come, riding parallel to the carriage way towards the gate.

'Oh, just look at that,' Bella said, pointing with her crop and proving to him that nothing could subdue her for long. 'Did you ever see such a vehicle?'

It was a high-perch phaeton painted in primrose yellow picked out with lines and scrolls in black. Its enormous wheels were yellow with red spokes. Sitting in it, reins and whip in hand, was Louis, Comte de Courville, resplendent in yellow driving coat with huge pearl buttons and a black and yellow striped waistcoat. Beside him sat a young lady in the biggest hat Bella had ever seen. It was yellow straw and quite two feet across. A huge feather flowed around its brim and touched her rouged cheek.

'Louis,' Robert murmured.

'Who is the young lady?'

'His sister, Colette. Have you never met her?'

'I do not think so, unless it was when I was very young.'

Louis had seen them and pulled his beautiful black horses to a standstill. 'Why, if it isn't Cousin Robert,' he said jovially, doffing his hat. 'And Cousin Isabella, too. How do you do?' His eyes raked over her as they stopped opposite the phaeton. 'You are in looks, I must say. Town life seems to suit you.'

'Thank you, Louis.' Bella had no intention of being cowed by him and looked him straight in the eye. 'You are looking splendid yourself.'

'Thank you. You have met my sister?'

'No, I do not think so. How do you do, Miss de Courville?'

'This is the heiress?' Colette asked her brother. 'Why, she is quite a sweet little thing.' She smiled at Bella. 'I feel so sorry for you, my dear, it cannot be easy…'

'What cannot?'

'Why, to be the wife of an army captain when you had

hoped for a fortune. Still, that is better than nothing, is it not?'

'Grandpapa is still very much alive, ma'am, and the speculation is premature.'

'Oh, people will always speculate, you cannot change that. Even Captain Huntley. If he is gambling that his lordship will be able to keep his word, he will come home by weeping cross.'

'I have heard that opinion voiced elsewhere today,' Robert said, smiling easily. 'And, do you know, I do not care. Fortunes, or lack of them, are not something that occupy my mind greatly.'

Louis laughed. 'Poor Isabella. You should have accepted me when you had the chance. Perhaps you will change your mind.'

'I do not think so,' Robert said coldly.

'And who are you to speak for her? I cannot believe this engagement of yours is anything but a hoax, otherwise you would have announced it. Waiting on his lordship before committing yourself, are you? Or the lawyers.'

Misty began to fidget with being kept standing and Bella was glad of the opportunity to turn and bring her under control. 'Robert, I think we should move on. We are blocking the way,' she said.

Robert seemed reluctant but as she had already moved away he was obliged to follow. 'I will fetch him a facer if he speaks to you like that again,' he said, as they rode.

'Oh, Robert, you do not have to take your obligations as my fiancé quite as far as that. I am perfectly capable of giving him the right about without your help.'

'As you were before, I collect.'

'I would have done if you had not stepped in.'

'It was what you wanted, you cannot deny that.'

'Yes, but…' She stopped, unable to tell him how horribly wrong it had all gone.

'But what?'

'We will say no more about it, if you please.'

'He is right, you know. About the announcement. It does look as though I am waiting for something…'

'In that case, you know what to do.'

'Make an announcement?'

'Certainly not. I did not mean that and you know it.' Bella was so upset she was hardly aware of what she was saying. 'Repudiate me. Find another young lady to escort about Town.'

'I cannot do that,' he said, horrified. 'Any more than I could quarrel with you.'

'Quarrel?' She laughed bitterly. 'We do nothing *but* quarrel.'

'It is not my wish, but you make it very hard for a fellow.'

'Then make it easy for yourself. Forget we ever made that foolish agreement. I shall go home to Westmere.'

'Bella, you can't do that. It would mean giving in to your grandfather and the tattle-mongers and proving Louis is right. He is only bluffing, you know. And what would we tell Mama? She thinks you have forgiven me.'

'I have.'

'It does not sound like it. I am truly sorry for causing you embarrassment. I have said so.'

'It is nothing to do with that and you know it.'

'Then what? Is it Edward and Charlotte?'

'Partly,' she admitted, assuming he meant Charlotte's outburst and Edward's condoning of it. 'I do not think I shall go the ball, it will be too mortifying.' She was near to tears.

He felt like yelling at her, taking her shoulders in his hands and shaking her until her teeth rattled. He wanted to shout, Forget Edward! Forget Louis! Look at me! They do not love you, but I do. I am here. I am waiting. But he did not. He simply trotted Nelson out of the gates and along Oxford Street to Holles Street, where he saw her safely inside and left with no more than a few polite words being said on either side.

He could not do as she asked, he could not find someone else to escort. It would be dishonourable and, besides, he did not want anyone else—there was only Bella. She lived in his heart and filled his thoughts. How could he have allowed it to happen? She had used him and, like a fool, he had allowed himself to be used.

If Bella wanted his brother, who was he to stand in their way? She had adored him for years and it was obviously what she had scheming for when she had asked him to bring her to London. He wondered what a man had to do to attract that kind of constancy.

Perhaps he should have told her the truth long ago. Perhaps he should have confessed that he wanted the engagement to be real and that marriage to her was what he wished most in all the world. He might have done if it had not been for that damned legacy. He could almost hate the Earl of Westmere for it.

He went back to his chambers, changed his clothes and set off for White's where he had arranged to meet George and Desmond. He would dine with his friends and spend the evening playing cards. Gambling was a serious matter and demanded his whole concentration; he would have no time to think of women and one young lady in particular.

They were halfway through pork chops, boiled capon in a wine sauce, roast beef and tureens of succulent vegetables, washed down with several bottles of red wine, when George mentioned the unmentionable. 'Your Miss Huntley is not at all as I imagined her,' he said.

'Oh, how so?' Robert said warily.

'Why, she is a beauty and clever, too. I thought she might be shy.'

'Shy!' Robert laughed harshly. 'No, she is far from shy.'

'Then shall we be seeing more of her out and about? Or are you going to keep her all to yourself?'

'No, not at all. In truth, she asked to meet you, Desmond.'

'Me?' he queried in surprise. 'Why, I am old enough to be her father and a confirmed bachelor to boot.'

'Oh, it is not your looks which attract her, my friend, but your intellect. Or rather the way you earn your living. She has ambitions to become a published writer.'

'Is that so? Is she any good?'

'I have no idea. I have seen nothing she has written. I gather she is saving that privilege for you.'

'Oh, no,' Desmond groaned. 'I suppose you said I would be only to pleased to read what she has written if you asked me.'

'No, she is perfectly able to ask you herself. I am simply to introduce you and leave you alone together.'

'Shouldn't risk that,' George said, grinning. 'Our Desmond has a way with the ladies. You might lose her.'

There was no fear of that, Robert thought. He had never had her to lose. He simply smiled. 'I'll take my chances. I have already told her Desmond is a gentleman.'

'You had better bring her to see me,' Desmond said. 'Does she have any of her work with her in London?'

'I really do not know. She only mentioned it in passing.'

'Mrs Huntley is bringing her to my mother's concert to-morrow night,' George said. 'You could meet her there.'

'Good idea,' Desmond said. 'But, Rob, I shall expect you to rescue me if it becomes too tedious.'

Rescue him? Robert thought. He could not even rescue himself. 'Very well,' he agreed. 'Now, do you think we could talk of something else? How is the new filly coming along, George?'

'She's a winner. I timed her over three furlongs and I could not believe how she covered the ground. With a light rider, she'll be unbeatable.'

'Let me know when she's running. I'll put a few guineas on her.'

'Ain't that your brother?' Desmond nodded in the direction of the door.

Robert, who had his back to the door, swivelled round to look. Edward, impeccably turned out in a black evening suit and pure white cravat, stood looking round the company as if searching for a familiar face. 'So it is.' He beckoned to his brother, who came slowly towards them, weaving slightly from left to right and back again.

'Unless I'm mistaken,' George said as they watched him, 'he is somewhat disguised.'

Robert rarely saw his brother other than sober and he was so far taken aback as to be embarrassed. 'Something's up,' he murmured, and rose to meet him.

'Robbie, been looking for you.'

'Now you've found me.' He looked back at his friends and shrugged his shoulders, then took Edward's arm and turned him back the way he had come. 'Let's find somewhere quiet.'

They found a corner in an alcove in the library and sat down. 'I'm foxed,' Edward said.

'So I see. It is not like you. What's to do?'

'Made a mistake.' He was trying hard not to slur his words and almost succeeding.

'Yes, you'll have a devil of a headache tomorrow.'

'Driven to it.'

'Oh.' Robert did not need to be told he was referring to Charlotte. He waited for his brother to go on.

'She will not let it rest. You would think she was marrying me only for my prospects, the way she keeps on about Westmere. The old man has made up his mind and there's no shifting it, and so I told her but she wants me to have him declared insane. I cannot do that, Robert. He doesn't deserve that, however muddle-headed he is.'

'You may not need to. I fancy Louis is intent on the same thing and he has no such scruples.'

'I am in the devil of a coil, Robert.'

'Your coming engagement, you mean? I never was able to understand why you offered for her.'

'I suppose I was overcome by her beauty and the encouragement of her parents, and before this business with Great-Uncle William, I had no reason to think she was anything but a charming young lady. And she professed to love me. Now I wonder if she is capable of it.'

'I should think that if you refused to make a push to secure the legacy, she will end the understanding herself. You are not officially engaged yet.'

'She is threatening to do that now. And saying she will tell everyone why.'

'Call her bluff.'

'I would be ostracised.'

'Not by anyone who knew the truth, you wouldn't.'

Edward brightened suddenly. 'You think not? It might almost be worth it to know that.' He paused and looked up into his brother's face. 'What do you think Bella would say?'

'About what?' Robert queried, suddenly full of apprehension.

'An offer, should Charlotte and I decide we should not suit.'

'I cannot speak for Bella, Teddy.'

'I know she would have chosen me when we were at Westmere if I had been free. I am ready to wager it was what his lordship intended all along. The legacy was never in doubt. He was simply trying to secure Bella's future under the guise of giving her a choice.'

'Aren't you forgetting one thing?' he said. 'I am engaged to Bella. Am I supposed to break that off, too?'

'Oh, that was never serious and you know it. She fastened

herself onto you for want of anyone else to stand buff for her and bring her to London. I could not and she has more sense than to ask James or Louis. Once I am free, she will admit that I was her first choice.'

Robert would not admit the truth of that, but he was in despair. He remembered the look Bella had given Edward when they had met in the park. It had been one of adoration, almost as if she had been telling him with her eyes that he was really the one. And there had been that admission that it was because of Edward she did not want to go to the Mellish ball.

How could he bear to release her when the time came? Edward would find a way of extricating himself from his commitment to Charlotte and then he would himself lose the only woman he had ever loved, ever would love. He could not stand in the way of her happiness.

'You don't truly believe the Earl can make you his heir, do you?'

Robert shrugged. 'It is a matter of indifference to me.'

'Then you will do the decent thing and make yourself scarce for a week or two?'

'Edward, I can't believe you mean that. It's the drink talking.'

'Indeed I do. Sober as a judge now, thanks to you.'

'And if Bella refuses you?'

'She won't. I can offer her everything she needs and wants—a home she loves, money enough to indulge any extravagance, a title…'

Robert stood up, controlling his anger with a great effort. 'I think you should go home and think about it more carefully when you have had a chance to get over your disagreement with Charlotte. Shall I call up a cab?'

'No, I have my carriage outside. Can I drop you off anywhere?'

'No, thanks. I plan to take some money off George tonight.'

'Then I bid you goodnight.'

Edward stood up and left, walking more quickly and steadily than he had when he had arrived. Robert smiled grimly as he watched him go, but he did not go back to his friends. He needed a walk, a very long walk.

It was not until a loud voice impinged itself on his senses that he realised he had wandered into one of the more unsavoury streets in the district. In front of him was a small crowd and in its midst a man standing on a cart. Robert stopped, wondering where he had seen the man before. He was no longer young, though his exact age was difficult to determine, a very big man with the craggy features of a seaman and the broken nose of a pugilist. His hair was plentiful, but pure white, not someone easily forgotten.

And then he remembered. It had been in Ely, the day he had gone to Westmere, the day that had changed his life. From being an independent, footloose man with no ties, he was now bound hand and foot.

'Are you men or mice?' the man demanded. 'Are you content that the landowners dictate who shall and who shall not sit in Parliament? Do you want your voice to be heard? If you do, you must learn to shout, shout your demands from the housetops. Do not expect the franchise to be handed to you on a plate. Those who hold the reins of power will not readily give them up. You must fight for what you want, fight with every weapon at your disposal...'

Robert, pushing thoughts of Bella into the back of his mind with an effort, stopped to listen. Where did the man belong, in the fens of Cambridgeshire or in London? Was he a Chartist or simply out to make trouble? He moved forward to hear more, but that was a mistake. The man beside him turned and, looking him up and down, instantly recognised him as one of the hated upper classes.

'We've a spy in our midst,' he shouted, grabbing Robert by his superfine coat sleeve and dragging him forward.

Resistance was useless, he had learned that in Ely. He allowed himself to be hauled to the front to face the man on the cart. Rough-looking though he was, the man's weather-worn face bore signs of intelligence and humour. He smiled at Robert, showing even white teeth. 'Well, well, well. Are you come to join the proletariat, sir?'

'No, I am merely a disinterested passer-by.'

'Disinterested, eh? How disinterested? Do you mean you do not care that some of your fellow men are being ground into the dirt?'

'No, I care.'

'Then perhaps we should adjourn to the hostelry on the corner and see if I can arouse your interest. What say you?'

'Delighted.' It was better than prowling the streets in moody contemplation of unrequited love and missed opportunities. Besides, he was curious about the man, who had jumped down from his perch and was elbowing his way through the bystanders towards him.

'Joseph Mostyn, at your service,' he said, holding out his hand.

'Robert Huntley,' Robert said, grasping the hand in a firm handshake. 'Captain Huntley, if that is of any significance.'

'The title is not, the name of Huntley is. Related to the Earl of Westmere, are you?'

'He is my great-uncle.'

'Oh, then you are one of old John's grandsons.'

It was in Robert's mind to berate the man for incivility towards his grandfather, but he decided against it. Instead he said, 'The youngest.'

The crowd made way for them as they turned in the direction of the tavern. 'Then it is unlikely you will make the next Earl of Westmere.'

'Impossible, I should say,' Robert said wryly, thinking of

Bella. 'But how come you know so much about the family? Do you come from Westmere?'

'I lived there many years ago before I went to sea.'

'I thought you had the look of a seafaring man. So how is it you are interesting yourself in the plight of the worker?'

'Life at sea palls in the end and I wanted to end my days on dry land. Only there was no place to come home to and the country was in severe straits. I had listened to Orator Hunt speaking and made myself known to him. You see the result.'

For some reason he did not fully understand Robert felt he was not being given the whole story, but he let it pass. There was no sense in antagonising the man who had only to lift a hand and his followers would tear the clothes from his back and beat him to a pulp. They passed into the tavern but the others stayed outside—on guard, Robert decided.

'Ale?' Joseph queried.

'Ale will do very well.'

And so they drank together and Robert listened to Joseph Mostyn talk. He put in a word of his own here and there, and by the time he made his somewhat erratic way home, he knew a little more about the aims of the Chartist movement but nothing more at all about Joseph Mostyn. But he had come to a decision.

Fight, the man had said, fight with every weapon at your disposal. He was a soldier, he should have thought of that for himself. Bella was a prize worth fighting for. She did not want a footloose erstwhile soldier, or an empty-headed Corinthian only concerned with enjoying himself. He had to make her realise there was more to him than that. He remembered her saying, 'If people who have been privileged all their lives were to take more note of the world about them, they might be more tolerant of others' misfortunes. And they might realise that there is more to life than enjoying oneself.' She was right. It was not enough to drift through life, a member of the privileged class. Privilege brought responsibility. He had learned that as a soldier and he should have remembered it.

He would become a Member of Parliament, have some influence on the way the government was run and try to do something for the labourers. Would Bella have him then? Could he convince her that he was worthy of her, that he did not need the Earl's legacy, did not want it, that he wanted her for herself? Was it too late?

Chapter Eight

Bella realised as soon as Robert had gone that she had ruined her only chance of happiness. She loved him with an intensity that was almost painful and yet she had deliberately and cruelly quarrelled with him. What had she been thinking of to send him away like that? Would he go?

Henrietta had not yet returned from visiting Lady Jersey, but as soon as she came back Bella decided she would confess that the whole idea of an engagement had been a ruse and beg to be allowed to go back to Westmere. She should have done it long ago, when it would have been relatively easy. Why hadn't she? Oh, she knew the reason well enough—she had been harbouring a faint hope that Robert would learn to love her as she had come to love him. That had been blown away and now there was nothing left.

Unable to sit still, she wandered into the garden to pass the time. The property had been unlet for some time and the gardeners had made little impression on the wilderness of long grass and overgrown shrubs, but it suited her mood. The sun, which had been shining fitfully, suddenly went behind a cloud and a swirl of wind blew round her, making her shiver. What a spring this was turning out to be! In Westmere the farmers would be cursing it and wondering if they would be able to harvest any crops at all, and the peasants would be hungry and discontented. Ellen had written that the riots had died down, but if things became any worse, there were sure to be more.

'I have another piece of news,' she had written. 'Mr Trenchard is to marry Mrs Clarke in the autumn, would you believe? They announced it soon after Mrs Clarke took the children home. While she was here she confided in me she had always had special feelings for Mr Trenchard and it was her dearest wish to marry him, but she was in despair when he told her he had offered for you. So, my dearest, you did the lady a favour, turning him down. I am sure she will make him a very good wife and the two little girls love her dearly.'

Bella was very pleased for Mrs Clarke and was quite sure she would make James a far better wife then ever she would have. The marriage would solve the problem of a mother for his children, but it would do little to help James's financial difficulties—Mrs Clarke was a widow whose only asset was a small cottage and possibly an annuity from her late husband. Bella sighed as she put the letter away. If it was a love match, as Ellen had said, then love would find a way.

She wished it could find a way for her. She had abandoned her grandfather, Ellen and the good people of the fens in pursuit of her own selfish pleasure, and that had turned out to be a dreadful disappointment. What had that strange woman said—that every act of selfishness hurts someone? She had hurt Robert, Cousin Henrietta and her grandfather, who must be feeling lonely without her.

He had only been trying to secure her future and the best thing she could do was to talk to him, tell him how she felt. He would understand and they could go back to having everything as it was. But even as she thought it, she knew nothing could ever be the same. She had grown up, turned

from a girl to a woman, and fallen in love, well and truly
in love. And it was nothing like she had expected it to be.

A few drops of rain sent her scurrying indoors. There was
still no sign of Henrietta and she decided to fill in the time
by writing to her grandfather, but it proved very difficult.
She did not know what to tell him, whether to say she was
unhappy and wanted to come home or whether to go on
pretending all was well. She tried to imagine his reaction to
the news that his plans for her had come to nothing and she
would not, could not, marry any of his great-nephews. She
left the letter half-finished and turned to her novel.

Here, at least, she could lose herself in the problems of
her heroine, whom she had called Juliana. Juliana had, by
questioning an old servant who had been pensioned off and
lived some distance away, discovered that her father, as a
very young man, had fallen in love with a young lady of
whom his family had heartily disapproved, being of a lower
social standing. He had given way to the pressures of his
parents and parted with her, not knowing she had been preg-
nant. Later he had married someone his parents had favoured, but it had not been a happy marriage and he remembered his lost love and regretted giving in to his
parents. And then he heard his lover was dying and rushed
to see her.

Bella sat for several minutes, staring at what she had written, but for once she did not feel the urge to write. The
muse had left her and she found herself gazing into space,
going over and over everything she and Robert had said to
each other. One minute he was the perfect escort, kind and
considerate, defending her against all comers, the next he
was berating her, accusing her of what? She did not understand what they had been quarrelling about.

It was all too much for her. Her head felt muzzy, like
cotton wool. Words went round and round in her head, dis-
jointed, isolated. Her eyes felt heavy, almost as if she had

drunk something noxious. It had felt like that when the old lady in the woods had given her that herbal drink. But she had drunk nothing.

When Daisy came in to turn the bed covers down and make up the fire, she found her mistress asleep at her desk. 'Miss Bella.' She shook her shoulder gently. 'Miss Bella, are you ill?'

Bella roused herself and murmured, 'So tired, so very, very tired.'

'I am not at all surprised,' Daisy said, 'racketing about town like you have been, staying up until all hours. Come, I'll help you to bed…'

'Cousin Henrietta…' Even speech was an effort. 'Got to tell her…'

'Never you mind about Mrs Huntley. I shall tell her you are asleep. She will understand…'

'Will she?' Bella muttered as Daisy helped her into her nightgown.

'Of course she will.' Daisy tucked the bedclothes round her charge and turned out the lamp. 'Go to sleep. There will be plenty of time to talk to Mrs Huntley tomorrow when you feel better.'

Would she? she asked herself as Daisy left, closing the door softly behind her. Would she ever feel better again? It was her last thought before she fell into oblivion, and she did not wake until gone noon the following day.

'Mrs Huntley has gone out,' Daisy told her when she brought her washing water. 'She said she had some calls to make and said you must be left to sleep. Do you feel better?'

'Yes, thank you. Did she say what time she would return?'

'No, but you are engaged to go out tonight and she asked for a light repast at five. You missed nuncheon—shall I bring something up on a tray?'

'No, I will wait for Mrs Huntley.'

But when that good lady appeared she declared she was exhausted and was going to lie down and rest until it was time to leave for the concert. 'I advise you to do the same, my dear,' she told Bella. 'You still do not look quite the thing. Are you sure you want to go out tonight? I could send our excuses…'

Bella knew Henrietta had been looking forward to the concert and, though in her present mood she would much rather have stayed at home, she could not deprive her hostess of the outing. 'No, I am perfectly well,' she said. 'Of course we shall go.'

As soon as they arrived at the Fulbright mansion, they were conducted to their seats in the overheated salon, and there was no time to engage in conversation—the concert was about to begin. Not until the intermission were they able to look about them and mingle with the guests. Henrietta knew almost everyone present and was in animated conversation with one of the ladies, who was escorting a whey-faced daughter, so Bella sat on a spindly-legged chair in a quiet corner where she could observe the different knots of people gathering to give their opinion of the music without the necessity to contribute.

'Bella.'

She looked up to see Robert standing in front of her, and her heart began to beat painfully in her throat. In spite of his beautifully tailored evening clothes and pristine cravat, he was looking gaunt, as if he had not slept, and she felt a pang of pity for him. 'Robert, I did not expect you to be here.'

He looked down at her, taking in the dark-rimmed eyes, the pale complexion, and concluded she was as unhappy as he was. 'Are you well?'

'Perfectly well. And you?'

'Oh, I am in plump currant, always am,' he said cheerfully. 'You remember Mr Norton, do you not?'

Bella had been so intent on studying Robert's face she had not noticed there was another man standing just behind him, waiting to come forward. She smiled and held out her hand. 'Why, Mr Norton, how nice to see you again.'

He took her fingers, bowing over them. 'Your obedient, Miss Huntley.'

'Do sit down. And you, Robert. Bring those chairs forward.'

'I will leave you to talk,' Robert said, as Desmond obeyed. 'Must make myself agreeable to Mama and our hostess. Please, excuse me.' He bowed and was gone.

With a sinking heart Bella, watched him make his way carefully between the rows of chairs to where his mother was engaged in conversation with Mrs Fulbright and George, and knew that their last quarrel had been final and irrevocable.

'Miss Huntley?'

She forced herself to pay attention to Mr Norton. 'I'm sorry. I was thinking that Robert does not look at all the thing.'

'Oh, that is nothing but lack of sleep. He stayed up late listening to some political speaker, so he told me.'

'Did he?' She was suddenly reminded of that meeting in Ely. Robert had been listening to that speaker, too. How long ago and far away that seemed now.

'Yes. He'll be right as ninepence tomorrow. It will take more than one sleepless night to bring him down. Strong as an ox and stubborn as a mule, that's our Rob.'

She smiled. 'I think it might be a family trait, Mr Norton.'

'He told me of your interest in writing, Miss Huntley.'

'Did he?' She was surprised. Robert had tried to dissuade her when she had spoken to him of it.

'What are you writing? A journal? Reflections? Poetry? Or something weightier?'

She laughed and it was the first true laugh she had managed all day. 'If weight is the measure, then I suppose it might be considered heavy, being somewhat lengthy, but if it is content you go by, then I suppose it must be called light. I have been writing a novel. It is nearly finished.'

'Oh, a rival to Miss Austen.'

'Oh, no, I am not nearly clever enough for that.'

'Would you like me to read it and give you my opinion?'

'Oh, yes, please.' Bella's eyes were shining with hope.

'Send it to me.' Desmond smiled as he extracted a calling card from a case in the tail of his coat. 'Here is my direction.'

Robert rejoined them as she was putting it into her reticule. 'I hope it was a fruitful meeting, Miss Huntley.'

'Yes, thank you, Captain,' she said, matching his formality. 'I am very grateful.' She looked up into his eyes and added softly, 'For everything.'

'Think nothing of it.' Her huge hazel eyes held him in thrall and it was a moment or two before he realised she was speaking. He pulled himself together.

'Mr Norton tells me you were listening to a political speaker last night. I did not know you were interested in politics.'

'Indeed I am. I have been thinking seriously about it.'

He could not have been very upset by their quarrel, she decided, if he found it so easy to find diversion almost immediately afterwards. 'And what conclusions have you reached?'

'That there are some things in life worth fighting for,' he said enigmatically. 'Do you not agree?' Why did she think his words were charged with tension? Why was he looking at her so strangely? Why was her heart beating almost uncontrollably?

'Indeed, yes.'

He smiled, aware that Desmond was listening to every

word. 'Then that is what I shall do. It might take time but, depend upon it, I shall win through.'

'I hope you may.'

'Thank you.' The orchestra was tuning up for the second half of the recital and they could not continue the conversation. He took her hand and bowed formally over it. 'Miss Huntley, I must bid you goodnight. Things to do. Come, Desmond.'

Desmond looked startled but stood up and took his leave of her. She forced herself to smile, but inside she was crying. Robert could not even bear to be in the same room with her and he was talking in riddles. What did he mean about fighting? They were always fighting. They struck sparks off each other whenever they met, like steel on steel.

She must stop herself thinking of him, put him right out of her head, concentrate on her book. How long would it take to finish it? If she really put her mind to it, three weeks, maybe a little less.

Robert and Desmond left the room with George Fulbright, who had taken his leave of his mother, just as everyone resumed their seats. Bella returned to sit beside Henrietta, but she did not hear a single note of the music. She was far away in the land of her imagination, shuffling her characters about, ordering their lives, rehearsing their dialogue in her mind. The applause signalling the end of the performance took her completely unawares and it was a moment of two before she remembered to clap.

Bella was still in her fantasy world as the audience began to shuffle out, taking leave of their host and hostess and standing in the hall waiting for carriages to be brought to the door.

Juliana's true father could hardly take the child home to his wife, she decided. No wife could be expected to accept her husband's bastard. But she was the daughter of his true love and because of that he loved her too; he could not abandon her or hand her over to others. He must find a way.

The inspiration came to her as they rode home. He must tell his wife she was the daughter of a dear friend who has died and named him her guardian. Then he could bring her up and watch her grow. Tomorrow, she would plead a headache and not go out and then she would finish it.

Having no engagements the following morning, Henrietta decided to stay in bed but Bella, who had woken with the dawn chorus, used the time to write. She was in the middle of writing a tearful reunion when the dying woman bequeathed his daughter to the man who had wronged her, and sniffing over it herself, when Daisy came to tell her Sir Edward was in the drawing room.

Reluctantly she put down her pen. 'Does Mrs Huntley know he is here?'

'I believe her maid has gone to inform her, but he asked for you especially.'

She tidied her hair and went downstairs, wondering what could be wrong. It was too early for ordinary morning calls and she could not think why he should wish to see her. She found him standing by the hearth, his elbow on the mantel shelf and his head down, staring at the fender. He looked up when he heard her step and, though he smiled, she was shocked by his appearance.

He was, as usual, immaculately dressed in riding coat and breeches, but as he had a very good valet that was not surprising. However, his starched muslin cravat was twisted as if he had been tugging on it while he waited for her and his face was drawn, his eyes dull. If she had not known better, she would have concluded he was suffering from an overindulgence of wine the night before.

'Edward, you do not look quite the thing. Is something wrong?'

'Nothing I should not have foreseen.'

'Oh, I am sorry.'

'There is nothing for you to be sorry for. I have been a fool and must do what I can to make amends.'

'I cannot imagine you doing anything foolish.'

He gave a strange laugh which grated on her ears. 'I think it was very foolish in me to imagine myself in love.'

'Oh, it is Miss Mellish who has cast you in the suds. I can only say I am sorry, Edward, but perhaps it is only a small thing and you will soon be comfortable with each other again. Grandfather told me that being comfortable was everything.'

'And do you believe that?'

'Perhaps,' she hedged. 'Is there anything I can do for you?'

'You could come riding with me.' He seemed to pull himself together and looked into her face, smiling in the old way.

'When?'

'Now. That is why I arrived early.'

She was wondering what to say in reply when Henrietta sailed into the room in a cream-coloured peignoir and with her lace cap on askew. 'Edward, why are you up with the birds? Is there something amiss?'

'No, Mama, I simply came to take Bella riding. Rob is away and—'

'I did not know that. Where has he gone?'

'He has not seen fit to confide in me.' There was something about the way he said that which made Bella wonder if it was strictly true.

'And where is Charlotte?'

'Her mama is taking her to buy a new gown for the ball. Colette has inveigled the Prince Regent to put in an appearance and though that is all it will be, five minutes at the most, the gown she has already chosen is not considered good enough and she must perforce have another, no matter what the cost. My presence was most definitely not required, and as I had no other engagement it came to mind that Bella might like to ride out.'

Henrietta turned to Bella. 'Would you like to go?'

Bella hesitated. Not long before, she would have been pleased at the prospect, but now she was not so sure. Apart from the fact that Miss Mellish would undoubtedly disapprove, Edward was in a strange mood and would more likely than not regale her with his complaints against Charlotte, which she did not want to hear. And he would begin apologising all over again for Charlotte's rudeness to her and she was tired of hearing it. On the other hand, he looked very sad and she really would like some exercise and fresh air, so she smiled. 'I should like it very much.'

Bella hurried to her room to change into her riding habit while he sent round to the mews to have Danny saddle Misty and the cob and bring them round to the front of the house.

In less than half an hour, she was in the saddle and riding beside him out of Holles Street and into Oxford Street.

'Shall we go to Green Park?' Edward suggested. His horse was a big bay and he seemed to tower over her. 'It is not so crowded and we might even manage a gallop.'

She understood he wished to avoid being seen with her, which was not flattering but perhaps sensible. If the gossips guessed he had quarrelled with Charlotte and saw him with Bella, it would not take much imagination to conclude he was angling after that legacy. Oh, how she hated that! If she had not loved her grandfather so much, she might have been tempted to think he was being deliberately mischievous.

'Very well,' she said.

Followed discreetly by Danny, they turned down Bond Street towards Piccadilly, riding slowly because of the crush of carriages which filled the road. Most of their occupants were out shopping and required their drivers to pull up out-

side the establishments they wished to visit, half blocking
the road so the two riders were unable to ride together and
certainly could not converse.

As soon as they entered Green Park, Bella was away,
cantering and then galloping across the green sward. Edward
followed, keeping slightly behind her until she pulled up
and slipped from the saddle at a stand of trees in the middle
of the park then turned to wait for him to join her. The
exercise had given her a good colour and her eyes were
shining with exhilaration; a few strands of hair had escaped
from her hat and blew across her cheeks. She brushed them
away, laughing. 'Oh, that was good.'

He walked his horse and stood beside her, the reins idle
in his hands. 'It is an age since I enjoyed a gallop more. I
had forgot how well you ride.'

'Why, thank you.' Bella smiled, genuinely pleased by the
compliment. 'It is a long time since you taught me.' She
paused, remembering him putting her on her very first pony
and leading her out along the bridleways around Westmere.
'You had endless patience, which was more than Grandfather had when he tried to instruct me. And then Robert
came, too, and no child could have had better companions.
I thought you were both so grown up. But, then, I suppose
you were, considering there is…how many years between
us?'

'Eleven between you and me,' he said. 'Nine between
you and Robert.'

'But you were always the sensible one, the one who bade
me take care, who would not let me take fences too high
for me. It was Robert who incited me to take my courage
in my hands and go for them.'

'Sensible,' he said, almost harshly. 'What a reputation to
have to bear, that of being sensible.'

She laughed. 'What is wrong with that?'

'Sometimes I wish it were otherwise, then I could snap my fingers at convention and do as I please.'

'I imagine that we should all like to do that sometimes.'

'I am persuaded that you have no compunction over it. It is why you asked Robert to bring you to London.'

'Whatever gave you that idea?' she demanded.

'He had no illusions about that inheritance when his lordship first spoke of it. He had ruled himself out, just as I had. And then suddenly he had offered and been accepted. He would never have thought of it himself.'

'I do not believe you have ruled yourself out,' she said, not wishing to pursue Robert's motives or her own. 'Not entirely.'

'Did you know the Earl had broken the entail?'

'No, I did not. And if he has, I wish he had not. It has brought nothing but heartache.'

'I am right, aren't I?' Edward persisted. 'About you and Robert. It is nothing but a hum. That is why he has gone into the country, to make it easy for you to break off your engagement.'

She had had no idea Robert had left Town. Was that why he had hurried away last night? 'His reasons are his own,' she said. She did not want him to be right; she wanted to stay engaged to Robert, to marry him. She wanted him to want it, too, and that was her dilemma. He did not. 'And why are you being so particular about it?'

'Bella, I must know.'

'Then you must ask him.'

'If that is his reason, you would be free to choose again.'

She gave a cracked laugh. 'Three down and one to go. James, Louis, Robert and now you. I assume that Miss Mellish has repudiated you and you are now making yourself eligible.' She waited for him to protest, but when he did not she added, 'Oh, no, Edward, I am not sensible, as you have just pointed out. I can and will reject you all.' She hauled herself back into the saddle without his help. 'If you do not mind, I should like to go home now.'

He remounted and followed her in leaden silence. Outside his mother's house, he dismounted to help her, holding out a hand to steady her. She thanked him stiffly and walked to the door, already being opened by the butler. She was not aware he had not followed her inside until she heard the door being shut and turned to find there was no one behind her but the servant. Slowly she made her way up to her room and flung herself across her bed.

Where was Robert? Her senses ached for him. Had he really gone away so that she could break off their engagement? How could he? And without saying a word to her first. But that was what she had told him to do, hadn't she? She had no cause to feel wronged.

In the next three weeks, she went out with Henrietta in the carriage, paying calls, going shopping, to Hookham's library, to musical evenings and routs, but he did not put in an appearance.

'Your ball gown arrived,' Daisy said, when she went up to her room to change to go to Almack's one Wednesday evening. 'Shall you try it on? It's lovely.' She took it out of its box as she spoke and held it up for Bella to see. The material of the open outer robe was the flimsiest gauze in a blue-green so pale as to be almost white, and shone with iridescence as Daisy lifted a handful and let it fall over the silk underskirt. Its bodice was decorated with tiny silk flowers and green velvet ribbons. 'Oh, go on, Miss Bella, let's see how it looks.'

In spite of her preoccupation, Bella could not resist trying it on. Although there were yards and yards of material in it, it was so fine it draped itself over her slim figure like softly moving water, moulding itself to every curve and flowing out around her ankles. Daisy's reaction was a long sigh.

'Oh, you look lovely, Miss Bella. You'll have all the young gentlemen fighting over you.'

She did not want young gentlemen fighting over her. She was tired of fighting, tired of tension and undercurrents, tired of this awful round of so-called pleasure. Hurriedly she pulled it off. 'Put it away, Daisy. The ball is a se'ennight away and we are wasting time.'

'What will you wear tonight?' Daisy asked, as she obeyed.

'Oh, anything. The blue silk.'

'That's awful plain.'

'I said the blue silk,' Bella snapped, and immediately regretted it. 'I am sorry, Daisy, I did not mean to fly into the boughs. Please, forgive me.'

'That's all right, miss. You are missing Captain Huntley, I don't doubt.' She gave Bella a knowing look which nearly had her in the trees again. She managed to control herself and allowed Daisy to slip the muslin over her head and do up the tiny buttons at the back. By the time her hair had been dressed and she had put on satin pumps and a matching three-quarter-length pelisse, she was feeling more herself. Picking up her fan, she went downstairs to join Henrietta, determined not to let anyone see how badly she was hurting.

'It is the outside of enough after all the trouble I took to obtain vouchers for us,' Henrietta said, as they set off. 'I'll wager Robert has gone to the country with George Fulbright, as he said he would. I am thoroughly ashamed of him and his Turkish treatment of you.'

'It is of no consequence, Cousin Henrietta, really it is not. And he did not say he would escort us. If you collect, he was against going.'

'I believe you have quarrelled again.'

'No, it isn't that…' Bella stopped suddenly. If she confessed now she would be sent home, and if that happened how could love ever blossom between them? She wanted

the opportunity to apologise, to put matters right, to tell him
how much she loved him, even if he did not return that
love, to ask his forgiveness. She must do that before she
was banished.

'What is it, then?'

'Perhaps he has gone away to let the gossip die down.'

'I should have thought there was a better chance of that
if he were to stay at your side and prove them wrong.'
Henrietta had her own ideas about what was wrong between
the young couple, but until one or other of them chose to
confide in her she would keep her own counsel. But she felt
like knocking their heads together, and would if that errant
son of hers would only come back from wherever he had
gone.

Almack's was disappointing, as Robert had said it would
be. It was stiff and formal and she was sure the young people who attended came only because it was expected of
them. She was asked to dance by several young hopefuls,
including Peter Collison, who returned to the subject of her
visit to his home to see his statue, but she was sure they
only made themselves agreeable out of curiosity. If Robert
had been there, it might have been different.

She missed him dreadfully, especially as she felt everyone
was looking at her, talking about her and that legacy, which
was like a millstone round her neck. She wished, with all
her heart, that she was not who she was, but some unknown,
the daughter of a parson or a scholar, or even a gentleman
of business, so that she could enjoy her Season and choose
a husband for herself. But, then, would she have been considered suitable for Robert?

It did not help when Edward arrived with Charlotte and
her mama. They crossed the room to greet Mrs Huntley,
which necessitated presenting Bella to Lady Mellish. 'I shall
look forward to seeing you at Charlotte's ball next week,'

she said, peering short-sightedly at Bella through her quizzing glass. 'It promises to be the event of the Season.'

'Of course, we are looking forward to it immensely,'
Henrietta said before Bella could reply.

'You expect Captain Huntley will be back in time to attend?'

'Oh, yes,' Henrietta answered promptly. 'He is away on
business but I know he hopes to be back for that.'

Lady Mellish smiled, inclined her head and drifted away,
followed by Edward and Charlotte. 'I hope you are right
about Robert,' Bella said, wondering if Charlotte knew
about Edward's ride with her in Green Park. She decided
probably not, for Charlotte was not the forgiving kind.

'Of course I am.'

Bella watched them chatting to those around them and
though they danced together twice, they seemed to have
little to say to each other and left early. Henrietta and Bella
followed soon afterwards. 'It is not the same without Robert,' Henrietta said, a sentiment with which Bella heartily
agreed.

But she had said she would put him from her mind and
she had to do so if she were to finish that novel. It was not
as easy as she had expected. There was the complication of
the laws of inheritance which she was not at all sure of. And
Juliana, when she learned she was illegitimate, must realise
she was an outcast from society and could not marry the
man she loved. She must send him away and make her own
way in the world. Would he accept that without being told
the truth? How should she end it? She did not like unhappy
endings as a rule, but this fitted in with her mood and she
cried as she wrote the last page, three weeks after the concert.

By this time she had confessed what she was doing to
Henrietta who, afraid she was falling into a decline, had
asked why she spent so much time alone in her room. Bella

did not tell her she had hopes of the book being published—
for some reason she could not explain, she felt that if she
did that Fate would find some way of dashing them. Henrietta smiled and asked no questions. If the girl was using
the writing as a way of expunging her despondency, then
why not? Putting it all on paper could do no harm and might
serve to make her see where her true happiness lay.

As soon as the novel was finished and had been checked
for errors, Bella packed it up and sent Danny with it to Mr
Norton's address, before she could change her mind. She
felt exhausted, drained of all emotion, as if she were just
recovering from a serious illness, and yet in some ways
elated. It was an achievement to have finished it at all, even
if he said it was dreadful. Now she must put it from her
mind until she heard from him. She went with Henrietta to
visit Lady Collison and view the wondrous figure of Bacchus far more cheerfully than she might otherwise have
done.

Having spent more than three weeks listening to Joseph
Mostyn speak all over the Midlands, where he attracted
great crowds, Robert rode south again. The man had a point,
but he did not think mere rhetoric would make the government or the landowners change their attitudes and he
guessed Joseph knew that, too. There was dissidence in the
air and undercurrents of violence which would erupt on the
slightest excuse. They matched his own feelings of anger
and helplessness. It was going to take years to make a difference. But he was committed.

He had taken the biggest gamble of his life by leaving
town. Edward would think he had done it to leave the way
open for him, and in a way he had. Bella had said over and
over again that she would not marry any of them and he
had been counting on her turning his brother down. He
could not declare himself to her, tell her his plans, ask her

to share his life, until she had finally and irrevocably put Edward from her mind. They had to start again with a clean slate.

He stopped at an inn when it grew too dark to go on and carried on next morning as soon as the cock crowing in the yard woke him. He arrived in London, tired and saddle-sore. He left his horse at the nearby stables, picked up his saddlebag and made his way to his apartments, thinking he would change his clothes and go straight over to Holles Street, but changed his mind.

It was late. His mother might have taken Bella out, and he needed a good night's sleep if he were to create the right impression and put his case properly. Not only that, he wanted to be sure she had not accepted Edward. He would go to Blandings House first thing in the morning and then go on to Holles Street.

He was met at the door by Adam. 'Good to see you home, Captain,' he said, taking his bag from him. 'You'll be needin' food and drink.'

'And a wash, Adam. Hot water, if you please. Any messages for me?'

'Several from Mrs Huntley, sir, wanting to know where you are. Sir Edward called, but he left no message—said it could wait. And Mr Norton said I was to tell you most perticler he needed to see you urgent.'

'Did he say what for?'

'No, sir. He said he'd be at White's most nights.'

'Then I shall not need supper. I'll eat at the club. Put some clean clothes out for me, will you? The mulberry superfine tail coat, I think, grey pantaloons and a clean shirt and cravat.'

Half an hour later, he was striding towards St James's, wondering what Desmond wanted with him. He had probably assumed that Robert had been with George at Newmarket and wanted to know how the filly had fared. But he would hardly have called that urgent.

He bounded up the steps into the club and found his way to the card room, where he fully expected to find his friend. He was greeted jovially by several acquaintances but there was no sign of Desmond. 'Anyone seen Norton?' he asked.

'In the library, I think,' one of the players said, before returning his attention to the cards in his hand.

Desmond was sitting in the depths of a wing chair, a glass of brandy in his hand and a manuscript open on his lap, which he was reading by the light of an oil lamp on the table by his elbow. There was no one else in the room. He looked up when Robert's shadow fell over him. 'Oh, Rob, there you are.'

'As you see, here I am.' Rather than call a servant, he turned and poured himself a glass of cognac from the bottle on the sideboard before sitting in a chair opposite Desmond. 'What's astir? Urgent, you told my man.'

'So it is. I'm in a devil of a coil.' He stopped, clearly embarrassed.

Robert sipped his drink. 'Go on.'

'It's Miss Huntley…'

'Bella?' He sat forward expectantly. Surely Desmond had not developed a *tendre* for Bella? He hadn't been playing fast and loose with her affections, had he? Or, worse, he had not offered and been accepted? He smiled grimly—that would put the old Earl in a spin. 'What about her? Spit it out.'

'You have heard the rumours?'

'Rumours. Oh, you mean about that legacy and what a money-grubbing fortune-hunter I am. Best ignored, and so I told Bella.' He paused. 'You don't believe that of me, do you?'

'Never gave it a thought,' Desmond said enigmatically. 'I was not referring to your motives, honourable as I am sure they are. Do you know what they are saying, besides the fact that the Earl is touched in the attic?'

'No.'

'That Bella is not his granddaughter at all but his love child, and he is trying to foist her onto whichever of his great-nephews is greedy enough to overlook the fact.'

Robert was appalled and furious. 'That's a damned lie! I'll call any man out who dares to repeat it.'

'Are you sure it isn't true?'

'Naturally, it isn't true. I have known Bella since she was a baby.'

'Not quite. I asked your brother. He tells me the first time you went to Westmere was for the Countess's funeral, when Bella was about two years old.'

'You spoke to my brother about it?' Robert did not know why that should fill him with dismay, but it did.

'Yes, why not? You were nowhere to be found. And what difference does that make?'

'None, I suppose. We have both known Bella all her life—she has grown up at Westmere. Do you think the Countess would countenance anything so outrageous as that? God, those gabble-grinders must be sick.'

'But why would they say such a thing if there was not a grain of truth in it?'

'I don't know.' He stopped suddenly. 'Oh, yes, I do. Louis is at the bottom of it. He cannot make his lawyers argue the Earl is out of his head and so he's trying a new tack by slandering him and disinheriting Bella.' He threw the rest of the fiery liquid down his throat and stood up. 'I'll make him withdraw. I'll break every bone in his body if he does not.'

'Sit down, Rob, I haven't finished.'

'There's more?' He sank back into his chair.

'I said I was in a coil.'

'So you did, but it is not your problem.'

'No, but this is.' He tapped the manuscript on his lap. 'It's Miss Huntley's novel. She sent it to me.'

'So?'

'Did she tell you what it is about?'

'No, a romance, she said—the sort of thing Miss Austen writes, I suppose.'

Desmond gave a wry smile. 'Not quite. I do not think Miss Austen would write so openly of illegitimacy, and if she did she would certainly not make her heroine a bastard.'

'Bella has done that?' he queried in surprise. There were hidden depths to Miss Isabella Huntley he had yet to probe.

'Yes, and done it extraordinarily well. There is no doubt the book would be a hit.'

'You are going to publish it?'

'If I were unscrupulous, I most certainly would. It would make me and her a great deal of blunt. But how can I? It is too close to home, almost as if she knew all about these rumours and was deliberately confirming them.'

'I do not believe it.'

'Read it yourself.' He closed the pages, retied the ribbon which bound them and handed them to Robert. 'And then tell me what I should do.'

Robert could not wait to get home, and the minute he had sent Adam to bed and closed the door on his chamber, he sat down to read. He was still reading as dawn broke. Desmond was right—it could have happened like that. Did Bella believe it herself? 'Oh, my poor, poor darling,' he murmured as he finished the last page. He had to go to her, tell her he was certain there wasn't a grain of truth in the rumours— and even if there were, he did not care a jot. He loved her for herself, not some legacy. He must make her believe it. But what to do about Louis?

As soon as he had breakfasted, he set out for Blandings House to confer with Edward. He found his brother alone in his breakfast parlour, munching toast and drinking coffee.

He waved at Robert to sit down and called for a servant to put out another place.

'Not for me,' Robert said. 'I had my breakfast hours ago.'

'Where've you been this past sennight?'

'Riding about the countryside. You made it clear you wanted me to out of the way to leave the field clear for you and, like a fool, I complied, but that's by the bye. I met Desmond Norton last night…'

'You know about that book, then?'

'Yes.'

'It puts an altogether different light on the Westmere inheritance, don't you think? If Bella is the old man's love child…'

'My God, you don't believe that, do you? It's obscene.'

'Robert, think back. Bella was two or three years old when we first met her and her so-called father never showed her an ounce of affection. Not surprising if she wasn't his daughter but his own father's by-blow. I wonder how the old man made him agree to pretend she was. To save the Countess pain, I shouldn't wonder.'

Robert could hardly believe what he was hearing. That his own brother should subscribe to that odious theory was horrifying. 'I do not believe it. The book is pure fiction— she made it up.'

'Is it? Where did the rumours come from? There must be some basis of truth in them—they have not been conjured from the air.'

'Louis did it to discredit the Earl and enhance his own chances of inheriting, you must see that.'

Edward laughed. 'Does it matter now? The old man's secret is out, Bella has confirmed it and she must be unbalanced herself to have done it. No one will have her now.'

Robert was becoming increasingly angry and frustrated. He had expected Edward to have some sympathy for Bella, especially after the last conversation they had had about her.

He had come to discuss ways of minimising the damage and was getting nowhere. 'I thought you loved her. You made me think I did not stand a chance. I left you to it. So, am I to assume that you have not offered for her?'

'You know, I very nearly did, but there is no need now, is there?'

Robert stood up so violently that his chair crashed back and fell over. He let it lie. 'I never thought the day would ever come when I would refuse to acknowledge you as brother, but I do now. If you do not want me to call you out, you had better keep out of my way in future.'

Edward laughed. 'Robert, do not be so melodramatic.' But before the words were out, his brother had gone, slamming the door behind him.

Robert dashed straight off to see Desmond. He found him in his office, sitting behind a huge desk littered with papers and manuscripts. 'My God, Rob, you look as though you are about to have a seizure,' he said, getting to his feet and pouring his visitor a glass of wine from a decanter on a cupboard. 'Sit down, man, sit down.'

Robert, who was breathless from the pace he had set himself, flopped into a chair and took the drink that was offered to him, almost throwing it down his throat and giving the glass back to Desmond, who refilled it and handed it back. 'I assume from your demeanour that you have read that manuscript?'

'Yes, I have. Desmond, you cannot publish it. It will crucify Bella.'

'Then why did she write it?'

'It's fiction, Desmond. I do not think she has connected the story with her own circumstances at all. It is all coincidence. I'll stake my life on it.'

'Then why do you want to suppress it? It could be published anonymously.'

'After all the rumours that have been going the rounds of

late, people will guess who the characters are meant to represent.'

'Pity,' Desmond said without rancour. 'I hate turning down something which shows such promise. What can I tell her?'

'Suggest she writes another, something different.'

'And if she sends it to another publisher, one who is not so scrupulous?'

'Is there another copy?'

'I doubt it. She hadn't finished it two weeks ago, there would have been no time to make a copy, but I have to return the original to her.'

'Tell her it's been lost, or stolen.' He grinned lopsidedly. 'That's true because I do not intend to give it back to you.'

Desmond sighed. 'What a waste!'

'But do it for me, my friend.' He stood up and held out his hand. 'And many thanks.'

They shook hands and Robert left, returning to his own home exhausted and drained. He had not been to bed the night before and the one before that he had been in an uncomfortable inn and had only dozed. He needed a few hours' sleep before he could think straight enough to face Bella.

He was woken by Adam pouring hot water into his bath by the hearth. 'Sorry to wake you, Captain, but if I hadn't you'd have slept all night.'

He sat up and ran his hand through his curls, blinking hard, wondering for a moment where he was. 'What time is it?'

'Eight. And you'd best eat properly before you go. There'll be nothing at Mellish House but titbits that won't fill a kitten.'

The ball! He had forgotten all about that. His mother and Bella would be there. So would Edward and Charlotte, and more than likely Louis, not to mention every tongue-wagger in the *haut monde*. He cursed aloud. It was too late to go to Holles Street. They would be in their bedchambers, dressing to go out, and would not welcome his arrival. He would have to go to that confounded ball and put a confident face on it. Bella would need his protection—there was no one else to support her. He clambered out of bed, flung off the underclothes he had slept in and stepped into the bath.

Bella was sure she would not enjoy the ball. Everyone would be talking about her and the Westmere legacy and how Robert had offered for her in order to gain it and had then had cold feet and fled to the country. Mrs Huntley was confident he would turn up. 'And I am not going to give the gossips any more fuel by staying away,' she had told Bella when she had suggested they should not go. And what about Edward and Charlotte? Would there be an announcement or not? And if there was not, Charlotte would blame her. Oh, what a bumble bath it all was!

She dressed half-heartedly, uncaring whether she looked her best or not, and Daisy's enthusiasm only served to dampen her spirits further. When she could find nothing else to do or say to delay her further, she flung her silk cloak about her shoulders and went downstairs to join Henrietta who was waiting impatiently in the hall.

'About time, too!' she said. 'Whatever have you been doing all this time, child?'

'There was a slight tear in the skirt of my gown. Daisy had to mend it.'

'How did that happen? Oh, never mind, let us be off. There will be such a line outside Mellish House it will be suppertime before we even get in the door.'

Bella thought she might well be right as they came to a stop at least a hundred yards from the entrance, while the carriages in front of them moved up one at a time and deposited their occupants at the open door, ablaze with light.

But it was all well ordered and they found themselves mounting the steps in less than fifteen minutes.

Lord and Lady Mellish and Charlotte stood greeting each guest as they arrived. Bella gave them a deep curtsey, but when she rose she found she could not move on because Henrietta had stopped to speak to Charlotte, who was dressed in rose pink silk. 'Has Edward arrived?'

'Oh, yes, he came very early to make sure everything is as it should be. He has been a tower of strength.' She was speaking to Henrietta but looking at Bella as she spoke, raking her with her eyes. If she meant it to be intimidating, she did not succeed. Bella had more pride than that. 'Of course, there is no sign of Robert.'

'Robert has important family business to attend to,' Henrietta said primly. 'But he will come if he can.'

There were others waiting to be greeted and Lord and Lady Mellish were already turning to them. Henrietta led the way into the ballroom.

The huge room was already crowded, the colours of the gowns so colourful, the lights so dazzling, and the excited chatter so noisy that Bella was almost overwhelmed. It was difficult to pick out anyone they knew, but there was no mistaking Louis, dressed in a green coat, primrose satin breeches and white stockings. The lace ruffles of his shirt-sleeves hung over his hands and his elaborately tied cravat sported a sparkling diamond pin. He was with Kitty O'Donovan which surprised Bella, considering the contempt in which Charlotte held the young lady. Nearby she spotted Colette and her mother, who sat bolt upright with her quizzing glass almost permanently glued to her nose.

Henrietta had seen them, too, and could hardly ignore them, so she went over to them, gave a stiff little bow and said, 'Good Evening, Elizabeth, Colette.' Then she made a beeline for Mr and Mrs Fulbright, trailing Bella in her wake.

'Henrietta, there you are!' Mrs Fulbright said. 'We had almost given you up.'

'A slight problem with Bella's gown.'

'And very charming it is, too,' Mr Fulbright said. 'You will be the belle of the ball.'

Bella smiled bravely in response as she took her seat next to Henrietta, conscious that Charlotte had finished greeting her guests and had entered the room on Edward's arm. Had they made up their quarrel? She hoped very much that they had—it would be dreadful to have that on her conscience as well as everything else.

'Miss Huntley, I would be honoured if you would stand up with me.'

She looked up in a kind of daze to see Peter Collison bowing over her, his hand outstretched. She rose, laid her fingers on the back of his hand and allowed herself to be led into a country dance.

After that she was constantly in demand and in any other circumstances would have been delighted at the admiring glances and the compliments she received. But in truth she was searching the room, looking for Robert. He would not have absented himself from tonight's ball if he had had any feelings for her. She had gambled and lost.

Chapter Nine

Robert stood in the doorway, surveying the colourful scene, searching for Bella. He spotted her at last, dancing with a pimply-faced youth who was several inches shorter than she was. She looked breathtaking in that gown. It was starkly simple, rippling about her as she danced, setting off her lovely figure and creamy white shoulders. The coronet of twisted flowers had fallen a little askew and gave her a mischievous, elfin look which made his heart turn over.

He could see Edward and Charlotte sitting with Lord and Lady Mellish. Charlotte's smile was stiff and Edward's expression severe. They did not seem to be the happy couple they ought to have been on what was supposed to be an occasion for rejoicing. But perhaps it was a good sign that they were still together. Affecting nonchalance, he strolled over to pay his respects to his host and hostess.

'You are very late, Captain,' Charlotte said, after he had greeted Lord and Lady Mellish and managed a curt 'Edward,' to his brother, who did no more than incline his head in reply. 'I was sure you had decided not to grace us with your presence.'

'I am sorry. I was detained on business.'

'Better make up for lost time,' Lord Mellish said jovially

as the music came to an end and the dancers began to move off the floor. 'Go and mark a few cards.'

There was only one card Robert wanted to mark and, having bowed to the Mellish group, he hurried to join Bella, who had returned her to seat beside Henrietta on the arm of the pimply youth.

Bella looked up to see him bearing down on them and her breath caught in her throat. She had always thought him handsome, but now she was aware of a new dimension. His black evening suit showed off his broad shoulders and long legs and the pristine whiteness of his muslin cravat enhanced his tanned features and dark hair. Her heart was pumping painfully and she clasped her hands together in her lap to stop them shaking.

'Good evening, Mama. Bella, your servant.' He made a flamboyant bow from the waist to both ladies.

'Robert I am extremely vexed with you,' Henrietta said. 'Where have you been?'

He smiled. 'In the country, learning politics.'

'Politics! In the name of heaven, why?'

'It seemed a good thing to do at the time. Very enlightening.'

'How very strange! But why now? Why disappear, just when I wanted you, just when Bella needed you most?'

He turned to Bella. 'Did you? I collect you sent me away, told me to leave you alone. I did not mistake your meaning, did I?'

'I…' She stopped, unable to admit just how deep her need was. 'I cannot, for a moment, believe you went away simply because I told you to go. There was more to it than that.'

'Perhaps.'

'Are you going to tell us what it was?' his mother demanded.

'Later.' The orchestra began playing a waltz and he leaned forward and, taking Bella's hand, drew her to her feet. Before she could protest that the dance was already taken, he had whirled her away past the young man who had come to claim her.

They danced in silence, each trying desperately to think of something to say which would not make matters worse between them, unable to confess their true feelings, seemingly unable to speak without quarrelling. Slowly, the feel of his body so close to hers, the strength of his hand on her back as he guided her, the warmth of him, the rhythm of the dance and his sure steps took over and she began to relax.

He felt the tension go out of her body and held her just a little closer than was considered proper, so that the scent of her dark hair filled his nostrils. 'That's better,' he whispered. 'You dance superbly well. Or is it simply that we were made for each other?'

'Made for each other,' she repeated, startled enough to look up into his eyes. They were dark and intense and searching her face, but he was smiling. Her heart gave a sudden lurch and she stumbled against him.

He caught her and whirled her round. 'Yes. Don't you agree? Perfectly in tune.'

'Oh, Robert, please, do not gammon me. I do not think I could bear it.'

'My poor darling, you have been having a hard time of it and Mama was right. I should not have left you to the wolves.'

'What wolves?'

'Edward, for one.'

She was astonished. 'You knew! You knew he was going to speak to me...'

'Of course. He told me he had made a mistake and wanted to put it right. He is the Earl's choice and he said he was yours, too, only you would not say so because of Miss Mellish, so I decided to leave the field.'

'Oh, Robert, whatever made you believe him?'

'You told me you loved him—fond of him, you said.'

'When?' She was genuinely puzzled.

'That day in March when his lordship sent for us and your horse threw you.'

'Did I?' she asked vaguely. 'If I did, I did not mean love in the sense of wanting to marry him.'

'You don't?'

'Of course not.' She looked up into his face and smiled tremulously. 'Oh, Robert, I have been such a noddicock...'

'But a lovely noddicock.'

They had reached the end of the room and he waltzed her straight out of the door into the hall. Taking her hand, he ran with her along the corridor and into the conservatory, where the humid heat met them like a wall.

'Where are we going?' Bella asked, allowing herself to be led.

'Somewhere private.' He pulled her behind a huge tropical vine. 'Somewhere where I can kiss you.' And before she could draw breath to protest he was doing exactly that.

She had dreamed of this, savoured the sensation of his last kiss, wishing it could happen again, and now it was happening again, heightened to a kind of ecstasy. Her whole body tingled, from the tips of her fingers, through her stomach and groin to the very ends of her toes. She was lost to time and place as she wound her arms around his neck and grabbed a handful of his curly hair, so that he could not have drawn back even if he had wanted to. Which he certainly did not.

His lips left her mouth and began exploring her cheeks and throat. 'Bella,' he murmured. 'Tell me I'm not dreaming. That you are in my arms, that you love me.'

'You are not dreaming. I do love you.'

'My, my, if it isn't the Earl's little by-blow,' said a laughing voice. 'I should have more care if I were you, Captain, or you will be tarred with the same brush.'

They sprang apart to see Louis, standing holding aside the greenery the better to see them. Robert turned on him, his fists clenched. 'You will take that back, de Courville, or I'll draw your cork for you.'

'Why should I, when it is the truth? My goodness, you seem prepared to go to any lengths to get your hands on the Earl's blunt, even to marrying the daughter of his *chère-amie*, but it will not serve, not now his secret is out...'

The blow that hit Louis was so sudden and so forceful that he crashed back among the plants with a noise that brought others running to see what had happened, including Edward and Charlotte, who helped him to his feet. He stood facing Robert, wiping blood from his nose. 'I might have known a common soldier would resort to his fists,' he said.

'Very well,' Robert said, controlling himself with an effort. 'Choose your weapons.'

'No! No!' Bella cried. 'Oh, please, do not fight.' Both men ignored her.

'Are you sure she is worth it?' Louis sneered. 'She is not the heiress you think she is, she's not even a true Huntley.'

Bella looked from one to the other in bewilderment. 'Robert, what does he mean?'

'Nothing.'

Charlotte's tinkling laugh penetrated Bella's confused brain. 'He means, my dear, that as the illegitimate daughter of the Earl's mistress, you have no standing, no rights, certainly no fortune. In fact, you should not be admitted to any respectable drawing room and certainly not to my ball, but Edward begged me, said it was not your fault...' She stopped and gave a high-pitched laugh. 'Now we see you in your true colours.'

'I don't believe you,' Bella's voice was no more than a whisper.

'Miss Mellish is mistaken,' Robert said.

Bella turned to Edward, who would not look into her face. Everyone was crowding round, their mouths hanging open. There hadn't been a story like this in Town in years and they were agog to hear more. Bella gave a sharp little cry of distress and, putting her head down, pushed her way through the throng and fled, ignoring Robert's sharp cry of, 'Bella! Come back!'

She hardly noticed Henrietta coming to see what the commotion was about as she ran like a wounded animal looking for some quiet place to hide. Through the corridors she darted, pulling open doors, not caring where she was going as long as it was away from prying eyes and cruel tongues.

She found herself out in the garden and sprinted for a summer-house she could see at the end of it. Unlike the garden near the house, it was not lit by lanterns. She opened the door and sank onto a bench in the comforting darkness, curling herself up in a ball, hugging her knees.

Darkness might conceal her body, it could not hide her thoughts. They whirled round and round in her head as she tried to make sense of what had been said. Was there any truth in the rumours? Was the Earl her father? That would mean the man she had always thought of as Papa was not her father but her half-brother. If so, her whole life had been a lie from beginning to end. And it seemed everyone had known it but her.

But had she known it? In the secret recesses of her mind, had she been aware that there was something different about her? Who was she? Who was her mother? Did Robert know the truth? How could he not have done when so obviously Edward and Louis and everyone else did? Just when she thought he loved her as she loved him and they might, after all, have a happy future together, it had all gone horribly wrong again. If he truly cared for her he would have come after her, knowing she would need comfort and reassurance, but he had not. He had believed Louis.

Why had he kissed her, then? Was it allowable to make free with a by-blow, as Louis had so crudely put it, when it would be considered highly improper and tantamount to a proposal when the liberty was taken with a real lady?

In the blink of an eye, she had gone from being the much-loved granddaughter of one of England's premier peers to a nobody, someone without an identity, just like the heroine of her novel. And like her heroine, she could not marry the man she loved because her shame would reflect on him. But that was a work of fiction and bore no resemblance to the truth. Had Desmond Norton revealed its contents, believing them to be true? Would he do such a despicable thing?

And then Bella remembered Charlotte hinting of other unsavoury rumours long before she had sent the book to Mr Norton. It was a terrible coincidence. She must get the man-uscript back. Today. At once. And then she must go home to Westmere and confront her grandfather. No, not her grandfather, the Earl of Westmere. He had been cruel to her, not only in keeping the truth from her but expecting one of his great-nephews, all unknowing, to marry her.

The night air was cool and she shivered. How long had she been in the summer-house? Minutes or hours? She had no idea. But, however long it had been, no one had cared enough to come looking for her. Wiping her face with the hem of her gown, she rose stiffly to her feet and peeped outside. She could hear cheering and clapping coming from the ballroom, but that was the last place she wanted to be, so she slipped through a side door and made her way up to the room where the ladies' cloaks and pelisses had been left. Finding hers, she slipped it on and went downstairs again.

The outer door was unguarded. The footman, who nor-mally stood by it, was on tiptoe at the ballroom door, watch-ing what was going on there. Probably Edward and Charlotte's announcement, she decided as she slipped out into the street.

It was just his bad luck that in dashing after Bella Robert should suddenly find himself face to face with the Prince Regent who had chosen that moment to arrive with Colette. It was a triumph on her part; she was as proud as a turkey-cock and was not going to forgo the pleasure of a grand entrance for anyone. She insisted on presenting Robert to His Highness, followed by Charlotte and Edward. Others crowded behind them and the general surge of the company carried everyone into the ballroom.

It took less than two minutes for Robert to extract himself, but that two minutes was long enough for Bella to disappear. While everyone crowded into the ballroom, he set out to search for her. She was not in any of the downstair rooms. He went upstairs, thinking she might be in the ladies' retiring room. He had expected to find a maid somewhere about, or other ladies coming and going, but the ladies were all in the ballroom and the maid had obviously gone to find some vantage point on the gallery. He paused only a moment before opening the door, but there was no one inside.

From there, he went back through the conservatory into the garden, just missing Bella who was entering the house by a side door. He spent half an hour in fruitless searching and was forced to conclude she had left the premises. The footman, now back at his post, assured him that no one had passed him. By now the Prince was taking his leave and the hall was once again crowded. Robert made his way over to his mother. 'Mama, I cannot find her. I do believe she has run away.'

'Oh, she can't have done! Where would she go? She must still be in the house.'

'I have looked everywhere.'

'The garden, then?'

'I've searched that, too.'

'Should we alert Lady Mellish or Edward?'

'No,' he said sharply. 'There has been enough talk already. I'll go out and look for her. She might have gone home.'

'On foot? In the middle of the night? She would not be so foolish, would she?'

'I believe she is desperate enough for anything, Mama. I could cheerfully strangle Louis and...' He had been about to say Edward, but knew that would hurt her and stopped himself in time. 'Will you make our excuses, say Bella is not feeling quite the thing and take the carriage home? I'll follow on foot.'

It was a matter of moments to put the plan into action. By the time Henrietta had called up the coach and set off, Robert was already scouring the streets. All in vain. There was no sign of Bella. He returned home as dawn lightened the sky, to find his mother pacing the floor in the hall. She swung round as he entered but when she saw he was alone her shoulders slumped and she sank into a chair.

'Robert, what are we to do? What can we tell his lordship? She was in my care...'

'She might be trying to get back to Westmere. I'll saddle up and check the coaches. It will be quicker on horseback.' He stooped to put his hand on his mother's shoulder. 'We'll find her, Mama.' And then he was gone.

He ran all the way to Albany and, arriving breathless at his apartments, found Adam already up and about. 'Mr Norton's man came with a message,' he said, following Robert as he bounded up the stairs. 'He has Miss Huntley safe and—'

Robert stopped and turned so suddenly that he collided with Adam and nearly sent both of them tumbling to the foot of the stairs. 'She's with Desmond?'

'Seems so,' Adam said. 'He said to get over there as soon as may be, for he don't know what to do with her.'

'I'll wager he doesn't,' he said with a wry smile. 'I'll go at once. You go to Holles Street and tell Mrs Huntley that Miss Huntley is safe and I will be bringing her home.'

The two men went downstairs again and parted at the street door. Ten minutes later Robert was hammering on Desmond's front door. It was immediately opened by the young man himself.

'Where is she? Is she still here?'

'Yes. Come through.' Desmond led the way. 'She arrived about an hour ago, demanding her manuscript back.' This last was said in a whisper as he opened the door to the drawing room and motioned Robert inside.

Bella was curled up on the sofa covered with a blanket and was fast asleep. 'I had a devil of a job calming her down when I told her I didn't have the book. I gave her some brandy. She is obviously not used to it. Now what am I to do?'

Robert perched himself on the edge of the sofa and gently stroked Bella's tousled hair from her face. 'My poor, poor darling. It has all been too much for you, hasn't it?'

'It was a blessing there was no one on the street when she arrived,' Desmond said, still in a whisper. 'And a wonder she was not molested on the way.'

'Thank the good Lord for that. And my thanks to you, my friend. I am obliged.'

'Couldn't do anything else, could I? I had to get her off the street. And we still have to get her out without being seen. I might live it down, but I doubt she would.'

'She has worse things than that to contend with at the moment. We need a carriage.'

'You're welcome to my barouche. I'll go and harness it up myself while you wake her.'

As soon as he had gone, Robert turned back to Bella and

gently shook her shoulder. 'Bella, my love, wake up. Wake up.'

She stirred and her eyelids fluttered open and closed again. 'Leave me alone.' Her words were slightly slurred and he wondered if it was the effects of sleep or the brandy she had drunk.

'No, Bella, you cannot stay here. Come along.' He put his arm under her shoulder and forced her into a sitting position. 'Bella, we have to get you home.'

'Home?'

'To Holles Street. To Mama. She is distraught at your disappearance.'

She shook herself and pushed her hair back from her face. 'I am sorry for that, but I could not stay with all those horrible people…'

He pulled her towards him and cradled her head against his shoulder. 'No, I know. But it's of no consequence. We will defy them.'

'But, Robert, if it's true what they say…'

'It isn't.'

'You cannot be sure. I am not sure. I wrote that book…'

'I know. I have read it. Desmond gave it to me, asked me what he should do.'

'You have it?'

'Yes. It's safe from prying eyes. Now, come on, my sweet, on your feet.' He helped her to rise. She stood unsteadily, leaning against him. He chuckled suddenly. 'How much brandy did Desmond give you?'

'I don't know. A glass full. He made me drink it all. And then I think I helped myself to some more while he went to speak to his servant. I'm not sure. My head aches.'

'I'll wager it does. We'll walk up and down until Desmond brings the carriage to the door, then we must smuggle you out.'

He propelled her up and down the room several times

until she was able to walk unaided, though he kept his arm about her.

'Robert,' she said. 'What am I going to do?'

'First, I am going to take you home and Daisy will put you to bed, then I am going to Westmere to talk to the Earl. Then we will decide how to put a stop to all the tattle-mongering.'

Desmond reappeared before she could answer. 'I've got the carriage as near the door as I could. Miss Huntley, you would be wise to pull the hood of your cloak over your head.'

So they were ashamed of being seen with her, she decided as she obeyed. Robert was simply being his usual kind self. Was that why he had kissed her and all but proposed, because he was a kind man and no one else would? She could never accept him under those terms.

Desmond went out and looked up and down the street. There was a milkmaid driving a cow at the bottom end of the street, but it was otherwise deserted. 'Now,' he said, as the girl disappeared down the steps of one of the houses.

Robert scooped Bella up in his arms and in a couple of long strides was at the coach and setting her gently on the seat.

'You get in with her. I'll drive you,' Desmond said.

'Thanks, my friend.'

'I want to go back to Westmere,' Bella said as they rode. 'I feel safe there.'

'Safe? You are in no danger, Bella. Malicious tongues cut, but they do not kill. They will soon have something else to talk about.'

'Tarred with the same brush,' she murmured, thinking of Louis's words.

'What do you mean?'

'You. You will be tarred with the same brush if you continue to champion me. If I had known about…you know…I would never have asked you to bring me to London. And your poor mama—people will talk about her, say she must have known all about it.'

'Fustian! You are distraught. You will feel better tomorrow.'

'How can you possibly know how I feel? How can you say it will be better tomorrow? You know how they love to gossip.'

He fell silent. He could have sworn that when they had danced together and he had kissed her, there had been an answering flicker, a meeting of souls, an affinity which went beyond mere dalliance. That kiss had been as real and meaningful to her as it had been to him. So why run from him? Did she think he cared tuppence who her father was?

A few minutes later they stopped outside the house in Holles Street. The door was flung open and Henrietta ran down the steps. 'You have her?' Then, seeing Bella, she said, 'Oh, my dear, how glad I am to see you safe. Come along in.'

Robert helped Bella to alight and then Henrietta took over, putting her arm round the girl and talking soothingly to her as she led her into the house and up the stairs to her room. 'Oh, what a fright you gave us. I was terrified. Robert searched everywhere for you.'

'Did he?' Bella asked vaguely.

'Of course he did, after he had got away from the Regent. Colette was determined on presenting him. And me, too. I never did think much of the Regent but tonight he tried my patience sorely. All those people mincing and primping, bowing and scraping, while you were heaven knows where…'

'I hid in the summer-house. It seemed like a very long time. No one came. Then I went to get my manuscript back from Mr Norton.'

They had reached Bella's room where Daisy was waiting.

Between them they helped Bella off with her bedraggled ball gown and stripped off her underwear. 'Now, you must have a sleep,' Henrietta said, putting her nightgown over her head. 'We'll talk when you wake…' She pulled the covers over Bella's trembling body and stooped to kiss her cheek, then, bidding Daisy watch over her, left the room.

She found Robert downstairs, pacing the drawing-room floor. He whirled round when he heard her light step. 'How is she?'

'Exhausted, but is it any wonder? Now I will order breakfast and you will sit down and tell me everything. Right from the beginning.'

Bella was woken by a thunderous knocking at the front door. It was a moment or two before she remembered where she was and what had happened. Robert had been so kind to her. He had not exactly said he loved her, which, she decided, was just as well, because there was no question of them marrying, not now, not after all the gossip. It would ruin him. She must go back to Westmere and remain single. The stigma must not be passed on.

She found herself suddenly thinking of the old crone in Westmere wood. She had said she would find happiness, which just proved what a poor fortune-teller she was. She seemed to know a great deal about the Earl, too. Had she known about her? Then there was Ellen. She would know the truth. The sooner she went back to Cambridgeshire the better.

She was in the process of climbing out of bed when Daisy flew into the room, bearing a jug of hot water. 'Miss Bella, the Earl's had a seizure. Spooner's been sent to fetch you.'

Bella sank back onto the bed as if she had been struck. 'He's not…not…'

'No, miss, he ain't dead, but he's asking for you. Mrs Huntley said I was to wake you and pack. She says she and the Captain will take us home.' She threw herself about the room, tumbling clothes from the closet and piling them into Bella's trunk, which was far too small to take them all because she had bought so many new garments.

Bella sat and watched her, unable to move, unable to take in this new horror. Henrietta came in and sat beside her, taking her hand. 'I'm so sorry you should have another burden to bear, my dear, but we shall perhaps find, when we arrive, it is not so bad, after all.'

'Yes.'

'Now, let Daisy help you dress.' To the maid, she said, 'You do not need to pack all that. It can follow later or remain here until Miss Huntley returns. Just essentials.'

'Yes, Mrs Huntley.'

'I do not want Robert to come,' Bella said dully. 'Make him stay here.'

'I need him, child, and, besides, his lordship asked for him, too. And Edward and Louis.' She paused to search Bella's face. 'I'm sure it is all a hum, you know.'

'What is?'

'That dreadful rumour. Don't give it another thought.'

The clouds dispersed as the coach, with Robert riding alongside, leading Misty, travelled north, and by the time it arrived in Westmere the following afternoon, the sun was shining and it was a glorious day. 'Why, it's May already,' Bella said in wonderment, noticing the hawthorn blossom in the hedges and the growing crops in the fields.

'Of course it is. Sunday, the nineteenth—had you forgot?'

'Yes. Life is so different in town; it is not governed by the seasons in the same way as it is in the country. And so much has happened, I was hardly aware of time passing.'

'You will doubtless be glad to be home.'

'Yes. But that sounds ungrateful and I do not mean to be.

You have been so very, very kind and I have not deserved it.'

Henrietta laughed and patted her hand. 'Robert told me all about it.'

'He did? Oh, can you ever forgive me?'

'I already have. It is done and forgotten. Now we must concentrate on what we find at the Hall.'

'Yes.' Now they were close, concern for the man she had always considered her grandfather put all other considerations to the back of her head. They were not banished, simply left to lie dormant. Father or grandfather, he had brought her up with kindness and love and she could not dismiss that, neither could she forget her love for him, whatever he had done.

On the surface, nothing at Westmere seemed to have changed. The hall, the servants, the furniture, ornaments and pictures were exactly the same as when she had left. The part of the house which was occupied was polished and welcoming. Ellen was waiting to embrace Bella and it was to Ellen they turned for news of his lordship, almost as soon as they had divested themselves of their outdoor clothes and were sitting in the small parlour and tea and cakes had been brought.

'The Earl had a seizure two days ago,' she told them. 'We thought at first it was fatal, but he seems to have made a slight recovery which has left him paralysed down his left side. He could not speak at first, but today we have been able to understand a word or two and Doctor Graham thinks the signs are hopeful. We have been warned not to do or say anything to upset him.'

'But I can see him?' Bella queried.

'Of course. You are the first person he asked for.'

Bella rose to go to him and Robert stood, too. 'I'll go alone,' she said to him. 'If he asks for you, I will send someone to fetch you.'

'Very well.'

She left the room. It was so very difficult to keep Robert at arm's length, when all she wanted was to be held close to him, to feel the security of his arms about her, to be loved by him. But it was not to be and she must remain cool and detached until she could decide what she was going to do. And that largely depended on the Earl.

She crept into the darkened bedroom and towards the bed. He lay propped on pillows, one side of his mouth pulled down and his eyes closed. His arms lay on top of the covers, the skin wrinkled and mottled. He looked pale and shrivelled, much smaller than the big man he had been only a few weeks before. She went and sat on a chair by the bedside, reaching out to take his right hand.

He murmured something unintelligible, his head thrashing from side to side as if in the grip of a dream. Then one eye opened; the other fluttered and closed again. 'Fanny?' he queried, grasping her hand. 'Fanny, is that you?' His grip on her hand tightened and there was more muttering. The only distinct words she heard were 'sorry', 'wrong' and 'all wrong', interspersed with grunts and groans. And finally she caught the word 'forgive'.

'Grandpapa,' she said, raising her voice a little to make sure he heard her. 'It's Bella. Don't you know me?'

'Fanny?'

'No, Bella.'

He turned his head and looked at her as if seeing her clearly for the first time. 'Isabella. Good…girl.'

'Is there anything I can do for you?'

'R-read to…me…' Every word was an effort. 'There.' He waved his right hand in the direction of a table where lay a book. 'C-can't…abide…ol' B-Batters…'

'She does her best, Grandpapa,' Bella said, moving across the room to pick up the book and returning with it to her seat.

'Young…Robert with…you…'

'Yes, and Cousin Henrietta.'

'B-best of the bunch…'

'Who? Robert?'

'Yes. M-made…that an-anoun…' The word escaped him and he stopped speaking.

'Not yet,' she said. She was on the point of telling him she did not think she would marry at all, but remembered Ellen's stricture that he was not to be upset. 'When you are better.'

She did not want to talk about Robert for fear of blurting out everything that had happened in London, all her apprehensions and doubts, all the questions which dominated her brain, even in the midst of her concern for the old man. 'I'll read to you, shall I?' It was a small volume of Shakespeare's sonnets, which surprised her. She had never known her grandfather liked poetry. Perhaps it had been Ellen's choice. She let the small volume fall open at the bookmark and began reading.

'When to the sessions of sweet silent thought
I summon up remembrance of things past
I sigh the lack of many a thing I sought,
And with old woes new wail my dear time's waste.
Then can I drown an eye unused to flow
For precious friends hid in death's dateless night,
And weep afresh love's long-since-cancelled woe,
And moan th'expense of many a vanished sight.'

She looked up, her eyes filled with tears, and realised he had fallen asleep. Replacing the bookmark, she shut the book and put it back on the table, before creeping from the room.

The rest of the family had arrived while she had been upstairs and were gathered in the drawing room. Edward was there with Charlotte, Louis, as much the tulip as ever, with his mother, and James, who was complaining that he need not have been sent for.

'No expectations,' he said, looking pointedly at Bella. 'And it ain't the best time to be leaving the farm. The labourers are making threats and if they know I'm away, there's no telling what they'll do. All week there have been outbreaks of rioting in Norfolk and they're coming closer. Last week it was Norwich and they had to call in the cavalry to clear the streets, yesterday there was trouble at Feltwell where they destroyed the land drains and at Southery they attacked Robert Martin's farm, and that's not above a dozen miles from Eastmere. It's far worse than it was in the early part of the year. If the old man's making a recover, then I'll be off back.' No one tried to dissuade him and he left, taking the smell of the farmyard with him.

'Thank goodness for that,' Louis said, fluttering his perfumed handkerchief after his cousin. 'And I do not know why you two are here,' he added, addressing Edward and Robert.

'Sent for, same as you,' Edward said.

'Well, I hope the old fellow is not going to go on about marrying the chit for the legacy again, for if he does I shall tell him straight I know his little game and it won't serve. I will not have his by-blow foisted off on me.'

'You need not worry about that, Comte,' Bella said, maintaining her dignity. It was all she had left with which to fight. 'I have no intention of marrying any of you. You will have to scrap over the legacy among yourselves.'

'Bella!' Robert exclaimed. 'I thought—'

'I mean it. Not even you, Robert. Now, if you will excuse me, I have things to do.' And with that she turned her back on them and went in search of Ellen. If it were not so tragic it would be laughable, and if she were writing it as a work of fiction she would certainly have played on the humour of the situation. It would be funny and serve them right if there was no legacy, except a house needing thousands spent on it and land that was prey to constant flooding. Only it was not at all amusing when you were in the middle of it and your heart was breaking.

Ellen was in the dairy, helping one of the daily women churn butter. She stopped when she saw Bella and took off her apron, leading the way into her own small sitting room which was at the back of the house and looked out over the garden, just beginning to show the colour of summer flowers. 'How is he?' she asked as they sat on opposite sides of the hearth. The fire was unlit and had an arrangement of blooms in front of a screen to hide the empty grate.

'I can't believe how small and helpless he looks. In a matter of weeks he has gone from being the grandfather I knew, strong and dependable, someone I could lean on, who would keep me safe from harm, to a wizened little man.'

'He is very old, my dear. You cannot expect him to last for ever.'

Bella smiled wanly. 'Do you know, I thought he might? That's why I did not take too much notice of him when he said I must marry one of his great-nephews. It did not seem to me to be something I need rush to do.'

'But you chose the Captain.'

'Yes, so that I could have a Season with Cousin Henrietta, nothing more. Was that very selfish of me?'

'No, of course not.'

'It was and I have been punished for it.'

'His lordship would have been taken ill whether you were here or no. You must not blame yourself.'

'It isn't that, it's something far worse. There was a scandal…'

'Scandal? Good heavens, child, what have you done?'

'Not me. Grandfather.' She paused to catch her breath, before continuing. 'Years ago.'

'Oh, that has resurfaced, has it?'

'So it is true. I am not the Earl's granddaughter.'

'Of course you are. Who did you think you were?' She stopped speaking to peer into Bella's face. 'Bella, what is it? You look as though you had seen a ghost.'

'Tell me the truth, Ellen. You must know it. They are saying...' She gulped and rushed on. 'They are saying I am his lordship's...' She did not want to say the word 'bastard'. Instead she said 'natural child'.

'What?' Ellen was visibly shocked. 'Who is saying it?'

'Everyone. Louis. Edward. Even Robert believes it, though he is doing his best to avoid the subject.'

'Oh, my poor, poor darling,' Ellen got up and went to sit beside Bella, taking her into her arms and rocking her back and forth, just as she had when she had been a baby and needing comfort. 'It is a lie.'

Bella looked up into her face. 'Are you sure?'

'I am absolutely positive. I was there when you were born and all through your mother's pregnancy.'

'Then why is everyone saying such terrible things about me?'

'It is the way half-truths become twisted with repetition,' Ellen murmured.

'Half-truths? Then there is something...'

'You are not the Earl's love child.' Ellen paused and then, as if making up her mind, went on more firmly, 'Your father was, so rumour had it at the time, which was hardly surprising considering how alike he and Henry were, though only the Earl knows the full story.'

'Papa! Tell me what you know. Everything.'

'The Earl left the house in a hurry one day and was gone nearly a week. I am talking about nearly fifty years ago, you understand. When he came back he had a little boy with him, two years old he was. He said the child was the off-spring of a distant cousin who had died and left him in his care. He insisted the boy should be brought up as his son, though the Countess never really took to him and I was employed to bring him up. Like my own, he was. I loved him dearly though he was a difficult child, always aggressive and apt to fly into the boughs for no reason. And when Henry was killed… I told you about that, didn't I?'

'Yes.'

'As soon as he was old enough he married the daughter of a physician, simply to get away from home. It was a disaster. The poor girl loved him to distraction, but he did not know how to cope with that; he had always held himself aloof from any close contact. He was cruel and violent. I lost count of the number of miscarriages she had but they killed her in the end.'

'Papa married again.'

'Yes, and this time he was the one to love. It is strange how in so many marriages one loves more than the other— one gives and the other takes. Marguerite d'Orsen, your mama, was French, as you know. She was very beautiful and dressed superbly well. Your papa begrudged her nothing. Whatever she wanted, she was given. Then you were born. Oh, I loved you from the first, and was overjoyed when I was told I could be your nurse.

'Your mama loved you, too, but your papa was insanely jealous of anyone who came between him and his darling, even his own daughter, and to please him she kept you at a distance. I thought she should have been stronger and stood up to him, but I never said so. They would have sent me away if I had and I couldn't have borne that. When she died, giving birth to a stillborn son, he went mad with grief.'

'Oh, that explains so much,' Bella said. 'I wish I had known.'

'You were only a little girl. When he followed her to the grave two years later, your grandfather brought you up. He always adored you. That was why he wanted to be sure you would not want for anything after he had gone. Your father could never have inherited and neither could you. I suppose he saw it as the solution for you to marry one of your second cousins.'

'But it has caused so much trouble and brought out the worst in them. Only James has had the sense to back out of it and I admire him for it.'

'And Robert?'

'I don't want to talk about him.'

'Why not? He is the one, isn't he? He is your true love?'

'All the more reason to send him away. There is still a stigma attached to me.'

'Don't be foolish, child. It was not your fault.'

'That is not what society thinks and what society thinks is important. I can never marry.'

'Of course you can.'

'No.' Bella stood up. 'I will go up and sit with Grandpapa again.'

'Very well. But I must caution you against saying anything to him of what I have told you. It could be fatal.'

'I won't. Now I know the truth.'

She slipped from the room and along the corridor into the great hall, intending to speak to Henrietta, but there was no one in the drawing room, except Elizabeth who was almost the last person she wanted to talk to. She withdrew and made for the staircase. On the way she passed the library whose door was open. Charlotte was sitting at her grandfather's desk. She had one of the drawers open and was riffling through its contents. She looked up suddenly and spotted Bella standing in the doorway.

'What are you doing?' Bella demanded. 'You've no business in here.'

'Oh, yes, I have.' Charlotte's tone was belligerent. 'It's the only way. If the old man did break the entail, then there must be some documentary evidence to prove it. And he must keep his will somewhere.'

'I imagine his lawyer has both in safe keeping,' Bella said coldly. 'And he is not dead yet. Or even dying. He is making a recovery, so you may return to London and leave us in peace.'

She surprised herself with her calmness. It was as if, knowing the story of her father, knowing she had no legal right to anything, it had washed away all her doubts and brought about a clearer understanding of why people behaved in the way they did. Knowledge of the past brought a greater grasp of the present.

She watched as Charlotte got up and marched past her back to the drawing room, no doubt to share grievances with Elizabeth. Then, fetching the key to the west wing, Bella wandered slowly up the stairs to the old schoolroom to stand for several minutes in front of the portraits of the two boys, one the true heir, the other an impostor, but so alike that no one could deny they were related. Her father. He had been the love child but who was his mother? Fanny? Fanny who? Her grandfather had called her Fanny. Asked for forgiveness.

'Bella.'

She swung round to face Robert. 'What are you doing here?'

'Looking for you. I seem to have done a great deal of that lately. Are you avoiding me?'

She turned back to the pictures so that she did not have to look at him. Seeing his beloved face weakened her resolve, turned her legs to jelly, made her want to cry. And she must not cry. She must not. 'I am trying to avoid everyone. Then I can give no offence.'

'You do not offend me.' He gave a short prickly laugh. 'Except by tarring me with the same brush as the others. I

thought I was different. It was me you turned to when you
needed help, remember?'

'That was a mistake.'

'A mistake?'

'Yes. I should have stayed here with Grandpapa. And by
the way, the gabble-grinders are wrong—he really is my
grandfather.'

'I never doubted it. Not that I care one way or another.'
He wanted to reach out and take her in his arms, but she
was standing so rigidly stiff he knew it would be a mistake
to touch her. With an effort, he managed to keep his hands
glued to his sides and talk to the back of her head. 'Bella,
please, listen—'

'No. I do not want to hear. Don't you see? Nothing has
changed.' She swung round to face him, her eyes twin orbs
of misery in a face so pale it was almost transparent. 'Leave
me alone, Robert. Go back to London. I do not want you
here.'

So vehement were her words he took a half-step back-
wards as if he had been struck. Then he pulled himself together. 'When I kissed you, you did not try and stop me.
You said you loved me…'

'I…' She faltered. 'I was confused and didn't know what
I was saying.'

'You do not mean that.'

'I do mean it, I promise you. I am tired of all this argument and bickering. It was why I asked you to take me to
London. I did not realise it would continue there, only
worse. I meant it when I said it was a mistake. I should
never have gone against Grandfather's wishes…'

'You mean you would take Edward.' What would she say
if she knew what Edward had said after he had read that
manuscript? But he could not tell her, it would hurt her too
much.

'No, of course not. I told you, I will not marry any of

you. And as soon as Grandfather is well enough, I shall tell him so.'

'Then when I kissed you…'

'It meant nothing, either to me or you. Forget it.'

He reached out to take her shoulders in his hands and was astonished when she slipped through them, ducked under his arm and made for the door.

'Bella!' he called after her, but she had gone, racing down the stairs and along corridors only she knew. He tried to follow but took a wrong turning and wasted several minutes going up and down the vast house before he found more stairs and the way down to the ground floor. He had played all over that house as a child and could not understand how he had forgotten the intricacies of its strange architecture. But she was nowhere to be seen in the habitable part of the house and none of the others admitted to seeing her.

'I expect she is with her grandfather,' his mother said. 'Let her be, Robert. She has had enough for one day. You will see her tomorrow.'

Bella did not put in an appearance at supper and he could barely swallow for the tumult in his breast, and the conversation of the others was all on the legacy and their individual prospects until in the end he pushed back his chair and stood up. 'Damn the inheritance!' he shouted. 'Damn your greedy eyes, all of you. Begging your pardon, Mama, I did not mean you. I'm going out to find more congenial company.' And with that he stormed from the room and went out to the stables, where he had Nelson saddled and five minutes later was riding out along the drive towards the road.

From her window, Bella watched him ride away, and with him went her hopes, her love, her happiness. She stood, framed by the window, a pale, mournful figure in a white cambric nightgown, her dark hair flowing over her shoulders, but he did not look back.

Chapter Ten

Robert spent the evening drinking at The Crown in Downham Market and half listening to the locals airing their grievances, mainly over the perfidy of the gentry in hiring a Bow Street runner to infiltrate a gang of poachers in order to inform on them. He had apparently been very successful because the poachers were now in gaol. The other half of his brain was busy with the problem of Bella.

Why had she lumped him together with his cousins, as if his motives were as tainted as theirs? He didn't care for the legacy; he had more in common with those working men who shouted so loudly for bread or blood. He loved her— was that not enough?

By midnight he had been ready to curse all women and was also very drunk, so when the landlord asked him if he required a room, he thought, Why not? It would save rousing the household and disturbing his lordship. Was the old fellow about to hand in his accounts? Or was it all a hum? It was only Bella who was keeping him in Cambridgeshire, no one else. He should have stayed and told her what was in his heart before he left, but she had been so adamant that she would not marry any of them, he had been too hurt and angry to behave rationally.

The landlord was busy when he went down to breakfast the following morning and he was given no time to enjoy his meal. 'We're expecting the magistrates and the overseers here for a meeting, sir,' he told Robert. 'They come every Monday morning.'

The magistrates began to arrive while he was paying his account. 'The men are on the march from Southery,' he heard one of them say. 'They're in an ugly mood.'

Robert did not want to be caught up in a riot. He had to return to Westmere and make Bella listen to him. He had to convince her that the manner of her birth was of no importance to him. He loved the person she was. As he left, he heard the magistrate ordering someone to ride to Upwell to ask Captain Lee to mobilise the yeomanry as men were on the march from Southery and other villages in the area. He could see the riots escalating until the whole countryside was in flames, including Westmere. The Earl, the largest landowner in the area, would not be immune from the rioters' anger and Bella and his mother were there, possibly in danger. He sprang into the saddle and rode hard for Westmere.

Bella rose with a leaden heart and no appetite for breakfast or company. Her grandfather, she was told by the nurse who had been employed to watch over him, had passed a peaceful night and was still sleeping. Robert had not been back all night, Bella learned from Sylvester, who had been assigned to look after him in the absence of Adam Gotobed who had been left behind in London. The others, more used to Town hours, were not yet astir and she was glad of that— she had no wish to hear any more of their bickering.

She smiled ruefully. She was home again, she could do all the things she liked doing without the stifling restrictions imposed by London Society. She could ride out alone and go for walks and no one would raise an eyebrow to stop

her. Putting on a cloak over her plain jaconet round gown
and a sturdy pair of half-boots, she set off across the park.

Why had Robert stayed out all night? Had he gone listening to political meetings again? If James was right, he
did not need to go far to hear those. The agitation was on
their doorstep. Perhaps he had ridden back to London after
all, but she told herself he would hardly do that without
telling his mother.

Without quite knowing how she arrived there, she found
herself walking along the edge of the wood, which set her
wondering about the old lady who lived there. She turned
and struck off along the path and there it was, the tiny cottage and a wisp of smoke coming from the chimney. The
door was opened as she approached.

'You're back, then,' the woman said. She seemed even
more bent and worn than before and the sacking apron she
wore was stained with some kind of juice.

'Yes.'

'You made your choice?'

'No.'

'That's a whisker.'

She should have realised it was useless to lie. The old
woman knew what had been going on, though Bella had no
idea how she did it. 'It is not. I am not accepting any of
them. Grandfather may do as he likes.'

'He'll do that whatever you say. William Huntley always
did like to have his own way.'

'How do you know so much about him?'

'Oh, I know.' The old woman tapped the side of her nose
with a long bony finger. 'There isn't much I couldn't tell
you about him.'

'Then tell me.'

'No, it is for him to speak of it.'

'He can't, he's had a seizure. He is hardly coherent, but
he keeps talking about someone called Fanny.'

'Fanny.' The woman repeated the name in a whisper.

'Yes, and asking forgiveness. If I could find her, perhaps—'

'No, no, my dear,' she put in before Bella could finish. 'Let it lie. The past is past. Best forgotten.'

'But you do you know who she is?'

'Was,' she said flatly.

'Oh.'

'Tell me about the young man.' The woman briskly changed the subject. 'The one you are trying to convince me you have not chosen.'

'I love him.'

'And…'

'I cannot marry him.'

'Why not?'

Bella paused. How could she tell this stranger that her blood was tainted, that whoever married her would always be surrounded by gossip, especially if her grandfather kept his word and made him his heir? She could just imagine the whispers… 'I have my reasons.'

'Fustian!' The woman sounded angry. 'Does he love you?'

'I do not know. Perhaps he does, a little, but—'

'Then what has reason to do with it? Happiness is elusive, child. Like a butterfly, you have to catch it when it settles or it will be off again, out of your grasp. Tell him how you feel, explain, let him make up his own mind. If he finds your reasons so compelling he is not worthy of you.'

'But he has gone. He went out last night and did not come back. I don't know where he is.'

'He will return.'

'Are you sure?'

'Naturally I am. Did I not tell you I had the second sight?' The woman smiled; it made her look years younger. 'Go on, my dear, don't waste time talking to an old crone like me. Tell him what is in your heart. He will never know if you don't, will he?'

Impulsively Bella leaned forward and kissed the old lady's cheek, before turning to go back home.

'Come back and tell me the outcome,' the old woman called after her, though the voice had a catch in it, and if Bella had looked back she would have seen her rubbing her face where the kiss had landed.

All her cousins except James and Robert, who had still not returned, were gathered round the table in the breakfast parlour, all talking at once, arguing about the inheritance. They were like vultures, waiting for the old man to die, and Bella could not bear to stay in the room with them. Making her excuses, she went out into the garden.

It was a fine, warm afternoon and the gnats were flying. She sat on a bench and watched the swallows swooping to catch them, almost at peace with herself. When Robert returned she would tell him what was in her heart, and if he rejected her, then so be it. She would have made her attempt to catch the butterfly but if it slipped through her fingers, it would not be for want of trying. And at least she would know.

Hearing the sound of a horse approaching, she sprang to her feet and ran up the path and round the side of the house to the front with his name on her lips. But it was not Robert arriving, but James. He was driving his dilapidated gig in which sat Mrs Clarke with her arms round both girls.

'Where's Robert?' he demanded, almost before he had come to a stop.

'I don't know.'

'Damnation! Beg pardon, Bella, but I had counted on finding him here.' He held out his hand to help Mrs Clarke to alight, then lifted the girls down. 'It's mayhem in Down-ham Market—has been since early morning. There's hundreds of men and women on the rampage, looting and threatening the inhabitants with guns and pitchforks. If it spreads, Eastmere could be next. I'm fearful for the children. If you could keep them until the danger's past, I'd be obliged.'

'Of course. What started the riots off again? I thought the magistrates had promised a rise in the poor allowance last March.'

'They didn't keep their word. I said they wouldn't, didn't I? And it's the farmers who suffer, not the magistrates.'

'What will you do?'

'What can I do but try and reason with them, and if that doesn't work, I'll have to give them money.' He laughed harshly. 'I wouldn't mind but they only spend it on drink.' He turned to the little girls and kissed each one on the top of her head. 'Be good, now.' To Bella, he said, 'When Robert comes back, send him to me, will you?' Then he clambered back into the gig and was gone.

'I should have gone back with him,' Mrs Clarke said, watching him go. 'I could have helped, but he would not have it.'

'He was, no doubt, thinking of your safety.'

'They think that just because he's kin to the Earl he's wealthy, but you know that isn't so.'

Bella sent the children to the kitchen. 'Cook will find you a drink of cordial and some cake,' she said. 'And ask her to send refreshments to the little parlour, too.' She turned to Mrs Clarke. 'I have not seen you to offer my felicitations on your engagement, ma'am. I wish you happiness.'

'Thank you,' the woman said, brightening a little.

'What started the riots off again?' Bella asked, leading the way to the parlour.

'The price of flour and bread and low wages. It isn't James's fault, Miss Huntley, he can't afford to put up the wages. If they ruin the farm, they'll never be paid, but they simply won't listen. I am afeared for James…'

'Oh, surely they would not harm him,' Bella said, as a maid arrived with a teatray and set it down on the table.

'If only the Captain had been here. Could he not be sent for? He's a military man, they might listen to him.'

'They might,' Bella said doubtfully, as she handed her guest a cup of tea. 'But I have no idea where Robert is.'

She had hardly uttered the words when they heard sound of a cantering horse. Bella ran to the window. 'It's Robert,' she said, watching him dismount and fling the reins at a stable boy who had run out to meet him.

'Thank the good Lord,' Mrs Clarke said and, picking up her skirts, ran out to the hall just as Robert entered by the front door.

He had intended to prise Bella away from his relatives and speak to her alone, and was disconcerted to see Mrs Clarke. He stopped and bowed to her. 'Your obedient, ma'am.'

'Robert, there has been trouble at Downham,' Bella said, following Mrs Clarke. 'James is afraid it will spread to Eastmere. He brought Mrs Clarke and the girls here for safety.'

'James needs help, Captain,' Mrs Clarke said. 'He cannot hold them off alone.'

He sighed heavily. Was he to be frustrated at every turn? 'Then, of course, I will go to him.'

'Oh, thank you, sir,' Mrs Clarke said. 'I am sure the men will attend to you.' And then she began quietly weeping. Bella put her arm about her to comfort her.

Robert turned to Bella, searching her face, trying to read her expression, but her wide hazel eyes were telling him nothing except her concern for Mrs Clarke. Now was not the time to speak of what was in his heart. Instead, he said, 'Has there been any trouble here?'

'No, Robert, nor likely to be.'

'All the same, it would be as well to be prepared. Put up some barricades on the approaches and put a lookout somewhere to warn you, so you can bring all the servants inside. Ask Edward to organise it. I'll be back as soon as I can.'

Bella followed him to the door. Catching elusive butterflies was the last thing on her mind, but she was reminded of it when he smiled ruefully at her. 'We'll talk when I come back. Don't do anything foolish. Stay here.'

She laughed shakily. 'Where would I go?'

'I mean it.'

She stood and watched him canter off down the drive, then turned back into the house. She must have patience.

Robert's route to Eastmere took him back through Downham Market, and by that time the marching rioters had arrived and been joined by the locals. The place was a seething mass of angry humanity, men and women brandishing guns, waving clubs and pitchforks and shouting that they would have justice or die. Again and again he heard the cry, 'Bread or blood!' Besides bludgeons, many of them were carrying sacks of flour, cloth-wrapped cheeses and sides of pork they had obviously looted. One had a huge barrel of beer, from which he was refilling the mugs of those who came to him. Many were already very drunk.

He was inclined to ride straight through them but his way was blocked, and unless he rode miles out of his way there was nothing he could do but sit impatiently while an overseer addressed the crowd and tried to persuade them to disperse. 'We mean to see the magistrates,' one of their leaders told him, 'so just you stand out of our way.'

'You can't all get in to see them.'

This was patently obvious. There were, according to Robert's swift calculation, upwards of fifteen hundred men and women crammed into the market-place and the roads around it.

'No. A deputation.' A group of men stepped forward. 'These men to speak on our behalf.'

'Very well.' The overseer led eight men back to The Crown where they disappeared inside. A few minutes later they came out, punching their fists in the air in jubilation. Once back in the market square they clambered onto boxes and their leader addressed the crowd. 'Two shillin' a day and flour at two shillin' and sixpence a stone for those with large families.'

It was something, but less than they had hoped for. There was a low murmuring and then someone shouted, 'What about our men in chokey?'

They had no answer to this, but the magistrates, who had been unwise enough to leave the safety of the inn and follow the delegation back to the market-place, were spotted and the crowd turned on them, demanding the release of the poachers. Robert watched in surprise as the justices fled back into the building, but the rioters did not stop there. They followed them inside, chasing them out again. Then they began systematically breaking up the public house, taking everything that was eatable and making the publican give them several gallons of beer.

Robert was appalled and helpless. They wouldn't listen to him, he had yet to prove himself their champion, but he remembered that Joseph Mostyn was due to speak at a meeting in Peterborough that evening; he had, in fact, half promised to attend. The rioters might listen to him. There was, of course, the possibility that Mostyn might incite them to further violence, but he did not think so. He turned his horse away from the Eastmere road towards Peterborough.

The day stretched endlessly for Bella. Her cousins had hardly welcomed Mrs Clarke and were not inclined to make conversation with her. Indeed, Louis hardly disguised his contempt and Elizabeth sat fanning herself as if she were hot. Edward continued reading his newspaper and Charlotte had picked up a book of verse and was flicking its pages without interest. Bella could hardly blame the poor lady when she said she would go to the kitchen and see how the children were faring, and stayed to help Martha.

Bella's escape was to sit with her grandfather, who was sometimes lucid and recognised her and sometimes took her for the mysterious Fanny. He seemed to be reliving an episode in his youth. Even his voice sounded younger at these times, though taut with misery. At other times he returned to mumbling and thrashing about, his right hand describing circles in the air, his left useless on the cover.

The Earl's dinner was brought at three o'clock and she watched for a while as the nurse spoon-fed him, but realising it was demeaning for him to have her see him like that, she left and went downstairs. Robert had not returned and there was no news from Eastmere, but a man passing by had stopped and spoken to one of the estate workers and told him that Downham Market was in ferment. He related the events of the morning, but it seemed that, far from quieting the mob, the concessions had incited them to further outrageous acts of plunder. They had attacked the flour mill, stolen flour, bread, cheese and meat from shops and some had stormed the gaol in an unsuccessful effort to set the poachers free.

'The militia be there now,' the man went on, 'laying about them with the flat of their swords. The market is a battlefield. I never saw so many broken heads.'

All this was faithfully repeated to Spooner, busy in the stables, and he repeated it to Bella, who had gone there to ask for Misty to be saddled so that she could go riding. 'You mustn't go out, miss, there's no telling where they'll strike next.'

She conceded he might be right. 'The man didn't say anything about Eastmere, did he?'

'No, miss. Only Downham.'

'He didn't say anything about Mr Huntley or the Captain, did he?'

'No, miss. Ain't they come back?'

'No.'

'There's no cause for worry, Miss Bella. The Captain can handle himself, being a military man.'

She gave up the idea of going riding and returned to the house to find Edward and Louis arguing as usual, this time not about the legacy but whether or not they should take the threat of violence seriously. Louis, encouraged by Elizabeth who was terrified that it was the beginning of a revolution like the one they had had in France, was advocating returning to London. 'It's the seat of government,' he said. 'And a big city. The rioters will never take it.'

'No, but I think we should do as Robert suggested and prepare to defend the house,' Edward said.

'What good will that do against thousands intent on our blood?' Elizabeth demanded. 'Louis, I insist you take me home. I do not want to die in this dismal place. The house is not worth it.' She shuddered. 'I never did like it, so cold and inconvenient, not to mention miles from civilisation.'

'Now I have seen it I have taken an aversion to it,' Charlotte said. 'It is tumbling down. Let the mob have it. I do not care. Let us go to Palgrave Manor, it is a far more amenable place. And if the troubles spread, you should be taking steps to prevent the mob doing damage there. It should be your first consideration.'

Bella looked from one to another, and could not refrain from smiling. Cowards all. They would make a colourful set of characters for her next novel, a humorous one, poking fun at greed and ostentation and overweening pride.

'Mama?' Edward queried.

'I think perhaps Charlotte is right,' Henrietta said. 'But we cannot leave Bella here alone. She must come with us.'

'Oh, no, I could not leave Grandfather and Ellen and Mrs

Clarke, besides all the servants. And Robert will be back directly.'

'Robert!' Charlotte said, giving Bella a look of sheer venom. 'It would not surprise me if he were on the side of the rioters. In any case, if he is so keen to inherit Westmere, let him look to its defence.'

'Bella, please, come with us,' Henrietta said. 'It could be dangerous for you.'

'It is too late to go tonight in any case,' Edward said. 'By the time we have finished supper, it will be growing dark. We'll go tomorrow morning. Perhaps Robert will be back by then. He might persuade Bella to leave.'

'He will not,' she said firmly. 'My place is here.'

Supper was eaten in a subdued atmosphere, and though an attempt was made to amuse themselves for the rest of the evening with cards and music it was not very successful and they all retired early.

Bella did not immediately get into bed, but stood at the window, gazing out across the flat fen countryside. The windmills on the distant drains were still turning; she could hear the hoot of a barn owl and a dog barking in the village. She found it hard to believe that out there the country people were in a rage of such proportions they were prepared to destroy property, loot and perhaps even kill. Was Robert among them? She doubted if they would listen to him if he tried to dissuade them from their violence.

He would not be wholehearted in his condemnation of them, she was sure. Charlotte could even be right and he was helping them. Was that why he had not come home? Was that his way of proving to his cousins that he had no interest in the Westmere legacy? And now it looked as though the others had decided they were not interested in the responsibilities that went with owning it either. They had been fighting over something not one of them truly wanted. She was the only one who loved the place, but it could never be hers. She was a nobody and perhaps she should be standing beside the rioters, demanding rights she could never have.

Sighing, she returned to her bed and fell asleep at last, dreaming of her mother, who had not been allowed to demonstrate her love for her.

As soon as breakfast was over the following morning, Louis went to the stables to order his carriage to be prepared. Elizabeth, Charlotte and Henrietta told their respective maids to pack, while Edward went round the house checking windows and doors and instructing Jolliffe and the footmen what to do. Then he sent Danny on the cob to find out what was happening in the countryside and if it would be safe to venture beyond the park gates.

Danny returned with the news that all was quiet, even in Downham Market, where the day before Mr Dering had recruited a band of special constables and, surrounded by mounted militia, read the Riot Act. 'The troops arrested some and the rest went back to their homes,' he said. 'Though they'll be lucky if the constables aren't knocking on their doors before today is out.'

'And Eastmere?' Bella asked, thinking of James and Robert. They were all gathered in the great hall, surrounded by trunks and bags, ready to leave.

'Quiet as the grave. Mr Trenchard said he'd be obliged if you'd keep the girls another day, just to be on the safe side.'

'Of course I will,' she said.

'Then let us be gone while we can,' Louis said.

'Are you sure you will not come with us?' Henrietta asked Bella. 'I hate to leave you. I think perhaps I shall stay.'

'If you do, then I shall have to stay, too,' Edward said.

'No, no, there is no need,' Bella said. 'Truly there is not. We are perfectly safe here and I must wait for Robert.'

'Robert is not at all dependable, you know,' Edward said. 'He might not come back here. He might go straight back to London.'

'He will come.' She spoke with more certainty than she felt. But he had to come back, he had to come because she had so much she wanted to say to him, so much to explain, so much to ask. And if there was any affinity at all between them, he must know that. He must.

She watched the two carriages leave, travelling together for safety's sake, though they would part when Edward turned off for Palgrave and Louis went on to London. Now she was alone with her grandfather again, just as she had been at the beginning of the year, and it was as if the last month or so had never happened. She knew she would not now be expected to marry any of her second cousins, which was ironic when she thought about it. Her first choice, made in desperation, would also be her last.

She went to tell the Earl they had gone, a piece of news he received with a grunt which might have been a chuckle. He reached out with his right hand and grabbed hers, pulling her towards him. 'You've more guts in your little finger than the whole lot of them put together.'

She was surprised he had managed a whole sentence which was intelligible to someone listening carefully and used to his manner of speech. 'Thank you, Grandpapa. But you do Robert an injustice.'

'Oh, he really was your choice, was he? I thought you were bamming me just to spend a few weeks in Town.'

'You knew?' she said in surprise.

'Of course. You were too anxious to keep it a secret.' He paused. 'But your chicks came home to roost, ain't that so?'

'Yes.'

'Where is he now? Gone back with the others, has he?'

'No. I don't know where he is.' Bella decided to say

nothing of the riots, which might upset him and set back his recovery, which today seemed to be remarkable.

'Gone to find consolation, no doubt.'

'Oh, Grandfather…'

'He cannot inherit Westmere, you know. I never broke the entail.'

'Oh.' She paused to let that sink in. 'Why did you say you had?'

'I did not. I left them guessing. Naturally, Edward will inherit the title and the estate, but without money he will be hard put to keep it going.'

'But Louis thinks he is the heir.'

He laughed. 'His mother has brought him up more French than English, and in France you can inherit through the distaff side which you cannot do in England. I believe that is how his father came into his lands. Louis will, in due course, discover his mistake.'

'What did you mean when you said "without the money"?'

The old man smiled. 'Have you ever wondered why there are so few great houses in the fens?'

'I suppose it is a little isolated.'

'True, but it is also because until the fens were drained there were not enough farms to support them and even now, with good agricultural land instead of bog and marsh, the rents are insufficient to maintain a large estate. And the present state of agriculture and the demands of the labourers are making things worse. The estate is in decline and I am glad I shall not be here to see its demise.' He smiled crookedly. 'Someone is going to have a rude awakening.'

'Oh, Grandpapa,' she said, full of pity.

'But it needn't worry you. The bulk of my fortune is not part of the estate, never has been. I inherited it from my maternal grandfather and I may do with that as I please. I have had to use some of it to maintain the house and land,

but the rest has been well invested. Put together, the inheritance of house, estate and investment would be sizeable.'
He paused to regain his breath and she helped him to drink
a little water from the glass on the bedside table. 'I thought
you would choose to marry Edward and then the whole lot
could be left to him and you would be taken care of.'

'But you said it would be my choice.'

'So I did. And I will not go back on my word. The title
and estate will go to Edward, I cannot change that, but the
rest will be left to the man you choose to marry.'

'Oh, Grandpapa…'

'It is Robert, is it not?'

'Yes,' she murmured.

'Where is he?'

'I am not sure. I think he is with James.'

'Then you are wasting time talking to me. Go and find
him.'

The old lady in the woods had said something very similar, she remembered. 'And then what?'

'Good God, girl, you don't need to me to tell you that,
do you?'

She smiled and bent forward to kiss his cheek. 'I love
you, Grandpapa.'

He still had hold of her hand. He lifted it to his lips. 'So
like her,' he murmured. 'So much like her…'

'Fanny?'

He looked startled. 'What do you know of her?'

'Nothing. You said her name several times when you
were ill.' She paused to look at him. 'She was my grandmother, wasn't she?'

He looked into her eyes and saw nothing there but loving
trust, and his anger turned to a smile. 'Yes.'

'What happened to her?'

'I don't know. We parted.' He released her hand. 'Now,

off you go before the same thing happens to you. Bring that young man back, I want to see him.'

Bella left him and went to change into her riding habit. Misty needed some exercise, and now that the riots seemed to have died down it would be quite safe to ride to Eastmere.

Riding along the towpath, she was reminded of the meeting she had come upon in Ely. Had that been the beginning of it all? She did not think so because there had been trouble in other places before that. Why had James been spared when there had been every indication that the rioters were on their way to his farm? Robert. Had Robert managed to turn them away from there? Why had he not come straight home?

It was midday and James was in the yard, feeding his pigs, when she arrived. He quickly stopped what he was doing to meet her at the gate. 'What's wrong? The girls? Rose?'

'All safe and well,' she assured him. 'I'm looking for Robert. Have you see him?'

'Are you mad, to ride out alone? Don't you know there's been a riot?'

'Yes, but I was told it was all over, and I must find Robert.'

'He was here, but he's gone now. Back to Westmere, I shouldn't wonder. I'm surprised you didn't meet him on the way.'

'I came round by the river. Did the rioters come here?'

'No, Rob persuaded them to leave me alone, though it was touch and go. He went out just after breakfast to find out the lie of the land and if it was safe to leave me. He came back to say there had been another march from Southery to Downham this morning to demand the release of the men who were arrested. This time they had guns, as well as pitchforks and staves, and there was a man among 'em who drilled them like soldiers and taught them how to meet a cavalry charge. They dispersed when the magistrates agreed to release all the men who had been arrested. Lily-livered lot...'

'Who, the rioters?'

'No, the magistrates. It'll set a very poor example, you know. The labourers will think they can do just as they like, and when the men are re-arrested, there'll be more trouble. Now, get you on home before it starts. I ought to stop and escort you, but—'

'Oh, no need, James, no need at all. I'll catch Robert up.' She wheeled her horse round and set off again, trotting her horse along the lanes, rehearsing in her mind what she would say to Robert when she found him. Riding round the countryside, taking on mobs single-handed—hadn't he any sense at all?

Bella entered Littleport with nothing on her mind except Robert and what she would say to him. But she wouldn't tell him what her grandfather had said—she wanted him to want her for herself, not that hated legacy. She imagined him kissing her again and this time there would be no interruptions and she would not slip from his grasp and run away. He would tell her again that he loved her and she would make it plain how she felt about him.

She savoured it for a moment, but then the reason for all that had happened forced itself into her consciousness. She would have to explain the truth about her grandfather and the mysterious Fanny. What would Robert say to that? He would understand, wouldn't he? What if he did not? What if he repudiated her, was repulsed by the truth? What had the old lady said? *'If he finds your reasons so compelling he is not worthy of you.'* She pushed her shoulders back and lifted her chin. If that was so, then he was not the man she had taken him for and she was better off without him.

She was forced to draw rein when she found herself surrounded by a gang of belligerent men, who grabbed Misty's bridle and came so close the poor mare was terrified and began sidestepping and prancing to avoid them. 'What do you want?' she demanded, trying to control the horse, but with little success. 'I have nothing to give you.'

'No?' sneered one. 'Lady like you, out on your own. I can think of something. Very tasty.'

Even from her seat above them, she could smell the drink on their breath. 'No. Leave me alone.' She lifted her crop, intending to make him let go of the reins, but he simply laughed and caught it. Misty, normally so placid, reared up on her hind legs, snorting with terror. The man who held her reins was forced to release them, but it was too late. The little mare was too terrified to answer Bella's tugs on her mouth and began prancing in a circle and throwing up her hind legs. Bella struggled valiantly to keep her seat, while the men looked on without lifting a finger to help.

Some called out in admiration of her skill and courage, others laughed in an embarrassed way and urged her to 'Go to it, wench.' But Misty won in the end by pitching Bella over her head onto the hard-packed road.

She came to her senses, lying on a bench, in what she took to be an inn. There was a woman bending over her, bathing her head with a wet cloth. Behind her, peering at Bella as if she were a prize exhibit in one of those fairground shows, were several men, those who had stopped her, she assumed. She struggled to sit up but was overcome by dizziness and sank back again. 'Where am I?'

'In The Globe, missy,' the woman answered. 'I'm Mrs Johnson. You've had a nasty fall.'

'Thanks to them,' Bella said, glaring at the men. 'They stopped my horse. Did they take me for one of the farmers?'

'No, a gentleman's daughter by the look of you.'

'So, if I am, is that any reason to panic my horse?'

'They are upset,' Mrs Johnson said. 'Hungry, not able to make a fair living, and the likes of you riding round the countryside dressed in your silks and feathers on an animal worth more than they can earn in a year…'

'That's no excuse.'

'Not an excuse,' one of them growled. 'A reason. What money have you got with you?'

'None. I did not think I would need any.'

'Then the horse it must be.'

'Then how am I to get home?' It was strange how unafraid she was. It was as if she were another person, not Miss Isabella Huntley but a disembodied being who was simply looking on from the fringe, completely disinterested. It must be the bang on her head, she decided.

'I doubt you can ride,' Mrs Johnson said. 'Rest awhile and we'll send for someone to fetch you.'

'She can't stay here,' one of the men said. 'We'll be starting our meeting soon.'

'Take her upstairs,' said another. 'Put her to bed.' And he gave a great guffaw of laughter.

'Tek no note on 'em,' the woman said, taking Bella by the arm. 'We'll go into the kitchen and leave them to it. You'd like a cup of tea, wouldn't you?'

Bella allowed herself to be led away, wondering how she could escape. Not through the front of the house, that was certain judging by the sound of men's voices as they gathered for their meeting. They were rowdy and all trying to talk at once. Once or twice Mrs Johnson and her husband went through with jugs of beer, and when the door swung open Bella could hear them arguing. 'It ain't no use us talking to the farmers unless we can make them listen. Where's Mostyn and that other fellow…?' The door swung shut again as Mrs Johnson returned.

'It is getting very late,' Bella said. 'My family will be worrying about me.'

'I durstn't let you go, not till they'm finished their meeting.'

Bella realised she was virtually a prisoner and they would decide what was to be done with her in their own good time. What would they do about her disappearance at Westmere? Would they even know she had disappeared? She was the only one in residence and no one, except perhaps Ellen, would question where she was. And Robert, if he had gone back there, but James might have been wrong about that.

How long would these men keep her? What would they do to her? Would her dead body be found tomorrow, flung in a ditch somewhere? And she would never have the chance to tell Robert how much she loved him, to feel his arms about her, his lips exploring hers, his voice half mocking, half gentle, telling her she was a lovely noddicock. And what a noddicock she had been!

The meeting in the next room was breaking up. There was cheering and shouting as they spilled out into the street and then one of the men came into the kitchen. 'You'm to keep her here,' he said. 'We've got business to attend to. When we've done with it, we'll take her home.' He looked hard at Bella. 'And don't you go thinking we don't know who you are. The old man will pay dear to have you returned to him.'

'He's ill,' she said. 'He doesn't know what's been going on.'

'But you do and you know how valuable you are to us. Sit still and be good and no harm will come to you.'

'They'll be out looking for me.' She prayed it was true.

'Here?' he queried with a laugh. 'I don't think so, do you?' And with a final instruction to Mrs Johnson not to let the wench her out of her sight, he followed his companions out into the street.

Those left behind did not need to see to know what was happening. The sounds were frightening enough, confirmed by other customers of the inn who came in from time to time. 'They're on the rampage and no mistake,' one said.

'Everyone has to give them money or they have their house entered and ransacked. There's no one dare gainsay them.' Another came in later with the news that the men were searching the town for more guns.

'They're mad,' Bella said to Mrs Johnson. 'What can they possibly hope to gain?'

Just before midnight a crowd of men returned to the public house, carrying guns, barrels of gunpowder and shot which they proceeded to distribute. This was far more serious than a rising of discontented labourers—people could be killed and maimed. She had to escape, to warn Robert and James. They would know what to do.

While they were absorbed in their task, she slipped past them into the street. There were men and women everywhere, most of them drunk, all armed with something—sporting guns, old blunderbusses, spikes and pitchforks. A wagon hitched to two heavy horses stood ready to move off. A heavy fowling gun had been mounted on it, its long muzzle poking over the end like a cannon. They hardly noticed her as she turned into the yard to look for Misty.

'Where do you think you're a-goin'?' a voice demanded, just as she was untying the mare from the stall where she had been put.

She whirled round to face one of the men who had captured her earlier. 'Home,' she said, standing her ground.

'You go when we say so.' He reached out and grabbed her arm. 'Seems we can't trust you to stay put, so you'll have to come alonga us.' He dragged her to the wagon and, lifting her up without ceremony, dumped her in the back of it, telling a young lad who sat there with a box of shot to tie her up.

'Where are you taking me?' she asked, as the cavalcade moved off and he set about fastening her hands together. She noticed that one of them was leading Misty, no doubt with the intention of selling her.

'Ely.'

'Ely?' She was dismayed. No one would ever think of looking for her there.

They moved slowly, gathering more people as they went until they were like an army on the march. If she could only give the young lad the slip, she might be able to disappear into the crowd. She wriggled about, trying to loosen her bonds. It was then she saw someone else lying in the bottom of the cart. He was a big man, old too, with craggy features and a shock of white hair. He had obviously been injured for there was a dirty bandage about his head and one arm hung uselessly at his side.

'What do they mean to do with us?' she whispered, trying to remember where she had seen him before.

'Me? I'm supposed to speak out on the labourers' behalf. You, judging by your dress and bearing, are a lady and, I imagine, are to be a hostage.'

'Oh.' Her voice faded with disappointment as she recognised him as the man who had been talking to the labourers in Ely. 'You are one of them.'

'No,' he said. 'Like you, I am a hostage to fortune. I came, hoping to calm them down and make them see reason, but my ideas and theirs no longer coincide.'

'So they did that to you?' She indicated his injured arm with a nod of her head.

'No, the militia.' He chuckled suddenly. 'That's the penalty of being big—you make a good target.'

'They shot you?'

'No, it's a sabre cut.'

'I'm sorry. Is it very bad?'

'Bad enough. Why, thinking of escape, are you?'

'Why not?' She peered over the side of the cart to get her bearings. 'This road goes through a wood soon, if we could get into that without being seen...'

'How? Your hands are tied.'

'If you would be so good as to untie them,' she said, hitching herself closer to him, 'I could jump over the side.'

'You're a game one and no mistake,' he said, picking at the knots that tied her. It took a long time because he had only one good hand, and she became very impatient.

The cart rumbled on and the mob grew more and more noisy. The road suddenly became darker as the overhanging canopy blotted out the moon. Because it also became narrower, closed in as it was by trees, the marchers moved forward, leaving the wagon to follow with only a handful of people for an escort.

Bella, free at last, watched the young lad at the back of the cart. He had been given a flask of drink and was sitting with his legs swinging over the back, laughing at something one of his fellows had called out to him. Bella's companion, whispered, 'Now!' And the next minute he had bundled her over the side.

She landed on hands and knees but quickly rolled into the cover of the trees. Looking back, she saw the old man silhouetted against what little light there was as he, too, jumped into the road and joined her. Breathless, they crouched side by side as the cart rumbled on.

'Are you hurt?' her rescuer asked, noticing that she was rubbing her knees.

'Nothing of consequence. What about you?'

'This infernal wound has opened again.'

The only doctor she knew was in Ely and she began to wonder whether he would not have been better staying in the cart, especially when she realised it had stopped. They were too far away to hear what was being said, but it was obvious they had been missed. Any minute now the men would fan out, searching for them.

Then she thought of the old lady and her herbs and potions, only a quarter of a mile from where they were. 'I know someone who might help,' she said. 'Can you walk?'

'It's my arm that's damaged, not my legs,' he said, grumpily. 'And the sooner we get out of here, the better. Lead on.'

Behind them she could hear shouting and the sound of men beating the undergrowth with sticks. Bella led the way, praying their pursuers would give up and return to their fellows. She turned off the path and plunged among the trees, hoping her sense of direction would not fail her and they would soon come upon the old woman's cottage. Her knees were hurting her and the man behind her was grunting with pain.

A few minutes later they came to the clearing and saw the lighted window of the hovel. 'You'll be safe and looked after here,' she said, as he stopped to hang onto a tree trunk with his good arm, too exhausted to go on. 'The old lady is a herbalist.'

She put his arm about her shoulder to help him the last few yards. The door was opened before they reached it and the old lady stood on the threshold, silhouetted against the light that streamed out.

'My friend is hurt,' Bella called out to her. 'Will you help him?'

'Bring him in.' She turned back indoors and Bella put the old man's arm about her shoulder to support him. Once inside, he sank into a chair. The woman bent to look at him. 'My God, Joseph Mostyn.'

'You know each other?' Bella asked, looking from one to the other.

'Did. Once,' the woman said. 'Married to him.'

He looked up at the sound of her voice and his eyes widened in surprise and then he gave a quirky laugh. 'Fanny, as I live and breathe.'

Fanny! Bella looked from the old man to the woman. She was standing, arms akimbo, looking down at him. Could it be? Fanny was a common name. But this one knew so much about the Earl. Her grandmother? She had reacted strangely when Bella had mentioned the name earlier, but had intimated that Fanny was dead.

Suddenly the woman began to laugh. 'Do you want me to take a look at that arm?' she said to Joseph. 'Or will you be tainted by my touch?'

'Oh, get on with it, woman,' he said.

'You're Fanny,' Bella said, as the woman went to work. 'You're my grandmother.'

The woman smiled without looking up from her task 'That's right, my dear. Not a pleasant surprise, is it?'

Before Bella could frame a reply, they were shocked into silence by the noise of someone approaching the cottage. 'Were you followed?' Fanny asked.

'Might have been,' her husband grunted. 'And I'll tell you this. If I'd known who she was, I'd never have helped her get away.'

'Gammon! It wasn't her fault. Innocent child, she is.'

'I didn't mean to get you into trouble, ma'am,' Bella said. 'But if the men find us…'

'Here, get into bed.' She grabbed Joseph by his good arm, bundled him into the bed and heaped blankets, quilt and clothes over him, covering him completely. 'If they find you, you're to act the drunk,' she hissed at him. 'Too drunk to speak to anyone.' Then she turned to Bella. 'You put my apron on and a shawl over your head. Dirty your face a bit. Granddaughter you are, granddaughter you shall be.'

Bella hardly had time to remove her riding coat and stuff it into a cupboard by the hearth, grab the apron and shawl from a hook behind the door and put them on before there was a loud knocking on the door and a man yelled, 'Open up, whoever you are.'

Fanny glanced round the room to make sure everything looked as it should and went to open it.

Chapter Eleven

Robert was in despair. He had been riding about the countryside, on an increasingly tired horse, looking for Bella for hours. How could she have disappeared so completely? If she had been thrown into a ditch somewhere, her horse would have come back on its own. It was long past midnight and the night was as black as pitch and he had found no sign of either her or the horse.

Having brought Joseph Mostyn to Downham Market, he had left him haranguing the crowd, trying to dissuade them from joining the men from Southery and marching on Littleport, and had ridden to Eastmere to help James. In the event, only a handful of men had come to the farm and they had been easily dissuaded from doing any damage, though he had been obliged to give them every penny he had had on him before they had been persuaded to go home.

No one else had come and when it seemed that all was quiet, he had galloped back to Westmere, only to discover everyone had decamped either to Palgrave or back to London. All except Bella, he had been informed by Miss Battersby who had run out to the stable yard as soon as she had seen him arrive.

'Then where is she?' he demanded, cursing his uncaring

relatives for abandoning her and then realising with a jolt of guilt that had been exactly what he had done.

'I don't know. Her horse has gone.'

'You mean you let her ride out alone with the whole country in ferment?'

'We would not have allowed it if we had known, but she did not tell us.'

'Where could she have gone?'

'I don't know. She might have gone to Eastmere.'

'But I've just come from there.'

'Could you have missed her on the way?'

'It's possible, I suppose. I'd better go back.'

'The Earl has been asking for her. And you, too, but we dare not say anything to him.'

'The old man will have to wait.' Impatiently Robert had turned round and rode straight out again without dismounting.

He retraced his route to Eastmere, but no one had seen Bella. James said she had been there looking for him, but had set off for home immediately and it had still been daylight then. He had thought she would be safe enough, going home along the towpath, and he had had work to do or he would have accompanied her.

It was no good railing against James, who had his own concerns, and, to give the man his due, he had offered to help look for her and so had Spooner and the other estate workers when he went back to Westmere by the towpath route and discovered she had not returned.

Deciding he would be safer dressed as a labourer than a gentleman, he changed out of his riding coat and breeches into a fustian coat and trousers borrowed from Spooner, and set off once again. Apart from the problem of searching in the dark, he had to be careful about asking strangers if they had seen a young lady on a grey horse. It would not do for the dissidents to know the granddaughter of the Earl of

Westmere was missing; heaven knew what fate they would dream up for her if they found her first.

Where was she? If anyone had harmed her... He could not bear to think of that. She must be safe, she must be with friends. The alternative did not bear thinking of.

He heard the army of marchers long before they came into view, shouting and singing drunkenly. He dismounted and pulled his horse behind a hawthorn hedge at the roadside and watched as they drew near and passed within a few feet of his hiding place. There were hundreds of them, walking several abreast, filling the road. Some of them were armed with guns, others carried farm implements and bludgeons. They had a wagon loaded with a duck gun and behind that a boy riding a horse. A grey mare!

It was all he could do to stop himself from rushing out and confronting them, but he knew that would be foolish in the extreme. He waited until they had passed him, then he tethered his horse in a nearby meadow and joined them. Impatient as he was, he knew he must do nothing to alert the marchers to a stranger in their midst.

It was daylight when they reached the outskirts of Ely and were confronted by a magistrate who had taken his courage in his hands to meet them and ask what they wanted, but the man driving the wagon insisted they should go into the market-place where they made the usual demands for a rise in wages and cheaper flour, to which they added a demand for beer at tuppence a pint.

But Robert was not concerned with any of that. He had inched his way into the crowd until he was standing next to the boy who holding Bella's horse. 'Nice little mare,' he said, nodding towards it. 'Yours, is it?'

'Nah, I'm minding it.'

'Who for?'

'Don't know.'

'It wouldn't be a young lady, would it? A pretty young lady.'

'Don't know.'

Robert produced a sovereign from his pocket and held it out. 'You can have this if you can tell me how this horse came to be here.'

The boy looked at him suspiciously. Robert didn't look like a labourer, didn't speak like one either, and yet he was wearing labourer's clothes—there was even a tear in the pocket of his coat. 'Hey, you i'n't one o' them there Bow Street runners wot they sent down to spy on us, are yer? 'Cos if you are…'

'No, boy, I am not a runner, or a spy, I promise you,' he said. 'But I have to help the lady, the one who owns this horse. She is…' He paused and smiled. 'My girl. You understand my meaning?'

'So what?'

'There's a guinea in it if you tell me where she is.'

A guinea was a fortune. The lad grinned as he grabbed it and bit on it. 'She was in the cart…' He nodded towards it.

'Was? Where is she now?'

The boy shrugged, more intent on the negotiations which seemed to be taking place between a group of magistrates and the rioters' leaders. 'Dunno. Got out somehow. They did look for her, but it was dark and the guv'nor said we was wastin' time and we had the horse, so he bid a few men to stay and search for her and the rest on us to come on.'

'You mean she jumped out?'

'I s'pose so.'

Bella could be hurt, she could be dying in a ditch. Or recaptured by those left to search for her. 'Where was this?'

'On the bend in the road by Lord Westmere's covert.'

'Good.' Robert produced a second guinea. 'Now I need that horse to get back there.'

'Oh, I don't know about that. They'd tan my hide if I was to let it go…'

'Say it was startled by all the crowds and the noise and panicked. You couldn't hold it.' He smiled and ruffled the boy's grubby curls. 'If not, I'll take you to the magistrates and charge you with stealing it.' It was an empty sort of threat, he decided, considering what was taking place all around him. The mob had tired of negotiation and were rushing away to do more damage. He did not wait for the boy to come to the same conclusion but seized Misty's reins and leapt into the saddle, only to be reminded most painfully that it was a side-saddle. With only one foot in the stirrup, he turned and rode hell for leather out of the town, past The Lamb and out onto the Littleport road.

He knew the place well enough. There was a footpath through the wood which led to the house and, naturally, Bella knew it, too. Clever girl. She might, even now, be safe at home. She would be glad to have Misty back, though. He smiled. Bringing the mare back might find favour with her. And he needed something to mitigate his Cavalier treatment of her.

He dismounted with a gasp of relief when he reached the spot where he had left his own horse and untied it from the hawthorn bush, which set the dogs barking in a nearby farm. He heard a window open and someone tell it to shut up, but no one came to investigate. Whoever it was, he was not going to risk meeting with the rioters. Robert led the horse back onto the road and mounted, leading Bella's mare.

Five minutes later he found the spot where she must have jumped. The ground was trodden down as if a crowd had been milling about. He examined the area carefully, imagining how she would have jumped and where she might have landed. One of the bushes was broken. He bent to look more closely and saw blood, a large patch of it. She had been hurt!

His heart began to hammer as he looked for more signs. There they were—spots of blood, one after the other, a perfectly clear trail. And there was a piece of silk, just the colour of her riding habit, caught on a bush. He rushed forward, almost on his knees, following the trail along a narrow path through the wood. And then it came to a sudden stop.

He went forward, hoping to pick it up again, but there were no more signs. Had she suddenly stopped bleeding? Had she been caught and carried away? Or had she simply lost the path? He went back to where he had seen the last spot of blood and wandered round and round in an ever-increasing circles, trying to pick up the trail again. And then he saw it. Blood smeared on a treetrunk and a torn linen handkerchief caught on a branch. He looked round him and there, not fifty yards away, was a tiny cottage with smoke coming from its chimney.

He walked cautiously forward.

'Tell me about you and the Earl,' Bella asked. Fanny had put on her best old crone's voice, petulant and quavering, to convince the men who had come to the cottage that there had been no fugitives there and that they had no right to frighten a poor woman with their shouts and threats when all she wanted to do was live in peace.

'That's my granddaughter,' she had said, when they had demanded to know who Bella was. 'She's a few pennies short of a shilling, but a good girl all the same.' Bella had blackened one of her teeth and tousled her hair before Fanny had let them in, and she had grinned at them, pretending to be simple.

They had been uncomfortable in the presence of lunacy and had hurriedly begged her pardon and left, telling Fanny that if she saw a big man with a mop of white hair and a young lady full of airs and graces, they should not let them in for they were dangerous. Fanny had said they would not entertain such people and Bella had grinned even more widely and sidled up to one of them, frightening him so much he had jumped a good foot out of her way and had made for the door, with the others behind him.

It was after the men had gone and their laughter had died down that Bella asked her question. 'I am not blaming anyone, you understand, but I simply must know the truth.'

Before she answered, Fanny went over to the bed to make sure Joseph was asleep, then she said, 'Sit down, child. You deserve to know what happened, though it is a sorry tale, to be sure.'

Bella sat on a stool beside the hearth while Fanny took the kettle and made herbal tea for them both. Then, mug in hand, she sat in the only other chair in the place. 'Where to begin…' She paused, her eyes unfocused as if she were in another time and place. 'My father was a country lawyer…'

'From Westmere?'

'Huntingdon. But don't interrupt or I'll never be done. It's hard enough as it is.'

'Sorry.'

'Joe Mostyn was a handsome man. Everyone said what a good match it was and, though I could not say I loved him, I liked him well enough. We were married in…' She stopped to think of the date. 'Seventeen sixty or thereabouts. He was the Earl of Westmere's steward. Not the present earl, of course, but his father. We lived in a house on the estate. Three years we tried to have a child, but none came. It made Joe bitter. He… No, I will not go into that, except to say he was not always kind to me. Not his fault. I do not blame him.

'I often saw Lord Huntley, the Earl's heir, round and about and he would come to the house to see Joe and talk about what wanted doing on the estate. And sometimes the two of them would go shooting or fishing together. One day, someone came from the house with a message for the young lord and I went to the fen to take it to him, expecting to find Joe with him. But Joe had left him. I learned afterwards he often used his days out with his lordship as a cover to go off enjoying himself with... Oh, never mind. I stopped to talk to William and somehow it went on from there.

'The two men would leave together, but as soon as Joe had gone off, William would come back to our house. We fell in love.'

'Oh, it was love, then.'

'Of course it was. I knew it was wrong and so did he, but young men in those days, especially aristocrats, took mistresses whenever they felt like it.'

'Was he married?'

'No, not then. But, of course, marriage between us was out of the question. He had to marry his own kind, someone his parents had chosen for him...'

'Surely he objected to that?'

'No, why should he? It was what happened.' She laughed, a dry rasping sound which was without humour. 'I discovered I was increasing while he was away on his wedding trip.'

'What did you do?'

'There was nothing I could do. I pretended the child was Joe's, though I knew it was not.'

'And Joe found out?'

'Yes. When William returned, I went to find him, to tell him. I don't know what I expected him to do, but not what happened. Joe overheard us. He lost his temper and attacked William, broke his nose and made such a noise, everyone came running. Joe was dismissed. He joined the navy. There was no question I could be allowed to stay in our house, nor even in the village. William arranged for me to go to a nunnery hundreds of miles away to have my child. After that he washed his hands of me. The Earl, his father, told me that if I ever tried to return, I would be declared insane and put into an institution. He could easily have done it, too.'

'Oh, I am so sorry. But surely no one could say you were insane when you were not?'

Fanny smiled. 'I think I was a little mad. I was certainly desperate. William had given me a little money, but that was soon spent on lodgings, food and clothes. We were starving. I was near to dying and so…'

'You came back.'

'William's father had died and he was now the Earl. He would not answer my letters, I knew that, so I wrote to Joshua Battersby, one of his lordship's tenant farmers…'

'Ellen's father?'

'I asked him to give his lordship a letter from me and do his best to make sure he read it. And he did. William came to see me. It was a terrible interview. I was living in a dreadful hovel, far worse than this, and I could see him recoiling at it. But he was man enough to realise he could not leave his son in such circumstances. He said he would bring him up, provided I relinquished all claim to him and never told him who I was.'

'You agreed?' Bella could not believe her grandfather could have been so unfeeling.

'I had no choice. I wanted what was best for my son. The Earl bought him with a purse full of guineas. It was enough for me to set myself up in a little shop, selling herbs and potions. I had learned about them while living with the nuns. I never saw Charles again.'

'You poor thing. I am so sorry. I never thought of Grandpapa as a cruel man.'

'Don't blame him too much. He was a man of his time, his behaviour was no worse than hundreds of others. And he brought Charles up as his son, in spite of the opposition of the Countess, and that could not have been easy.'

'When did you move back here?'

'Two years ago. I'm getting old and I wanted see you before I died. I did not intend to make myself known to you, simply to make sure you were happy, but…' She shrugged her shoulders. 'Events have overtaken us, haven't they?'

'Does Grandfather know you are living so close?'

'No. Nor must he.'

'Why not? He is sorry. I am sure he would like to tell you that.'

'Too late. I told you before, the past is done with, and seeing him again won't change it. Your happiness is my only concern.' She stopped and looked into Bella's face. 'This man…'

'Robert.'

'A good man, is he?'

'Yes. The best, but…' She stopped and turned her head to listen. 'I thought I heard a sound.' Her voice was a whisper. 'There's someone outside. They've come back.'

Fanny stood up and picked up a shotgun which was propped in a corner. 'We'll soon give them the right about. Open the door and keep behind it.'

Bella obeyed. She could not see who was there but she saw her grandmother lift the gun and take aim. 'Get out! Get away from here. Leave us in peace or you'll have a stomach full of shot to take home with you.'

The man stood his ground. 'I'm looking for a young lady…'

'Yes, I know, your friends told us. There's no young lady here, only me, my drunken husband and my granddaughter.'

'Oh, I'm sorry I troubled you.'

Bella held her breath. She knew perfectly well it was Robert outside the door, but something stopped her from revealing herself. What would he say when he learned she was the granddaughter of this strange peasant? The knowledge was still so new to her that she could not take it in. She needed more time.

'Huntley?' The name was said by a masculine voice behind her.

'Joe, is that you?' Robert asked, evidently surprised. 'What are you doing here?'

''Tis a long story.' He pushed past Bella and took the gun from Fanny's hands. 'That's no way to welcome a friend. Invite him in.'

Robert stepped forward and then he saw the girl. She was filthy, her hair was matted, and she was wearing a riding skirt which looked as though it had once been good but was now torn and smeared with blood.

'Bella?' He could hardly believe his eyes. 'It is you, isn't it?'

She gave her wild-eyed idiot's laugh, revealing a black tooth. He recoiled and she stopped laughing. 'See what a girl has to do to survive these days.'

Fanny looked from one to the other. 'Am I to assume you are Captain Robert Huntley?'

'At your service,' he said, ducking his head below the lintel to enter the cottage. He stood looking about him, longing to take Bella into his arms and shake her, to stop her looking at him like that, as if she were afraid of him, keeping him at a distance.

'Sit down, man, sit down,' Fanny said, as Bella slipped into the lean-to at the back to wash her face. 'You, too, Joe. You shouldn't have got out of bed.'

'What, and let you shoot my friend! Women have no business handling guns, especially old women. In any case, I am recovered enough to travel.'

'You don't need to go, not if you don't want to...'

'Will someone tell me what has been going on?' Robert asked as Bella returned from the bedroom, her face clean and her teeth sparkling white. She had brushed her dark hair and it was spread about her shoulders, making her look very vulnerable and infinitely beautiful. He reached out and took her hand.

'I was captured by the rioters and put in a wagon,' Bella said.

'So I discovered. I've been looking for you the whole night.'

'Have you?'

'Do not sound so surprised. Did you think no one would care when you disappeared? Everyone has been searching for you and worrying about you…'

'Grandfather?'

He smiled grimly. 'No one dared tell him you were missing.'

'Oh, I am glad. It might have made him worse and as no harm had come to me…'

'You escaped.'

'Yes, with Mr Mostyn's help. He was hurt, and so I brought him here to…' She paused. He had to know sooner or later. 'To my grandmother, who is also his wife, though I did not know it then.'

'Go on,' he said quietly. 'Tell me the whole.'

So the tale was told and when it was finished she waited for Robert's reaction, waited for him to drop the hand he held so tightly, to take his leave on some pretence or other, but he did not. He laughed. 'What a bumble bath!' He hugged her to his side. 'Now what?'

'I think you should take Bella home,' Fanny said. 'She is exhausted. Time enough to talk later.' She smiled at the young man. 'You be good to her, do you hear? I want to know she is happy, and if I hear anything to the contrary, I shall put one of my witch's curses on you.' And when he laughed she added, 'And don't think I can't.'

They left hand in hand, found their horses and set off, riding side by side. 'Now what?' he repeated.

'I think I shall be a famous novelist,' she said lightly. 'Isn't it strange how that book I sent to Mr Norton was so very near the truth? Only it wasn't me but my father who was the love child. Do you think I knew, deep down inside me?'

'No, you just have a vivid imagination, that's all, and you know that's not what I was asking. I want to know what you mean to do about our engagement.'

'What engagement?'

'Bella, do you want me to pull you off that horse and spank you?'

'Try it,' she said, and dug her heels in. He caught up with her when she dismounted in the stable yard, but by then everyone had heard them arriving and were crowding round, wanting to know if she was hurt, where she had been, where he had found her. He answered as briefly as he could and then scooped her up in his arms. 'Miss Huntley is exhausted,' he said. 'You'll hear all about it soon enough.'

He carried her indoors and straight up to her room where he laid her gently on the bed.

'Robert,' she protested, 'you should not come in here.'

'I shall go where I please and I am not leaving until you tell me what I want to know.'

'And what is that?' She looked towards the open door, expecting Ellen to come bustling in to send him away, but there was no sign of her.

'Will you marry me?' He sat on the edge of the bed and took her hand in both of his.

'You do not have to marry me,' Bella said. 'Our engagement was meant to be a hoax after all. You knew I could not hold you to it, I said I would not. Grandfather knows about it and he hasn't broken the entail. He told me so and though I do not think he will leave me penniless, I have no right to expect—'

'What has that to do with anything?'

'Everything. Were you not listening when I told you about Mrs Mostyn and Grandfather?'

'Oh, I was listening. And I repeat, what has that to do with my asking you to marry me? I love you, you goose, and what happened in the past, or what your grandfather does with his legacy, has nothing whatever to do with it. I want to marry you and if we have to live in a hovel in a wood, why, so be it. We shall contrive to be happy.'

'Do you mean that?'

'Do I look as though I am joking?'

'Oh, Robert!'

He smiled. 'Am I meant to take that as an affirmative?'

'Oh, yes, please.'

He bent and kissed her very gently, very lovingly. 'Now, go to sleep. I could do with some myself. Later, I will go and see his lordship…'

'He knows,' she murmured, her eyes already closing. 'I told him I loved you.'

'Oh, Bella! If I were not so tired, I really would spank you for leading me such a dance.' But she was already slumbering and he stood up and crept from the room, closing the door softly behind him.

The Earl of Westmere lived long enough to see them married, though he died in his sleep before she could tell him she was expecting his great-grandchild. By that time Edward had married Charlotte and, though he became the next Earl of Westmere, he never took up residence. The house was sold and used as a boarding school. His lordship divided his fortune between his great-nephews, though a considerable portion went to Bella for her own use. Louis went to France to reclaim his father's estate where he met and married the daughter of another returning émigré.

James married Rose Clarke, and Joseph Mostyn and Fanny went to live in Peterborough together, where they were able to visit Robert and Bella from time to time at their country house not far from Westmere, where Bella settled down to await the birth and write her second novel.

Little Robert William Huntley was born in May 1817, amid great family rejoicing. He had no title and could have no expectation of inheriting one, but Bella was convinced he would be a great man and earn untold honours. 'How can he do anything else?' she asked her husband mischievously when he was at last allowed into her bedchamber. 'With two such gifted parents?'

'A renowned authoress and a rising Member of Parliament,' he said, sitting on the edge of the bed and ignoring the nurse who clucked disapprovingly. 'He could have done worse.' He smiled down at his lovely wife, propped up on pillows, cradling their child, and his heart nearly burst with love and pride. 'But in his mother he could certainly not have done better. I love you, Mrs Huntley.'

'And I love you, Mr Huntley.' And then, seeing the nurse's face turn scarlet with embarrassment, they burst out laughing. But there was nothing out of the ordinary in that— their house always rang with laughter.

*   *   *   *   *

Historical Note

Although Westmere and Eastmere do not exist and the characters in my book are all fictitious, including Joseph Mostyn, the riots at Downham Market, Littleport and Ely really did take place. Over eighty of the rioters were arrested and tried in Ely, five of whom paid the supreme penalty and were hanged; forty-eight were transported to the colonies for varying terms and the rest either sent to prison or fined. They gained nothing by their protests.

MILLS & BOON®

Makes any time special™

Mills & Boon publish 29 new titles every month. Select from...

Modern Romance™   Tender Romance™

Sensual Romance™

Medical Romance™   Historical Romance™

MAT2